Praise for SS Turner's first novel, *Secrets of a River Swimmer:*

"S.S. Turner has written a profound story that is about all our lives. He has found the connection that makes us all the same, while remaining unique. His words will resonate with every reader as they see themselves, find themselves embedded in them. You will not escape, you will not want to escape from the depth of your own world he reminds you is yours to be lived, to survive and thrive. I am honoured to have read an advance copy of *Secrets of a River Swimmer* and cannot recommend it highly enough."

– Heather Morris, #1 *New York Times* bestselling author of *The Tattooist of Auschwitz*

"This is a beautifully written, almost lyrical, account of one man and how the river saved his life – quite literally . . . It's magical at times, tragic at times, laugh out loud funny at times. It not only entertained me, it uplifted me."

– *Long and Short Reviews*

"This is an amazing story full of heartbreak, full of hope, and ultimately full of inspiration."

– *Literarily Illumined*

The Connection Game

The Connection Game

SS Turner

Gramarye

Gramarye Media
1270 Caroline Street
Suite D120-381
Atlanta, GA 30307

Copyright © 2022 by Simon Turner
The Library of Congress Cataloguing-in-Publication Data is available upon request.

Gramarye paperback ISBN-13: 978-1-61188-337-4
Fiction Studio Books E-book ISBN: 978-1-945839-72-6

Visit our website at www.GramaryeMedia.com

First Gramarye Printing: February 2023

Printed in the United States of America
0 9 8 7 6 5 4 3 2 1

Also by S.S. Turner:

Secrets of a River Swimmer

Keeping Watch

In the morning
When I began to wake,
It happened again—
That feeling
That You, Beloved,
Had stood over me all night
Keeping watch,
That feeling
That as soon as I began to stir
You put your lips on my forehead
And lit the Holy lamp
Inside my heart.

-Hafiz

CHAPTER 1

When I think of my husband, I picture a restless meerkat sentry in my mind. He was on the lookout for intruders at the gate from the moment we moved into the little flat under the stairs. We only lived there for a year and a half, but it seemed like an eternity. If you could see photos of us before and after we moved there, you'd be shocked. We weren't far off a normal family of four when we arrived, but now, well that's a long story.

There's a photo of my husband on the front page of that newspaper on the table—some journalist must have found it on social media. What a telling shot! Of course, he's staring out the little flat's one and only damned window, no doubt searching for answers as he loved to do. No, the photo doesn't do him justice. He was much more than a meerkat on watch. I need to keep reminding myself that when that photo was taken, he was a mere shadow of the man he once was, the man he was when I met him all those years ago.

My name is Bell, well Belinda if I don't like you, and Bell if I do. Let's go with Bell for now, and I'll let you know if we need to change that. We should be fine if you agree to listen without judgment. I can't stand people who think their view of the world is the only right way of seeing things. And besides, there's no point you even pretending you are listening to me if you are secretly judging me, my husband, my family.

So what can I tell you about me? Well, I grew up in north London in an area called Rickmansworth. My family was working class, so we lived in a small house near a railway line on the cheapest street in our postcode. The railway line was the one and only reason we were able to afford to live there. But we were happy and had all we needed. We had a little garden out the back of our house that ended at a huge wall and dropped around ten yards down to the railway line below. That wall was the source of many of my childhood memories. My sister Angie and I frequently climbed it and watched the trains speed past below. There was something therapeutic about watching them heading toward their destinations. We believed they were all traveling somewhere better, and often told each other stories about the eccentric passengers on board. One of the recurring characters we enjoyed discussing was Mr. Nincompoop who was always in a rush to get to wherever he was going, even if he kept forgetting where he was going, and he often did. We often imagined Mr. Nincompoop was calling out for answers about his destination as he rushed past us. Sometimes we'd shout out destinations for his benefit like Make-Believe Land and A Better World, and sometimes we'd royal wave at him like the Queen and then giggle at our silliness.

We were a family of four. My father was a miner who worked away from home for many months each year, and my mother stayed at home to look after us, more out of necessity than choice. My sister Angie and I found magic in all the small things and developed a wonderful bond from a very young age. When we weren't climbing the garden wall, we were creating vast worlds for the fairies we were certain lived in our garden to inhabit. We once lost touch for a while, but Angie remains my closest friend to this day.

Now as I look back, my childhood was pretty uneventful. Happiness is not a good story in itself, so sorry about that. But thank god I had such a solid upbringing given what was in store for me. Strong foundations become necessary when the earthquake arrives.

After school, I decided to study hospitality at University College in London. I wanted to meet people with different backgrounds and experiences but without traveling too far away from Angie, who was still at high school in north London. UCL seemed like a great match since most of their students are international. It was a good decision, and a wonderful time in my life. My course had fifty people comprising twenty nationalities in it, so my perspective on life expanded on a daily basis.

It was a surprise to discover I was popular with the opposite sex. I was so used to hanging out with my sister that I wasn't even aware how men would regard me when I started spending regular time with them. And regard me they did. I found myself being inundated with requests for dates from the men on my course. It was quite a shock at the time. I remember an Indian fellow named Nisheth tried to serenade me while I was walking home one day. His attempted rendition of "Angels" was so bad it was charming. But he wasn't the right man for me, as was the case with all the men I knew back then. I gave Nisheth and all my other would-be suitors conciliatory hugs and thanked them for their friendship. That was back in the day when people understood subtleties. None of them genuinely thought we were stepping into friendships, but they gracefully pretended we were for the greater good. It seemed so much kinder than delivering the brutal truth about my lack of feelings toward them. Maybe I've always been a little afraid of hard truths.

In those days, I couldn't have put into words what type of man was right for me, but I was certain I'd just know when the right man arrived in my life. I was right.

One day after lectures, a few of us were celebrating at a little UCL bar called Kaleidoscope. I was unusually tipsy as we had recently finished exams and were about to have a few weeks off university. I ordered a large round of drinks for our group at the bar. The bartender handed me a tray full with our drinks, and I turned around to make my way back to the group. At that very moment, a girl I recognized as one of the too-cool-for-school UCL students somehow walked straight into me and my drinks tray went flying. The glasses ended up broken all over the floor, and most of the drinks found their way into my hair or onto my dress. It was one of those moments in life you just have to laugh about.

Out of nowhere, a man emerged by my side. He helped steady me, and then started picking up the tray and broken glass. I was discombobulated by the chaos, so my memory of this moment is a little hazy, but I do remember the exact words that followed.

"I wish I could have been the one you walked into," he said.

"Why?" I managed to blurt out.

"The other girl was moving 25 percent faster than me so this accident would never have happened if it were me in her place," he stated. "This is on her, not you. No one needs to move that fast in a bar."

I laughed nervously thinking he was cracking an intellectual joke, and it seemed very funny in the circumstances.

Before I could say anything else, this mysterious man was standing at the bar ordering drinks. And he miraculously ordered all the drinks I'd just dropped on the floor. He returned to my side carrying the full tray of drinks.

"Right, where are you sitting?" he asked without fanfare.

"Are they for me? How did you know my order?" I asked, confused.

"I'll explain it some other time," he answered with a smile.

His words "some other time" filled the air around me with anticipation. *Why on earth did he think we'd be seeing each other again?* I wondered.

I led him toward the table we were sitting at, and with surprising grace he deposited the drinks tray at the table without a word. The rest of the group stared at him as though he was an unwelcome intruder there to upset the group dynamics, but he smiled it off. He stood tall as though he was meant to be standing exactly where he was, and it was hard to argue with him.

"How can I ever thank you?" I asked, suddenly nervous.

"No thanks required. It was my pleasure to almost bump into you," he answered with a dangerously charming smile.

And then he walked away without another word.

In that moment, the course of my life changed forever. Benny had entered my life in all his glory. Of course, I had no idea that day in the bar, as I didn't see him again for a long time after our initial meeting. I did think of him though, a lot. I'd never before met a man who'd made such a uniquely powerful impression on me, and the longer I didn't see him, the more my mind built him into the man of my dreams. But as I didn't know how to contact him, I also started to think of him as the one who got away. Angie teased me about it to no end. She started referring to him affectionately as "Long-Lost Bar Hero." I didn't find it funny.

Then one day out of the blue, Benny casually walked up to me at UCL as if running into each other was the most normal thing in the world.

"So, do you want to know how I knew your entire drinks order without asking?" he asked confidently without even saying hello.

"Go on, tell me how you did it," I said as teasingly as I could.

"I read your mind," he answered with the same deadpan certainty as when we'd last met.

"Really? So what am I thinking right now?" I asked.

"You're thinking how the hell did he read my mind," he replied with a half grin.

"So games aside, how did you read my mind?" I asked, genuinely interested.

"I didn't. I overheard you order. I was standing next to you at the bar," he stated without remorse or even a hint of humor.

Ordinarily I'd have been annoyed by this pointless little charade, but with Benny his behavior only seemed to amplify his strange charms. I could tell then that I was in trouble.

"How disappointing. So you don't have any superpowers then?" I asked.

"You're wrong there. How many people do you know who can remember a random person's ten-drink order perfectly without the help of pen and paper?" he asked.

"You're right. You are indeed the most unusual man I've ever met," I told him. I wasn't lying.

We became a couple soon after and were inseparable within a matter of weeks. I was hooked by Benny's extreme confidence and uniqueness, and he seemed fascinated by my "normalness" as he put it. Next to Benny's high IQ, I counterbalanced with high EQ. For Benny's lack of friends, I had an abundant social network that he shared. Compared with Benny's overconfidence, I brought a confidence deficit to the table. And in contrast to Benny's ability to say funny things,

17

I was a generous laugher who enjoyed supporting all things humorous. Everything existed in a delicate counterbalance within our relationship. We were a match made in a creative heaven, and it just worked.

Five years later Benny and I were married, and I became Belinda Basilworth. I always thought my married name sounded more like it was destined to be my name, as opposed to my maiden name, Belinda Harry. There was something about having a man's first name in my surname that never sat well with me. Maybe I'd been called "Dirty Harry" one too many times when I was growing up. Anyway, one year after our wedding day we welcomed our first-born into this world, a little baby boy we named Will. And he was followed three years later by the arrival of a little girl we called Wendy.

Despite Benny's uniqueness, we found ourselves in the wonderfully average position of being married with two children. We had officially become normal as Benny sometimes joked, although he often found the idea challenging.

"It's remarkable," Benny said to me one day. "When I walk around as a father of two, I'm hidden from the world. Being a parent is the ultimate disguise because people assume parents are normal, well-meaning people without delving deeper. What a useful unintended consequence of procreation."

"Maybe people make assumptions, but I love all that being parents brings us. I feel connected with the other parents, and our social life has never been better," I responded.

"But don't you care *why* our social life has improved?" Benny asked. "Doesn't it matter to you that it's all based on how things appear on the surface?"

"Not really, honey. I'm just happy to accept all the good stuff in our lives for what it is," I responded with a little sadness.

"But Bell, the truth is none of this is real!" Benny exclaimed as he pointed in all directions.

"The truth? The truth is we are a beautiful family of four and I love my husband and kids dearly," I responded. "That's as real as I know. Beyond that, not much matters, does it?"

"Let's keep running with this disguise then," Benny smiled as he took my hand in his. "Who cares what anyone else thinks. I'm content being a member of the unusually happy Basilworth family."

We were indeed happy, and we remained like that for a long time. Fifteen years to be precise. I know that because it was Will's fifteenth birthday a few weeks after we moved into the little flat. We stayed in that evening. Of course, we did—we stayed in a lot once we moved into the little flat.

CHAPTER 2

It's hard to explain how we found ourselves in that flat—the real reason. Everything had been going so well in our lives up until then. But first, you'll need to understand a little more about our lives before we arrived at the flat. What happened before holds the seedlings of what was to come next.

Benny had a successful career as a computer programmer, which he fell into when he was a student at UCL. His immense intellect was starting to be recognized even then. When Benny was in his second year at university, one of his lecturers asked him to help out with a technology company he was setting up as a personal endeavor. After a year of working together, Benny was so valuable to his lecturer's business that he offered him an equity stake along with a director role. It was the start of bigger things for Benny as he quickly built a name for himself in the industry. He was so talented at what he did that he was soon invited to help some of the world's most successful companies with their technology development. His IQ had always been extraordinarily high, but in the realms of computer programming he was able to create new dimensions that few people could even follow, never mind understand. That's why he was held in extremely high regard among the small group of people who *almost* understood what he did. He was a bona fide genius.

We were proud of him, but his family never fully understood the depth of Benny's talents, and what he could offer the world. However, it made us happy to know Benny was loving his success, including the large amount of money he was being paid. He always described it as gratifying to be someone who could make a difference and be recognized for it. I think his love of recognition came from his childhood. His father was apparently a domineering control freak who constantly demanded Benny prove his worth as a son and a human. Benny once told me the only time his father showed him any affection was when he won prizes, so he won prizes by the dozens. But I don't think Benny ever believed he was truly worthy in his father's eyes. That's another story, but suffice it to say, Benny was more focused on succeeding than anyone I've ever met.

My career in hospitality was also thriving in its own way. Since I was a child, baking has been a passion of mine. Something about creating luscious and generous food that dances with the senses makes me feel fulfilled. It's my way of sending love to the world. So I focused upon developing my baking skills early on in my career and I left the more business-focused aspects of hospitality alone. It was a great decision emotionally, financially, and from a lifestyle perspective as I've genuinely loved my career. Over time, I developed my own unique baking techniques that resulted in the creation of a successful range of luxury cakes and cookies. For many years, I sold my product range directly to the Harrods Roastery and Bake Hall in Knightsbridge, and I was often stretched to keep up with their ever-growing demand. I was shocked by how many people out there were prepared to pay ten pounds for a cookie, but I guess that's the power of a brand name like Harrods. At one point, I was even selling my cakes to a Michelin-starred restaurant, and my cheesecake developed a cult following of sorts thanks to a glowing endorsement by a celebrity chef who referred to me as the "cheesecake standard-setter." It was stressful but fun to be the best at what I did. Benny and I always had that in common.

Our children, Will and Wendy, led a charmed life for all those years. Will was sporty and had been accepted as one of the cool group of jocks at his expensive private school. As someone who came from a working-class background, I sometimes found the world of elite private schools hard to fathom. Something about the ignorant cocksureness of the young boys Will was friends with made me uncomfortable. One day, when I was picking Will up from school, one of his friends said to me, "Do you enjoy baking cookies for all the kiddies?" It sounds innocent, but it was laced with a less-than-innocent tone. I remember a time when children acted with more respect toward adults. I preferred those types of children. Benny had been to a top private school and always told me the positives far outweighed the negatives at these types of schools. Look at the statistics confirming how successful their alumni have become, Benny would argue. Sometimes I wasn't sure if it was Benny or his father talking to me. But I went along with it as I could see Will was happy and believed he was a part of something bigger than himself.

Wendy has always been more like me. She's quieter than Will and only speaks her mind around people she trusts. She was enrolled at the girls' equivalent of Will's private school, but at the last minute she asked if she could instead attend the local state school where many of her friends were enrolled. When she made her case to us, Wendy pulled on our heartstrings as only a daughter can. So we agreed to the change of school. I was secretly overjoyed, but Benny was openly concerned. He wondered how Wendy could possibly achieve the grades he knew she was capable of if she attended what he viewed as a second-rate school. I knew she'd do well regardless.

Benny's and my marriage thrived despite our extreme differences, or maybe because of them. I think the main reason for our relationship success was that we deeply respected each other. We each recognized that the other brought things to the table that each of us didn't have as individuals, and by combining our strengths we both benefited. Having said that, it was far from smooth sailing all the time. When we argued, and we did regularly, it was like World War III. In those less-than-perfect moments, our differences became weights around our necks which were hard to bear. Benny's fixation upon cold hard facts made him almost impossible for an emotionally aware person—like me—to argue with when tensions were running high. There were some times I didn't even think we were speaking the same language. But we always managed to somehow weather those storms, and the good times would return with a vengeance. We were well versed at laughing off our arguments when we were on the other side of them. I guess that's how all healthy marriages work.

I remember one particularly revealing argument we weathered a few years ago. It was about the best way to hang toilet paper. (Yes, you heard that right.) Benny insisted toilet paper should always hang forward at the front of the roll, and I suggested it should hang at the back. Rather than letting it go, Benny argued the advantages of hanging it forward as though his life depended on it.

"Of course, toilet paper should always hang forward!" Benny implored. "Anything less is at best dysfunctional, at worst uncivilized."

"Uncivilized? Are we talking about the same thing here?" I asked. "Just because I think toilet paper should hang backward doesn't in any way reflect how civilized I am."

"But consider how you're positioned on the toilet," Benny said while he pretended to sit on a toilet. "You don't want to have to lean forward any further than you absolutely have to when you need the toilet paper. Otherwise, you're wasting valuable wiping time. It's bloody obvious, isn't it?" As Benny acted out the role of the desperate toilet user searching for toilet paper in earnest, he looked ridiculous. My need to laugh was becoming overwhelming, but I fought against releasing it with all my might. I feared Benny would be upset if I laughed at him.

"Not everything is black and white, Benny, including the world of ass wiping. It's more of a brown zone," I smirked.

"Oh brilliant," Benny half smiled while trying not to laugh, just as I was. "Next, you'll be telling me you don't believe in using knives and forks!"

"Yes, that's exactly what I had in mind," I responded knowing the best way to turn our tide was to make light of the situation until Benny's inner giggle revealed its beautiful sound to the world. "Here's an idea: Let's start living like Tarzan and Jane. The only problem is we're in need of a back-to-front jungle where toilet paper can break Tarzan's all-so-important rules. Can you please point me in the right direction?"

Benny stopped his attack and started laughing, and I finally joined him. It was such a relief. It was always the way with us. Once Benny started laughing at our ridiculousness, we both knew we'd successfully made it through to the other side of the darkness, and the light always shone all the brighter from then on.

"Thank goodness I married a woman with a wonderful sense of humor who can deal with my back-to-front ways," Benny smiled. "We're lucky, aren't we?"

"We are indeed. Mr. and Mrs. Basilworth are a force to be reckoned with," I said as I gave him a hug.

We were a force to be reckoned with, and I doubt the world has met many couples like us before.

I'd rather stop our story there if I had a choice as what happened next led to us moving into the little flat. And at that point in our lives, we were happy, healthy, and wealthy. Of course, we didn't fully appreciate how lucky we were, but in hindsight we were nailing it.

CHAPTER 3

Benny always had a passion, no an obsession, for puzzles, mysteries, game shows, basically anything involving a problem looking for a solution. It's hardly surprising since he couldn't sit still unless his mind was engaged in an activity that distracted him from the mundanities of life. I sometimes wondered if he was looking for a distraction from himself. Anyway, around two and a half years ago Benny started watching that TV game show, The Connection Game, in the evenings. They always billed it as the world's hardest game show, which was like a red rag to a bull for Benny. The objective of the game is for contestants to find the connections between seemingly unrelated clues whether they be words, expressions, numbers, or pretty much anything. The game requires an ability to deconstruct and then reconstruct on multiple levels. To say it was "up Benny's street" would be an understatement. Whenever he watched it, he would jump up and down like a crazed madman when he knew the answers ahead of the other contestants. And he always did, every single time. That show quickly became a fixture in our lives every weekday evening. Benny insisted we eat dinner before or after the show to ensure it wasn't interrupted in any way.

They say passion is contagious—it was in our household. When they first watched an episode of The Connection Game, Will and Wendy had no interest in it whatsoever. Wendy described it as a bunch of old people with nothing better to do than desperately search for their one and only moment in the limelight in order to make up for all their lost opportunities. But over time, their father's passion for solving the unsolvable infected both of them. It happened slowly, like a frog sitting in gradually warming water unaware the water was approaching boiling point. The boiling point arrived a few months later. I couldn't believe it when one day I found Benny, Will, and Wendy simultaneously punching the air together because they'd solved a Connection Game question in record time as a team. I smiled at the time, but I remember feeling some unidentifiable unease deep within.

I'll never forget the conversation at dinner that evening.

"Dad, you were wicked. You are so much better than any player on the show. Isn't it time you show them what you can do in real life?" asked Will.

"What? You mean actually go on the show?" asked Benny, who seemed to have forgotten it was a real TV show with viewers apart from him.

"Will's right, Dad. You should definitely go for it. They announced the other day that they will soon be recruiting for the first-ever individual version of The Connection Game. They're searching for the one player in the country who is the best of the best. If that's not right up your street, everything I know is a lie. What are you waiting for?" added Wendy.

"What's the point? I'm happy playing at home with you guys. And besides, I know I'm good at the game. I don't need a title to tell me that," answered Benny with a smile that didn't quite extend all the way to his eyes. I knew he was lying.

"Two reasons, Dad. Firstly, you'll have fun, and you know it. I don't think I've ever seen you have as much fun as when you're playing that game. And secondly, the winner of the individual game takes home one hundred thousand pounds. Let me repeat that: one hundred thousand pounds. If you don't want that big pile of cash, I'll happily take it off your hands," said Will laughing.

Benny thought for a long moment.

"Bell, what do you think?" he asked, but I knew he'd already made the decision in his head to go on the show. Benny always pretended to check with me when he thought that's what I'd expect, but he must have been one of the world's worst actors.

"I think you should go for it if you want to," I answered like a fool.

So Benny applied to be a contestant on The Connection Game the very next day. The application process for the show required an IQ test, a recent CV, and the completion of a questionnaire regarding your personal interests. We all knew there was no way they wouldn't accept Benny on the program. It would have been like telling the Queen the royal family had no space for her.

Over the next few weeks, Benny was quieter than usual. We all noticed he had stopped watching The Connection Game in the evenings and was more focused on his passion for sudoku and crosswords. One of the things I've always loved the most about being in a family is knowing things about my husband and children without having to ask. There's something special about those known knowns that are beyond words. And knowing Benny as well as we did, we could all see he was nervous about whether his application for the game show would be successful. He was trying to divert his attention elsewhere as a coping mechanism. That meant it clearly mattered more to him than he'd like any of us to know. So we didn't ask.

When the letter from the TV studio finally arrived a couple of months later, Benny ripped it open like a hungry animal. He speed-read the letter, and then handed it to me.

"Good decision. I knew they'd do the right thing," he said with his most charming smile. In that moment, I remembered why I'd fallen in love with him.

CHAPTER 4

Benny was due to appear on The Connection Game six weeks after the letter arrived, and he was invited to meet the show's producers for a pregame briefing a week before the show. He was so excited. All of us were. And we all resumed watching The Connection Game every evening in preparation for Benny's appearance. If you'd seen us watching an episode of that damned show during the happy six-week window before Benny's TV appearance, you'd have thought we were watching the world's most exciting sporting match rather than a game show. There was all manner of jumping on the sofa and shouting at the television going on from the moment the game show host arrived on stage. What geeks we were. Happy geeks though.

When I say happy, we still had our moments as all families do. One evening, Benny figured out a Connection Game answer within a matter of seconds, but Will disagreed with him. Will thought he had also figured out the answer, and that Benny was blatantly wrong. All hell broke loose.

"So your clues to connect are: Why beryllium? Why carbon? Why gold?" read Morgan Hill, the Connection Game's host.

"Got it!" called out Benny within seconds.

"Me too!" shouted Will just afterward.

"Did you get: Why selenium?" Benny asked with gravity.

"No way, Dad. I got: Why Materion?" Will responded with equal seriousness.

"Please explain, Will," said Benny.

"Materion is the one and only company in the world that engineers products with a combination of beryllium, carbon, and gold, so it's the common denominator and the answer," responded Will.

"Wrong, wrong, wrong!" answered Benny with more force than was needed. "The answer is: Why selenium? Because if you line up the chemical symbols for beryllium, carbon, gold, and selenium, what does it spell?"

"You are so off track, Dad. I know I'm right on this one," Will stated with a shake of his head.

"Will, just humor me and spell out the damn chemical symbols," Benny insisted.

"OK, but only because you need to be taught some humility. The symbols are Be. . .C. . .Au. . .Se," responded Will.

"Well done. And what have you just spelled?" asked Benny.

"Because," Will responded as the realization hit home that Benny was right as always. It occurred to me it must be hard to have a genius as a father. The best Will could ever do was occasionally keep up with Benny, but the rest of the time he was destined to be left behind in his intellectual wake.

"It's the right answer to the question because the answer connects the clues. Can you see where you went wrong?" Benny asked.

"I'm not interested in this bullshit, you old git," Will seethed.

"You know you are," Benny continued, ignoring Will's desire not to be corrected for once. "Your problem was your answer presupposed a fact that wasn't given as a clue, and thus can't be right. You wrongly assumed you were looking for a company specializing in using those materials."

"Not any company, Dad—the one and only company on planet Earth. Don't you want to know how I knew that remarkable fact?" Will asked. It was hard to watch as he tried to prove his worth to his father who was still trying to do the same thing.

"Not really, Will, because it's the wrong answer, and wrong answers don't impress me. If you work your way backward, you'll always find the truth staring you in the face from amid the data," Benny responded.

"We all work our way backward because of you on a daily basis. How about we work our way forward one of these days!" shouted Will as he stormed off.

Benny and Will eventually made their peace, but that dispute was the beginning of an underlying competitive tension between the two of them that would flare up again once we moved into the little flat.

The pregame interview arrived in no time. Benny met the show's producers and they talked him through what was expected of him on the big day. They told him to smile when the red light on his panel lit up as it meant he was being filmed, and they advised him to use the audience to his advantage. They explained that having the audience behind you counted for more than most contestants could fathom, and that the vast majority of Connection Game winners had first won over the audience. "Yeah right, I'm sure I'll need *their* help," was Benny's sarcastic response. Of course, the producers were shocked, but they didn't know who they were dealing with. Most people didn't.

That evening at dinner Benny was less positive than we'd all expected he'd be after the preshow interview.

"How did today go?" I asked.

"Average," Benny responded.

"Were they too focused on the showbiz side of things for your liking?" I asked.

"No, it's not that," Benny stated.

"What then?" I asked.

"They seemed too focused on my background as a computer programmer. The degree of their interest didn't fully align with the show's objectives," Benny responded.

In Benny speak, it was the equivalent of saying his gut instinct was giving him a warning. Of course, Benny had no gut instinct. His brainpower was so overpowering that all his other senses were at its mercy.

"Could they have been trying to learn a little about you as a person?" I asked having watched too many Connection

Game contestant interviews to mention. "Maybe it was about preparing to ask you a question or two on the show that leads to an interesting answer. It's so awkward when that smarmy presenter asks a question that inspires a nothing response from a contestant. Like the time he asked the pink-haired lady who colored her hair, and she told him it was natural."

"Possibly. Maybe you're right, Bell," Benny said after a long pause.

I'll never forget those words because I rarely heard them. For Benny to concede I may have been right about something meant he was possibly feeling unwell.

"Moi? How could a mere mortal like me possibly be right?" I joked.

We all laughed but that conversation has stayed with me.

The next week was filled with anticipation. Will had arranged for T-shirts to be made for the three of us with "Benny Connects" printed on the front. Yes, I think I mentioned, we were a family of geeks. None of us would wear them in public, but we wore them at home and Benny loved it. I can't remember seeing him laugh as much as during those wonderful few days before the show. He found it particularly funny when I pretended to be a cheerleader for him in the Connection Game audience.

"Give us a B, give us an E, give us an N, give us another N, give us a Y," I called out one evening after dinner. "And what have you got? Only a bloody genius!" I jumped up and down like a teenage cheerleader much to the kids' embarrassment.

"You're too good to me, Bell. Thank you for being you," Benny said as he grabbed my hand and twirled me around the kitchen before dipping me backward. It was a glorious moment.

Anyway, the day of Benny's big appearance on The Connection Game soon arrived. When he awoke that morning, he put on his best suit and combed his hair, which was a first in the time we were together. I'd grown accustomed to his mad-professor look, so it was somewhat of a shock to see what a good-looking husband I had when his hair wasn't hiding his face. He reminded me of Rock Hudson when he was young and handsome. I remember feeling a tinge of sadness at the realization Benny was ordinarily so focused on hiding his beauty from the world. It was almost as if he was scared the world would see him for what he was and judge him for it.

"You're looking mighty fine this morning, Mr. Basilworth," I said. "I'd say you are dressed for success."

"Thanks, Bell. Getting dressed up was a precondition for all contestants. We all need to dress like average contestants on a game show, you see," Benny explained.

"Average is a good look for you, honey," I responded, but Benny's mind was already elsewhere.

We drove Benny to the production studio that was located in West London. I can't remember Will and Wendy ever being as excited before.

"Dad, promise me you'll mention my name on camera," pleaded Wendy. "And make sure you engage in some coherent chitchat with the host, Morgan Hill. I love him! Remember, our analysis showed the contestants who chat the longest with Morgan are 56 percent more likely to win."

Wendy was sounding more like her father in those days. I was living in a family of probability-focused data nerds.

"I'll do my best, Wend," smiled Benny, "but here's hoping I'm an outlier today in every possible way."

We dropped Benny off at the studio and wished him luck. Then we parked the car and entered the studio via the front door with all the other audience members. We had family-member passes, which allowed us to sit in the few front rows. While we were waiting for the show to start, we glanced around and noticed that the average age of the audience was around sixty or seventy. I wondered why it was that old people got to have all the fun. I guess the rest of us are all so busy being busy that we don't get a chance to do the things we want to. Well, at least we got to sit in the Connection Game audience as young people alongside the old people. It was a small victory for the Basilworths.

CHAPTER 5

The contestants were called onto the stage by a deep booming voice, which sounded like it was coming from the heavens above. Three contestants sat down at the table on either side of the host's chair in the middle of the stage. Benny was sitting on the far left next to an older woman who reminded me of Miss Marple, and she was sitting next to a thin muscular woman around his age. Benny appeared unusually nervous for a man of his innate confidence. He was fidgeting with a pen and avoiding eye contact with everyone, including us.

"Please welcome our host, Morgan Hill, to the show!" the deep voice announced over the loudspeaker.

The crowd applauded and Morgan Hill ran out to the front of the stage more like a rock star than a game show host. He waved at the audience as though they were old friends he adored and then took his seat between the two tables of contestants. Wendy had always fancied Morgan Hill, and we had teased her for it to no end in our household. I remember Will calling her "Morgan Hill's one and only devotee" and asking her if she dreamed of connecting with him in private. We all laughed at Wendy's expense, and she was embarrassed. On TV, Morgan Hill shone bright as though he was born and bred to host a game show with his slicked-back hair, always consistent suntan, and teeth as white as a moon-lit sail. Watching him on stage in person, I could understand Wendy's perspective a lot more. There was something attractive about the way he prowled around the stage like a leopard ready to pounce. His charisma was palpable.

"Here we are, the last game of the most epic series yet," Morgan said to the audience with a beaming smile. "And once again we're here to find that needle in a haystack, that four-leaf clover, that white cat in a snowstorm."

A green light flashed above the camera that was filming the audience. One of the producers had told the audience earlier we should smile or laugh whenever the green light came on. So laughter it was. But the green light inspired forced giggles in all directions that seemed way out of proportion with the only mildly funny joke. It was like arriving overdressed at a party to which you were only invited to make up the numbers.

"So who will today's winner be? As a reminder, this series' contestants are playing as individuals rather than in teams as was the case in previous series. We've changed the rules to allow us to find an individual stand-out performer this year. Call us selfish, but we want to be entertained by the best minds this country has got to offer," continued Morgan. "So let's meet our resident geniuses. On my left we have David, an engineer with a love of athletic robots; Margaret, a writer who believes ice cream is better for you than vegetables; and Henry, a translator who has eaten scrambled eggs in every country in the world."

A green light, a few giggles, and applause followed. Like the well-rehearsed performer he was, Morgan Hill left just the right amount of time for laughter to follow everything he said.

"And on my right, we have Veronica, a pilates teacher who can do the splits when juggling; Rosemary, a teacher who can recite every word of Homer's *Odyssey* while drunk; and Benny, a computer programmer who has never been beaten by a *Times* cryptic crossword."

The audience applauded but I laughed. We'd all racked our brains to think of a suitably humorous introductory anecdote for Benny. It was a part of the Connection Game's written application process. Will had initially suggested we go with Benny's ability to remember literally everything anyone ever said to him, but we agreed Benny would be best to keep that one to himself as it was such an advantage in the game. "Walk in as Clark Kent; fly out as Superman," Wendy advised at the time. So we came up with the cryptic crossword idea. It wasn't as funny as we'd have liked, but we couldn't think of any funny facts about Benny. He was always so performance focused.

As we sat nervously in the audience, we knew what was coming next: the first question. Even my hands were sweating as we watched from the audience. Benny was still looking less than comfortable, and the three of us were finding his stress contagious.

"Right, to the questions," started Morgan with a toothy flash of his smile. "Push your buzzer if you know the answer. And remember, knowing you know and thinking you know are very different things. But then again, so are winning and losing."

And so the game began. You can find the episode on-line but suffice it to say it was a whitewash. Benny got every single answer right on only the second clue, which had never before happened in the show's long history. His poor competitors were systematically dismantled like flies having their wings torn off in front of the nation. I'll never forget witnessing Rosemary, the teacher who could recite *Odyssey* while drunk, wiping away a tear from her eye toward the end of the game as she stared at Benny in disbelief. Her face was so expressive, and she gazed at Benny as though he were an alien who had invaded from another planet. We could all see she would have preferred if Benny had stayed from whence he came.

When the final bell rang, Morgan Hill appeared perplexed and less chirpy than usual. He looked as though he wasn't sure what to do next.

"Well, that's a Connection Game first," he eventually said to the audience. "I think we just watched history unfold, folks. Well done, Benny, what an incredible performance! Are you human? To the rest of you, I'm sorry you were up against this intellectual beast. On any other show, you may well have had a shot at winning. You were just unlucky to be competing today, but the rest of us should consider ourselves incredibly lucky to have witnessed such an awesome display of agile brainpower."

His words of consolation didn't seem to be helping. The other contestants sat motionless and broken. Rosemary's face told us all she was planning to get drunk again, but minus the *Odyssey* recital. And David, the engineer with the love of athletic robots sat awkwardly like the kid no one wanted to pick for the sports team. I didn't fancy his chances of any success with the ladies, robotic or otherwise.

I was so proud of Benny in that moment. I gazed at his handsome face from across the studio, fascinated by how he would react to his win. He was no longer nervous, but he wasn't as elated as we might have expected, given he was already being talked about on national television as the best-ever Connection Game contestant. What did I see in his face? Was it embarrassment? Or maybe it was the look of someone who had shared a deeply held secret with someone they weren't sure they could trust. Yes, that's it. He was uncomfortable to have shared the full extent of his gifts with the world. At the time, this didn't make sense even knowing Benny as I did. But with the benefit of hindsight, I'd say Benny was, as always, one step ahead of the rest of us. The line between good and bad can be blurred, so he was right to be cautious after revealing the true extent of his almost-supernatural talents to a world full of judgmental people. He knew there were eyes watching him from directions we didn't even know existed. If only I'd understood this at the time.

The cameraman focused in on Benny as the other contestants were ushered off the stage like the unnecessary props they were. Margaret was bringing up the rear and didn't appear ready for her time in the limelight to end, so a security person put his rather hefty arm on her shoulder to encourage her on her merry way. She was indignant but her Connection Game story had ended. A few production staff then started repositioning the stage for what was to come next. It was clear they wanted a longer-than-normal winner's interview with Benny, given the unusual nature of his win. Morgan Hill moved closer to Benny and sat in a chair next to him.

"Benny, what an extraordinary achievement. Are you surprised?" Morgan asked with interest.

"No," Benny responded.

"Why not?" Morgan asked.

"I have a unique ability to understand patterns," Benny answered in his normal matter-of-fact manner.

"Clearly you do, and on a monumental scale," Morgan responded. "Is this pattern-understanding skill a part of your career, or is it just the way you are in general?"

"Yes to both your questions," Benny answered. "I'm a computer programmer, so I use these skills every day. And they also feature in my spare time. I'm developing some software that identifies patterns in people so as to calculate what their true beliefs are, as opposed to what they tell the world they believe."

"How's that even possible?" asked an incredulous Morgan Hill.

"The data reveals more than most people realize," Benny responded with confidence. "Most humans only show the rest of us what they think the world wants to see from them. What lies beneath is a largely unexplored world that we know less about than space. And it's as complex as space. So I decided it was time to create some technology to uncover and explore the data below the surface of the human condition."

Benny's honesty always was a weakness. Why did he need to mention that damned side project of his? The rest of us hadn't given it a second thought when we heard he was working on this latest software project. He was always doing something like that, so it wasn't newsworthy in the world of the Basilworths. But there he was, telling the whole world about it on national television. For a genius, Benny was sometimes inconceivably stupid.

"How fascinating. You are a man of extraordinary talents," Morgan Hill responded.

"Thank you," said Benny.

"We need to wrap up the show, folks," Morgan Hill said with a particularly toothy smile. "Until next time, remember: The truth is out there—you just need to wear the right glasses to see it."

The audience applauded as though a rock god had just completed an encore performance. And then they started slowly filing out of the studio while gushing over what a fantastic show it had been. One older lady near me described it as "The Connection Game equivalent of Glastonbury." As we waited for the audience members to leave, I noticed Morgan Hill had turned his microphone off while he was talking quietly with Benny.

CHAPTER 6

Will and Wendy were so proud of Benny after his big win. Instantly, he went from being an uncool geek in their minds to a global superstar with a devoted fan base. Will started calling him Champ, and Wendy's social media posts suddenly became inundated with photos of her and Benny hanging out. She closely monitored the number of likes she received and told us that a photo of the two of them laughing together once generated over two hundred thousand likes. There were clearly a lot more people watching Benny's win than any of us could have imagined.

Then there was the money, of course. Benny's one hundred thousand pounds of winnings meant we could move into the type of house we'd always dreamed of, a large townhouse on a posh street in Pimlico. Even though we thought we were wealthy people at that point, we didn't feel so wealthy once we'd agreed to pay the astronomical market value our new home commanded. London property prices have a way of always being too high no matter how much cash you have. "We just have to accept that there's a long queue of Russian oligarchs wanting to live in London these days," Benny stated when we were coming to terms with the cost of the property purchase. So despite the game show winnings and the fact Benny was doing so well at work, we had to stretch ourselves with a big wad of debt to make the purchase happen. You only live once, was our thinking. And besides, we calculated we would be able to pay off the debt in around ten years if Benny's income kept growing the way it had started to. It was all so simple to us at the time.

I have a wonderful memory of our first evening in our new Pimlico home. The movers had just left, and we were surrounded by boxes in every direction. Benny ordered Indian takeaway, which we ate sitting on a picnic blanket in the middle of our substantial living room. He poured some red wine for all four of us.

"Can you believe we live here?" Benny asked as he swept his hand in a circular motion like a king presenting his palace. "What a journey it's been for the Basilworths."

"I love it here!" I responded. "I'm grateful you showed the world what you can do on that TV show. It's the beginning of great things for us."

"The world ain't seen nothin' yet," Benny smiled.

"Take it easy. I'm happy with our almost-but-not-quite-famous status," I laughed.

"I want you to know that I understand you three are pretty special," Benny said as he held his glass up for a toast.

"Everything good that's happened to me, to this family, is because of you three. I'll always remember that."

"Are you talking to us?" I joked.

"I am indeed. You mean more to me than you'll ever know," Benny responded, addressing me alone.

"You too, honey. I'm proud to be married to *the* Mr. Benny Basilworth of Pimlico," was my all-too-flippant response as I took a swig of wine. It was unusual for Benny to openly express his feelings, so I was a little speechless at the time. But his words have stayed with me and have gathered interest ever since. I'll hold onto that precious moment until I'm in my grave.

Do I need to go on? What's the point? The world will keep turning regardless, and our story will continue hovering in its alternate universe. Oh, who cares. I'm finding this surprisingly therapeutic to talk about, and I'm still OK with you calling me Bell.

A couple of weeks later everything changed, and I mean everything. The proverbial shit hit the fan while we were asleep at the wheel.

I was at the checkout in the Pimlico Sainsbury's having completed a big food shop for the week ahead. When it came to paying, I pulled out my debit card and touched it to the self-service payment terminal as I always did. However, this time the terminal returned the error message "no funds available." How strange, I thought, as I knew that bank account held a sizable amount of our cash. Oh well, I reasoned, I'm sure there's a simple explanation. So I tried another card, and received the same error message. I then tried all our debit and credit cards, and none of them worked. That's when it became clear that something was seriously wrong. Much to the shock of the checkout assistant, I had to leave my shopping bags behind in an unceremonious pile of unpaid-for confusion as I left Sainsbury's in a panic.

I called Benny straight away. At the time he was working in the office of a telecommunications company in Holborn, helping them on a large technology project. Everything Benny worked on in those days was mission critical, so I almost never called him at work. It was like interrupting Picasso in the middle of painting his latest masterpiece.

"Hey, honey," he answered with surprise.

"Hi Benny, listen, I discovered while food shopping that none of our credit cards are working, not one of them. The last time I checked our accounts, we were reasonably flush so it's beyond strange. Can you please check our online accounts?" I asked with as much calmness as I could muster.

"Roger, boss, checking now," he answered.

Then Benny went quiet for longer than I'd have liked. I paced up and down the street while I waited. Passersby gave me a wide berth.

"*Shit*," Benny said quietly.

"What's happened?" I asked.

"All our funds are missing, and in their place our credit cards are maxed out with debt," he answered. Time stopped in that moment.

"How is that possible?" I managed to ask.

Benny again responded with prolonged silence as his mind computed the possibilities.

"Someone has stolen our identity. We've been the victims of a sophisticated online fraud," Benny concluded confidently.

Everything changed in an instant. All our savings were gone, and worse than that, we became the proud owners of far more debt than we could possibly manage.

I'm sure you're thinking: Why didn't the banks compensate you for your losses, or the government, or some other safeguard in the system? Because surely there's no way something like that could happen to innocent people minding their own business.

We thought so at first as well. But then, we discovered that this particular online fraud attack was so sophisticated that the perpetrators had made it appear as though we'd spent the funds ourselves on a series of extravagant house-related purchases after we moved to Pimlico. They had somehow managed to rewrite our banking statements to corroborate this picture of decadent financial mismanagement. They even fabricated the purchase of a fifty-thousand-pound luxury hot tub against our names. As a result, when we applied to the powers that be for compensation, we were laughed off. I remember one government official saying to me "Word to the wise: take it easy on the spending from now on—relying on debt always ends badly." It was so frustrating as prior to buying our new home we'd been the world's greatest savers. We'd vowed to steer clear of debt at all costs and had avoided buying many things we wanted just to stay on the right side of the line. And yet there it was: an ugly pile of debt sitting on our doorstep insisting it belonged to us. It was the type of nightmare you think can't ever happen in real life. But happen it did.

Our initial reaction was to think through every situation in our lives that could possibly be connected with this catastrophe to try to figure out who had done this to us. We believed identifying the culprit would allow everything to go back to how it was. Benny's ability to solve puzzles proved useful on that front, and his conclusion came fast and simple. Someone watching him win The Connection Game had surely concluded we were the perfect targets for an online fraud because we were wealthy. Benny had been presented as a successful technology professional, and the whole world knew he'd won the hundred thousand pounds on the show. He also suspected he was a particularly attractive target because he was so focused on helping others protect themselves in the digital world.

"It's the equivalent of shooting the largest elephant in the wildlife park," Benny explained sadly. "I'm just a trophy for these people's mantelpiece." I remember picturing a miniature version of my husband sitting motionless on a mantelpiece with the words "World's Greatest IT Expert" underneath. I wondered if that was exactly how Benny would like to be remembered.

That moment took us from hero to zero in one fell swoop. We were forced to sell our Pimlico home at a large loss in a falling market, which meant we weren't able to repay all of the debt attached to the property. The combination of the remaining debt and all the credit card debt we'd been kindly laden with in the online fraud was too much for us to bear. And to add insult to injury, Benny's career fell apart at exactly the same time. Some loudmouth started telling everyone in the IT world that the great technology expert Benny Basilworth had been the victim of an online fraud. If Benny could be personally attacked like this, what sort of value could he add in the corporate world, those same voices asked. The problem was people love to watch when someone is being crucified, and Benny's crucifixion attracted a particularly large crowd thanks to his Connection Game success. It seemed to us that the world was relishing every moment of our demise. We'd become nothing but gossip fodder for malicious tongues.

Our downfall was too much for Benny to cope with. He started believing every doubt his father had ever had in him was justified. So I had to watch my poor husband's self-esteem disintegrate before my very eyes. It was incredibly hard to watch. He quickly transformed from being the overly confident man who had wooed me without trying to becoming an insecure and scared man who jumped at every shadow. At times, he reminded me of a lost little boy, and I wondered if he was regressing to a time in his life when his father's criticisms reigned supreme in his mind. So it's no surprise Benny's career fell apart during this time. No one wanted to hire a loser, and that's how the world viewed him.

Shortly thereafter, we were declared bankrupt as we couldn't service our debt and our income had fallen to almost zero. We had officially run out of options in the most inglorious of ways. The party had ended, and the hangover had begun.

We quickly discovered a whole world of government services created to deal with people like us, people who had fallen through the cracks no one knew existed. Dealing with our living situation became a priority since the moment we were declared bankrupt, we were essentially homeless. The day before we had to leave our Pimlico home, we trudged across to the housing office in Westminster to apply for welfare housing. It was a long and lonely march through a part of London where everyone appeared to be wealthy and happy in their beautiful homes. Sounds of carefree laughter echoed throughout the streets as we searched for that wretched office amid the rows of rich townhouses. The joyfulness around us rubbed our noses into the reality that we were staring down the desolate barrel of homelessness. When we finally found the housing office, filling out the application form for welfare housing was one of the hardest things I've ever done. We were basically admitting on paper that we were screwed. There was no hiding from reality from that moment onward.

And that's how we ended up in the little flat under the stairs. The welfare housing department was running particularly low in housing stock when we applied, so we were all out of choices. We were to be given whatever was available, and the little flat was our only option.

"How do you feel about windows?" cautiously asked the clerk dealing with our application.

How did we feel about windows? Well, that little thing known as daylight would have been nice to have, but we were beyond nice-to-haves at that point. I knew then and there that what was coming next was going to be even worse than losing everything. We were still a long way from the next trough in our lives. Once the paperwork was finished, the clerk handed us a rusty key and an address in Hackney.

"I hope you will be happy in your new home, best of luck," he said with a forced smile, which seemed to mask his true feelings. I sometimes wonder if he understood where he was sending us. He had a kind face, so I want to believe he didn't.

CHAPTER 7

Why is it the good moments in life take years to build toward, while the bad moments happen in an instant? Angie used to say, we all go up by the stairs and down by the elevator. I missed her in that moment. She was then living less than two miles away in a nice part of north London leading a happily normal life with her husband Michael and son Jasper. And there I was at the rock bottom of the pile. Mind you, I was still glad it was me in that position rather than her. Somehow, I suspected I deserved everything that happened in my life.

Our next challenge was to move all our possessions from Pimlico to the flat using public transport. Hackney is only a few miles from Pimlico as the crow flies, but that day it seemed as though we were flying to the moon. Benny's photographic memory of the London transport map meant we were painfully aware we had a journey involving multiple transport changes ahead of us. Benny calculated the fastest route to get there would be to catch the Victoria line from Pimlico to Oxford Circus, then to catch the Central line to Liverpool Street, followed by an overland train journey all the way to Hackney Central. Even amid the ashes of our lives, Benny's mind delivered the right answers like a well-oiled machine.

Our personal belongings had been unceremoniously dumped in the front garden of our ex-Pimlico home. The new owners had shown us a kindness by not throwing out our stuff the day they moved into their new home. I could just imagine their horror when they realized our remnants remained stubbornly in situ when they were starting a fresh chapter in their lives. So they'd moved our things into the garden to give us enough time to swiftly evacuate them. However, it didn't feel like a kindness when we returned to Pimlico to discover the London rain had soaked all our possessions through. Everything I touched was cold, wet, and soggy, which was how I felt on the inside. I was tempted to leave everything we owned where it was, but Benny's practical side once again shone through.

"Guys, we'll need certain things like laptops, video equipment, important books, and anything that's worth a decent amount of money," Benny stated. "But I also calculate that we only have one opportunity to collect our things. The probability is very high that by the time we return for a second load all that remains will have been taken by the local street sleepers. You may not see them often in a place like Pimlico, but believe me, they're watching our every move and are planning their collection mission right now. Let's sort out what we need so we can collectively carry it to the next place."

The idea that we were being watched seemed ridiculous, but I reminded myself we had already been the victims of a sophisticated holdup, so anything was possible.

"Your dad's right," I said putting a hand on Benny's wet shoulder. "We can transport all we need in one journey, and we'll no doubt be thankful for it at the other end."

"OK, but I call dibs on not carrying the sofa on the underground," Will contributed without humor.

After some painful sorting through of the sogginess that was our lives, the four of us picked up all we could carry, which wasn't much, and trudged toward Pimlico tube station like homeless ants in need of a new, more forgiving nest. I was struggling to walk as I'd filled a backpack full of all our kitchen and cooking utensils, which weighed a ton. I knew the other three would be more focused upon salvaging our technology, so practical considerations like eating lay firmly on my shoulders. As we walked away from our furniture and bigger items, something inside me died a little death. Everything seemed to be happening in slow motion like a poorly made music video from an earlier time when people lived harder lives. Benny's and Will's faces were the most telling of our situation. Benny's face was angry, crumpled, and forlorn, while Will's was indignant and insistent that this was all a terrible mistake that would be rectified shortly. Acceptance was nowhere in sight for those two, but Wendy and I were more circumspect. Maybe not having the weight of a male ego to add to the weight of our wet bags made our fall from grace easier to bear.

"Dad, let me carry the small backpack, you've got too much on your shoulders," said Wendy with notable kindness considering the stress we were all experiencing.

"Thanks, Wend," answered Benny as he handed it over without a second thought. No one asked me if they could help with my bag.

When we finally made it aboard the tube carrying our even wetter and smellier bags, it was absolutely rammed full of people. Of course, it would be. We were standing in the open carriage section lined with seated people on either side. All Londoners know there's an unwritten rule that when you catch the tube you must never ever make eye contact with anyone else around you. It's like one of the Ten Commandments for locals. However, on that day—of all days—we were surrounded by a group of rowdy lads wearing fancy dress. It looked as though they were on a stag weekend and searching for a booze-fueled fight. I stared at my feet willing them to ignore us, but of course they didn't.

"Haven't you heard of movers?" one of them sniggered with a posh voice in our direction.

We all pretended not to have heard, wished not to have heard.

"You'd think there would be a rule against homeless people bringing all their smelly crap onto the tube," said another posh twat nearby and was followed by harsh giggles from the whole group.

I glanced at Benny. The Benny I used to know would have confidently addressed the situation in short order.

Maybe a clever word or a swift punch to the stomach of our attacker would have smoothly ended our torment, but the man standing beside me did nothing while our dignity was brutally attacked. So the comments kept coming, and we all shriveled up on the inside like snails trying to find protection inside our broken shells. Will finally turned around and re-acted on behalf of the family.

"Hey mate, that's the worst haircut I've ever seen!" he said to one of the main perpetrators.

It wasn't exactly a line from *War and Peace*, but it worked for the simple reason it made everyone in the carriage laugh, myself included. There was a woman sitting nearby who had one of those contagious laughs that set everyone else off. She reminded me of a hyena.

Will was empowered by the laughter, even proud of himself. I was also proud of him in that moment as it was the first time I'd ever seen him stand up like a man. But then he continued.

"I think your hair style is known as Mr. Floppy in barber circles," Will said with a broad smile. "But in your case we all know it refers to something else."

The woman with the loud laugh was off again, this time even louder. Our tube carriage had become a stand-up com-edy show, and Will was the star. He glowed with thunder. It was a moment of sweet justice amid the chaos, but something inside me was slightly uncomfortable with the relish with which Will was destroying our posh attacker. The instant our tormentor became the butt of the joke, he turned bright red and as scared as if he was the one being bullied. I guess that's the nature of all bullies—they're all trying to exude artificial strength to overcompensate for their low self-esteem.

When we finally arrived exhausted at the address of our new abode, we thought we'd made a mistake. The address we were looking for was Ground Floor flat, 198C Urswick Road, Hackney. We could find 198A and 198B Urswick Road all right, but 198C was nowhere in sight. All we could see were some poorly maintained stairs next to the world's smallest window. It was only around six inches high and ran adjacent to the level of the footpath. And then the awful realization hit us that number 198C was in fact located under the stairs, and that dreadful window was to be our one and only source of daylight.

"We can't live down there, guys. I've known zoos with better enclosures!" pleaded Will.

"You may well be right, Will, but in this moment, we are all out of options. Do you understand? We must walk down those stairs no matter where they take us," I explained. "And besides, all being well, we'll be out of here in no time."

Benny remained quiet but he gave me a look that as much as said "Yeah right!" I understood then and there that I was the family's last parental source of hope as Benny had officially entered the land of hopelessness.

We walked down the narrow wobbly steps that were all but hidden by the larger, more functional stairs above. We arrived at a narrow front door with the number 198C on it—the *C* was swinging lazily on its side in a rebellious act of independence.

Benny pulled out the rusty old key the housing office had given us and attempted to open the door. It didn't fit properly at first, but after some jiggling around, the door creaked open. A putrid smell bombarded our senses before we could take a step forward.

"Gross!" whispered Wendy. "Is there a dead body inside?"

"I'm sure it's nothing a deep clean won't fix," I responded holding my nose. "It will do us all good to get our hands dirty."

I fought all my instincts to run in the opposite direction, took a deep breath, and stepped forward into the flat. It was the darkest place I'd ever entered, so I searched quickly for a light switch. You'd have thought they'd have put a light switch next to the front door, but the wall was bare. I turned on my mobile phone light and continued to search. Eventually, I found a light switch a few yards inside the entrance corridor and turned it on. A bright science laboratory-type light filled the corridor and made my eyes hurt.

"Are you all right, Mom?" called out Will from the door entrance. The three of them were still standing outside gingerly perusing the new frontier before them.

"Welcome home, team," I smiled at them with all the positive energy I could muster. It nearly killed me.

CHAPTER 8

The little flat was true to its name. It was tiny. There was a small kitchen and living area to the right of the entrance corridor, and three small bedrooms further along the corridor. It was lucky we had salvaged next to nothing as there was no space to unpack anything.

The flat's incumbent putrid smell was slightly masked by the copious amounts of disinfectant I washed it down with soon after we arrived. I decided if we were going to live in squalor, we were going to live in clean squalor. God only knows what went down in the flat before we moved there because those underlying smells that greeted us somehow lived on beneath the overpowering aromas of the disinfectant. And they popped up at the most unexpected moments, usually when we were in need of love and support rather than a reminder we were living in poverty.

The lack of windows was a monumental issue. When you take access to daylight away from a person, you take away their life. Any scientist will tell you humans are like any other mammal in that we need access to food, water, and sunlight. They are all need-to-haves rather than the would-have-been-nice-to-have light had become for us. It's important to remember this when you hear the rest of our story as it partially explains how our relationship developed with that tiny slither of window that was our one and only connection with daylight.

We each reacted to life in the little flat in very different ways. In hindsight, I think it showed us our personalities in ways we hadn't experienced before. Maybe that's the silver lining to our story: We were forced to learn new things about ourselves. By then, I was the only one who ever left the flat out of choice, and the children only left when they had school to attend. Wendy was still going to the same school, while Will was attending a local state school in Hackney. And Benny never left the flat. Ever.

I remember one weekend evening around a month into our time there when our differences were particularly on display. I'd cooked the best pasta meal I could manage with the basic ingredients I was working with, and we sat down to eat dinner as a family. Benny had started drinking beer for the first time since we'd been together, and let's just say he was making up for lost time.

"How's everyone's day been?" I asked cautiously, knowing full well none of them had left the darkness of the flat all day.

"Fucking brilliant!" answered Benny aggressively. "It's been another day in paradise."

"We are a lot better off than many people in the world," I responded as calmly as I could.

"I'm sure you're right, honey, but how many down-and-out unemployed people were making the big bucks, winning the world's hardest game show, and working their asses off before it all came to nothing? I'll give you a clue. It's a small number known as zero," Benny bemoaned.

"All we know is what we've been through, Benny. We can't generalize about anyone else because we'll never be able to live their lives. We should do the best we can with what we've got," I said.

"Rubbish. It's all in the data. The software I've been working on tells me what people are thinking and believing behind the bullshit they spurt out into the world. And do you know what most people are almost always thinking?" Benny asked with a vein throbbing on his forehead.

Wendy, Will, and I remained silent. When Benny was like this, we often were.

"They're asking themselves what's the maximum output I can receive from this situation called life for the absolute minimum input I can get away with," Benny continued. "In the language Wendy's pea-brained, social-media-focused friends would understand that translates into: give me, give me, give me."

"Hey, my friends aren't pea-brained," responded Wendy without conviction.

"Dad's right, Mom, humans are shit," added Will.

"Will, please don't speak like that. There are good people in the world," I added without as much belief as I'd once had.

"Yeah Will, shuddup your face. What do you know about humans?" contributed Wendy who was sounding more like her father.

"Let's talk about fairness," continued Benny after taking another large swig of beer. "I've been a contributor, a creator, an outlier all my working life. I've been swimming against the current of human laziness and complacency for years. And yet somehow, against the odds, I'm the one who's barely surviving on social welfare payments from the government while living in this shitty little flat below street level. How is that fair?"

We'd all become used to Benny's ranting and raving against the world, but he was particularly upset that day.

"Dad, would you please stop moaning about yourself. It's getting old," said my increasingly fiery daughter.

"How dare you speak to me like that. Go to your room!" shouted Benny.

"Gladly. Anything to escape the whole 'poor me' thing you've got going on. I'm more mortified for the rest of us than for you because we have to listen to your draining crap on a daily basis!" screamed Wendy as she stormed off and slammed her bedroom door shut.

Benny was shocked but Will laughed.

"What's so funny?" grimaced Benny.

"What she said. It's funny because she's actually right about something. Before you can tell me to go to my room, I'll save you the trouble. Would you like the customary door slam? I normally charge extra for that, but this is a special occasion since it's just another evening of grimness with the Basilworths," said Will calmly as he retreated to his bedroom.

Benny and I glanced at each other, but neither of us knew what to say, so we sat in awkward silence.

Benny left the table and walked over to the tiny window that provided a view of nothing more than the concrete of the footpath and the passing feet on the street above. He stood on tippy toes to gaze through that damned window, which was more like a small strip of glass than a real window. I knew he was trying to focus on what was happening outside the flat to help him ignore what was happening within the flat—that had been his modus operandi ever since we'd arrived. He remained standing at the window without moving for the rest of the evening. It was strange even by Benny's standards. I wasn't sure what he was staring at, but I was certain it had to be more than the passing feet as they surely weren't worthy of so much attention. However, Benny was mesmerized by something, and after a while he even calmed down. He didn't turn back around to talk with me again all evening. I went to bed knowing we were in trouble.

CHAPTER 9

From that moment on, Benny stared out that window like a zombie all the time. And when I say all the time, I mean *all* the time—every minute of the day and most of the night. There was just something about watching those feet walking past on the street that fascinated him.

The rest of us initially welcomed the distraction as it calmed him down, and it gave him something to focus upon apart from releasing his ever-growing anger. But quickly it became an obsession. Benny placed a chair under the window that he would stand on so he could look directly at the passing feet. Even from his higher vantage point he couldn't see much apart from the shoes and socks of all the passersby, so the mystery of what was so bloody interesting continued to grow.

The more Benny stared out the window, the harder it became for the rest of us to communicate with him. It had become the elephant in the room. So eventually, after being ignored one time too many, I decided it was high time the elephant was introduced.

"What's so interesting about the passing feet, honey?" I asked while holding my breath.

Benny kept staring out the window for a few minutes without responding, so I thought I had zero chance of getting a sensible answer out of him. But I was wrong, as I was on so many things.

"At first, it was therapeutic to watch the rhythm of the passing feet," Benny began with a more rational tone than I'd heard in a long while. "You see walking is a perfectly cyclical motion based upon generating forward momentum from energy that was previously flowing in multiple directions. It's a beautiful movement when you understand how complex it is beneath the surface at a level we simple humans can't or won't see."

Maybe I was tired, maybe I'd just had enough. But this explanation, calmly delivered as it had been, annoyed me. Here we were, languishing as a family in the depths of despair, and my husband had decided to focus on the beauty of the fucking walking motion.

"Really? Is that why it's so important for you to stand on that chair like a mute zombie day in, day out?" I hissed.

"Honey, *honey*," Benny said as he stood down from the chair, "there's more to it than you think."

He almost seemed to have returned to being a seminormal version of Benny for a brief moment, so I decided to shut up and let him talk.

"Go on," I said.

"OK," he continued, "well, I started to notice things about the passing feet. At first, it was the type of shoes, and then it was the walking style and what it implied about the person. After a while, I started to get to know each pair of feet based on the facts presented to me from the window. You'd be surprised how much I've learned about the people out there, shocked even."

"I can confirm I am indeed shocked," I responded.

"And then when I allowed myself to see the big picture, I started noticing patterns behind the foot movements," Benny continued oblivious to my taunt. "Juicy, predictable patterns. That army out there needs better training as any formidable enemy would be able to find them by watching their foot movements alone. But then again, formidable enemies are hard to come by in a world that is so dumbed down."

"Army?" I asked with panic rising within me.

"We can talk about that another day," Benny responded. "But for now, I'm just asking you to believe me when I tell you I'm doing important work here. It may not look like it to you, but one day you'll understand. In the meantime, please trust me."

"Trust you that this is important work? You mean watching passing, sodding feet on the street?" I asked with incredulity. "Quick, let's call the UN and tell them we're working on the next big thing: foot-watching. I'm sure they'll send out help right away knowing full well that passing feet are one of the world's greatest risks right now."

OK, so maybe my sarcasm went too far.

"Listen Bell, I'm sorry for how I've been behaving of late," Benny responded with less anger than I expected. "I know I've been difficult to live with, but this is different."

"Different how?" I asked.

"Different real," Benny answered without a second thought.

"The only thing that's real here is your insanity," I threw at him.

"Oh great, I go and trust you with the truth and you react by throwing it back in my face," he responded sounding more like the angry Benny we'd become so used to.

"Seriously, I think you need to see a psychiatrist. No, more than that, I need you to see one, right now," I stated.

Benny sat in silence. I knew he was dodging my words by not letting them enter his mind. It was a classic Benny move when we disagreed on something.

"And the other thing I need you to do," I continued, "is to start applying for jobs. Living on social welfare payments just isn't enough. In case you haven't noticed, we are barely able to put food on the table. It's time to get off your sorry ass and start looking after your family." I was clearly running low on empathy at that point.

In response, Benny stopped talking and turned his back on me. Who could blame him? His wife had just called him insane and useless. He returned to staring out his beloved window at the feet who couldn't upset him with words or emotions. And the message I received loud and clear was that the window was already more important to him than I was. We were officially in marital trouble in a way we hadn't experienced before.

I stormed off, but there was no space to storm to anywhere in that tiny flat. In the preceding weeks, I had been regularly leaving our hellhole to go for long walks in the outside world, which had become the one and only place of respite for me. So that's where I headed that day when I needed space from Benny's foot-watching and whatever he was becoming. I slammed the front door shut and marched up those wobbly steps to freedom. It tasted sweet every time I managed to get away from the little flat, and I breathed easier straight away. I walked for hours that day, and with each mile I relaxed a little more. By the end of what must have been ten miles of walking, I returned home calmer and exhausted.

Benny was still in his zombie-like stance on the chair when I returned. He had gone back to ignoring my very existence. While I was out walking, I decided I should have a chat with the kids upon my return as I was aware they must be finding life in the flat just as hard as I was. They were no doubt in need of some motherly love amid the train wreck of our lives. So I approached Will's door, which wasn't quite shut. In more normal times, we had a house rule that you only needed to knock if a door was closed, so I pushed Will's door open without knocking and walked in. I arrived just in time to witness Will punching the wall in his bedroom. And when I say punching, I mean really whacking. There was blood everywhere.

"Will, take it easy there!" I exclaimed as I put my arms around him in the hug position.

But he pushed me away. He was furious about something.

"What's the matter?" I asked.

"You wouldn't understand, Mom," was all he could blurt at me.

"OK, let me guess. Does it relate to your father?" I asked.

He calmed down for a moment and nodded.

"Does it relate to the fact that your father has become a London Foot Guard, but appears to have confused the term with someone who stares at feet all day?" I continued.

Just like Benny, the only way through Will's armor was to crack wise, so a light touch was my best shot at starting a conversation. It worked. Will laughed, and I knew we'd then be able to talk properly.

"What's wrong with him?" asked Will seriously.

"He's a broken man who is trying to prove his worth," was the best summary I could come up with.

Will nodded.

"Has he done or said anything in particular that has upset you so?" I inquired.

"Yes. He asked me to join him on his stupid foot-staring mission. He said he'll teach me things others will never comprehend, things that will make me worthy, things that will allow me to follow in his footsteps," Will explained.

"Oh right!" I responded with shock.

"I don't want to be remotely like him, Mom. He's a raving lunatic," Will said in a moment of honesty.

"I understand why you'd think that," I responded as I hugged Will again, this time successfully. I could relate to Will's dilemma. Benny had become a living blueprint of how I didn't want to live my life.

71

CHAPTER 10

Somehow, in the midst of our despair we fell into a rhythm of sorts. Routine makes time pass by more smoothly regardless of the context, so time marched forward.

Benny avoided the rest of us whenever he could, which meant most of the day apart from mealtimes.

Wendy purchased a goldfish that had become her one and only friend in the household. From the moment the fish arrived, she spent most of her time in her room, and she talked with that damned goldfish more than the rest of us combined. One day, when I was about to knock on her door, I heard her utter the words "I wish I was in there with you" to her goldfish. I wished the same wish.

Will became an expert at playing the angry teenager. He split his time between punching his bedroom walls and listlessly watching TV like an inanimate piece of furniture. When I tried to speak to him all I received as a response was a grunt, or a nod if I was lucky.

And me, well, I viewed my time in the little flat as penance. I let my social life and my baking business evaporate to nothing as I was painfully embarrassed by the dire state of our lives. The idea of even spending time with other humans had become foreign to me. I tried to bear our situation as gracefully as I could for the children's sakes, but I only came alive during my opportunities to leave our prison. The outside world became my one and only source of possibility and freedom. So I left the flat more and more frequently, and I got to know the streets of Hackney better than I'd ever have imagined.

Over time, Benny established an unsaid truce with the rest of the family based on the overarching philosophy that the less he saw of us, and vice versa, the better. To say verbal interactions were at a minimum would be an understatement, but one day a flare-up between Benny and Will occurred in which the truce was voided. Benny had started writing copious notes about the passing feet and was becoming increasingly excited by something as he wrote. He was punching the air like he used to when he was watching The Connection Game on a regular basis. The rest of us knew not to ask questions as we didn't want to know the answers.

Will had just returned home from school. We all suspected he was being bullied as he had a black eye and was looking sheepish. Every time I asked him about it, all I received were conversation-avoiding subject changes. However, I knew that by changing schools Will had gone from being a top dog in the cool gang to residing well and truly at the bottom of the heap alongside everyone who was perceived to be an outsider. He was clearly hating it. His posh accent no doubt made him an easy target in a rough area like we were residing. It was no surprise his anger was getting worse. In hindsight, I shouldn't have let sleeping dogs lie—it was bad parenting. If I'm honest, having witnessed Will verbally attack our tormentors on the tube a few months earlier, I struggled to imagine him being the weak and vulnerable one.

As was generally the case in those days, Will sat down to watch TV without a word the moment he arrived home. But on this particular occasion, he diverted his gaze away from the TV toward his father who was getting more and more excited about the "data" he was working on.

"Can't you see what you've become?" Will finally asked through clenched teeth.

"Go on, tell me, oh wise one. What *am* I?" answered Benny with more than a hint of sarcasm.

"You're just a waste of big old space in every possible way," stated Will.

Benny appeared to be engaged in a rare moment of self-reflection while he contemplated Will's attack, but appearances can be deceiving.

"OK, I get it. You're upset, I'm upset, we're all upset," Benny responded. "But with all you know about me as a person, all those data points you've been privileged to gather throughout your life, do you really believe I would be wasting my time on a fool's errand?"

"I do think that, Dad, because you've become a fool," Will stated calmly.

Benny was floored for a moment. For a man of his fragile to non-existent self-confidence, it was a hard blow to his nether regions. He took a deep breath before responding.

"Remember when we used to play The Connection Game together and I was a few steps ahead of you with the right answer? There were many times then when you thought I was a fool as well, weren't there?" Benny asked.

It was obvious Will didn't want to answer anything in the affirmative, but he almost managed a head nod.

"OK. So the game I'm playing now is exactly the same as The Connection Game," Benny continued, "but it's far, far more important. More important than you could possibly imagine. Will, I'm your father and I promise you there's more to what I'm doing than meets the eye."

"I'm struggling to believe that," Will responded.

"I know you are," Benny said. "So let me prove it to you in the same way I've taught everything else to you: by showing you. Evidence trumps theory every day of the week. I'll show you the evidence and you can then make up your own mind."

Will grappled long and hard with this offer, and I hoped he would say no. The idea of Benny teaching Will how to become a zombie foot-watcher was like a nightmare to me. But it wasn't my decision.

"OK, OK. Show me the evidence, but don't expect me to become your crazy foot-watching partner," Will eventually responded.

"Understood, son," said Benny with a rare smile.

I prayed that conversation would come to nothing, but Will was true to his word and started watching the bloody passing feet with his father. Our nightmare was to continue. They each had matching chairs set up at the window for standing on. Initially, barely any words were exchanged between them, but Will stood there next to Benny watching intently regardless. I suppose Will was only following his father's lead, but I was surprised he continued with it for more than a few minutes.

Then the whispering started. Benny would point out the window and whisper something to Will who would then watch intently at whatever mad thing Benny had highlighted. I wanted to shout out at them that it was rude to whisper, and by the way, they were only watching passing feet. But I didn't want to upset the nearly empty apple cart, so I let it be. And I somehow rationalized to myself that it was a good thing Benny and Will were talking, or at least whispering, again. After all, they were father and son.

With each passing day, Benny and Will spent more and more time together at that damned window, and their whispering had evolved into a two-way street. Will had become actively engaged in whatever they were doing, and he was asking Benny questions. I could see his interest had been piqued. I wanted to warn Will about what curiosity did to the cat, but this cat didn't appear to care anymore.

My walks in the outside world were becoming longer and longer while all this was happening. Something about Benny and Will uniting through their foot-watching endeavors made the little flat seem even smaller, even more insane. I sometimes wondered if the walls were shrinking. And with only two of the four of us now firmly residing within the realms of reality, I was aware the ratios were turning on me. It struck me that our household had become split between those who walked and those who watched the walkers—the participators versus the observers. Having listened to Benny's recurring rants for far too long I was starting to view both sides as armies of sorts. If it came to a battle situation, I decided I would fight with the walkers—they were much more my type of people.

I wanted to call Angie to tell her about the nightmare my life had become, but I never did. I'd stopped calling her since we'd arrived at the little flat. What a terrible sister I was. Why didn't I trust Angie enough to share the truth with her? Catching up with her would have been so easy. She was working as a nurse at Great Ormond Street Hospital, only a few miles away. With minimal effort, I could have walked to meet her for lunch one day and told her about the wrong turn our lives had taken. But I chose not to. It's hard to explain why. I think I didn't want her to picture me as anything but the confident big sister she'd grown up with. In hindsight, maybe I had some ego issues of my own to contend with. So I bore my pain alone, and my relationship with my sister withered.

One day, in an effort to escape Benny and Will's frenetic efforts to pull answers inward through the window, I walked all the way from Hackney back to Pimlico. It was like walking back in time to better days. As I walked up our old street, I imagined that the past few months had been nothing but a bad dream and that our lives were still thriving like the good old days. However, when I walked past our old house, it was quite different from how I remembered it. The new owners had repainted the front of the house and had landscaped the front garden. There was a neat row of flowers on either side of the front path, which had been planted according to color with yellow flowers closest to the path, followed by red flowers, then purple flowers, and finally pink flowers. It presented as far more cared for than when we lived there. I sat down on the street and cried. The buildup of all the pain and torment I'd been through hit me like a ton of bricks and the tears wouldn't stop.

An elderly man approached me and put his hand on my shoulder.

"It will be all right, sweetheart," he said kindly. "You let those tears out and I promise you everything will get better. A nice girl like you deserves to be happy."

I thanked him through my sobs, but I wasn't so sure he was right. I still had to return to the little flat where the inmates were running the asylum. My happiness wasn't high on their priority list.

CHAPTER 11

As they spent more time together watching the passing feet, Benny and Will resumed talking to one another like they used to. Their father-son relationship was clearly on the mend. It was rare for me to hear anything they were saying beyond their urgent whispers, but one day their excitement led to them raising their voices loud enough for me to hear their conversation.

"Yes, we were right!" exclaimed Benny. "Brown Suede is indeed an Abnormal, but a predictable Abnormal. Knowing this information will help us explain where Blue Joggers and Red High Heels fit into the system. I suspect they are connected with Brown Suede in some way, although Blue Joggers is more of a mystery."

"Agreed," responded Will. "Brown Suede is the key connector in this group and knowing he's an Abnormal allows us to solve for everyone else on this list. I suspect Red High Heels is also an Abnormal, and now Brown Suede has been labeled we can easily solve for her with some more data. She should be walking past at seven o'clock this evening, and she may give us enough data to work with. I can't wait to see if I'm right!"

My heart sank. My husband and son were officially talking crazy talk, and there was nothing I could do about it. It was a disaster. At dinner that evening I decided to confront them about it.

"What on earth is going on with all the foot-watching you two are doing?" I asked in both their directions.

"Will and I are taking forward the important work I've previously mentioned to you," answered Benny, sounding more like a corporate spin doctor than my husband.

"Once again, what is this important work?" I asked, trying to keep it together.

"You wouldn't understand, Mom," contributed Will with typical teenager finesse.

"OK, assume I'm an idiot then. Break it down into simple English," I said.

"All right, that's easily done," responded Will. "Well, the simplest explanation is that Dad and I are solving important puzzles that need to be solved."

Everything remained as clear as mud to me.

"What type of puzzles?" interjected Wendy with apparent interest.

"Bigger puzzles than you're used to, Wend. This one's above your paygrade," answered Will with his best condescending big-brother smirk.

If there was one way to inspire Wendy's interest it was to tell her she couldn't do something, and Will knew it.

"Oh really? We'll see about that, you cheeky bugger," Wendy responded.

"No, we won't. This is something only Dad and I are qualified to do," taunted Will, knowing it was a checkmate move.

"Sod that. I'm joining you at the window tonight. I want you to show me what the hell it is you're doing no matter how mental it is," responded a fired-up Wendy.

One more domino was wobbling as Wendy had officially applied to join the foot-watching army. The ratios were conspiring against me as though they were preordained to side with the foot-watchers. A few tears welled up in my eyes, but I was beyond letting them come out. I wondered if Benny and Will would use crying as a data point in their "important work."

Benny and Will were back in position at the window straight after they'd inhaled their dinner. They were genuinely excited about watching the street for their expected data point, and their excitement was starting to colonize the limited air in the little flat. Admittedly, excitement is a better energy than the previous combination of depression and anger, but I was becoming more and more terrified of my foot-watching family.

Like a slow-motion car crash, Wendy pulled a chair over to the window and took her position beside Benny. He had now recruited one junior foot-watcher on either side. Benny stood tall on his chair like a tribal chief watching out for other tribes in the vicinity who may be dangerous. Once again,

I prayed common sense would prevail and Wendy would make a swift exit from the crazed scene. But she didn't. Much like Will's recruitment process, she initially stood quietly observing the passing feet on the street above. Then Benny and Will shared the occasional whisper with her to which she nodded with interest. Even I could see that their passion for whatever they were doing was as infectious as a deadly virus. Wendy was a sitting duck. I was sorry for both of us.

At around seven o'clock that evening, Will and Benny became excited and again raised their voices loud enough for me to follow what was happening. They were counting down to something.

"Four, three, two, one, and eureka!" shouted Will.

"There she is!" joined a euphoric Benny. "Red High Heels is walking up the street toward us with her typical urgency. Now, if she crosses the street in around ten steps, we'll have all the evidence we need to prove she's an Abnormal and is somehow connected with Brown Suede. You know you want to cross the road, honey!"

The three of them lurched forward toward the window like lost souls in need of redemption.

"Six steps, seven, eight, nine, and yes, there she goes across the street. Put it there, baby!" exclaimed Will while high-fiving Benny.

Even I could see Wendy was feeling left out during the celebrations. She put both her hands in the air to belatedly join in the high fiving action with both of them. If it weren't such a disturbing moment, I'd have been overjoyed to see the three of them bonding again as a family. But the reality was it was a ghoul show, and I had no intention of buying a ticket.

It struck me that one of the reasons Benny and now the children had become so obsessed with the passing feet was that feet are much easier to get to know and understand than people—they lack internal emotions so they can be explained by their external movements. Yes, my family was rejoicing in being able to find meaning in the foot movements because they were far more explicable than the inexplicable chaos of the human world. As these thoughts formed, I noticed a seed of empathy growing inside me. I quickly asked it to leave the building. It must have been the conflicted joy of watching the three of them celebrate together like a loving family. I reminded myself I was the last remaining sane person in the household, and I intended to keep it that way.

So Wendy officially became one of the foot-watchers that evening. And from then onward, the three of them became inseparable as a foot-watching team. They would stand at that window for long days and nights at a time looking for answers to their strange riddles. Sometimes I wondered if they were even taking toilet breaks. And I couldn't remember seeing any of them leaving the flat for weeks on end.

Around then, Benny instructed the children to take "a little time" off school to further their home education. In other words, he wanted them to stand next to him on their respective chairs to stare at the passing feet through our ridiculously small window. That was the education plan he thought would provide them with the life skills they'd need as adults. Of course, I didn't agree with him, but I was too tired to fight any more. So the kids left their schools without my input or agreement. That's how we rolled as a family in those days—my opinion was worthless.

As I watched on with growing unease, I noticed the three of them were starting to develop individual roles within their little team. Benny was the team leader and would focus on strategy development as well as team management. Will was the data analytics expert and was compiling copious spreadsheets of information he would in turn analyze to death. And Wendy soon became the audio-visual expert. She used her iPhone and laptop to create videos of the passing feet that she'd in turn analyze in slow motion and from different angles. Their team dynamic worked remarkably well. In fact, I'd never seen a team work together as such a well-oiled machine before. I watched on from the sidelines as they high-fived and cheered with increasing regularity. The pangs of jealousy grew inside me.

CHAPTER 12

Gradually, like an old pair of boots left at the front door that no one can remember who owns, I became an outcast in my own home. The bond between the three foot-watchers grew stronger with each passing day, and they all but forgot about my futile existence. My escapes from our prison by way of long walks continued to provide welcome respite, but returning home was becoming harder for me. I began to dream of permanent escape from the little flat, from my family, from everything about my life. Running away wouldn't have been hard since my family wouldn't have noticed my exit from their lives. I even constructed a rough plan in my mind as to how I'd execute my escape plan. It was so simple. I'd tell the three of them I was off to the shops and then I'd never return. I'd walk until my legs couldn't walk any further, and then I'd ring Angie just so I could hear her beautiful voice. I'd explain everything to her and ask for her forgiveness for losing touch. Beyond that, there was a gigantic void where my life had been, but I knew everything would be all right.

While this seedling of an idea was growing in my mind, another somewhat shocking development in our family dynamic emerged: the three foot-watchers were starting to have genuine fun in their demented endeavors. They could often be found giggling hysterically like Mad Hatters who'd founded their own exclusive tea party. I'm sure the little flat had never witnessed so much uncontrollable laughter before. It was hard for me to watch being the outsider I was—and it made me angry.

"Hey guys," Benny enthused with his minions one evening, "did you hear Blue Joggers bought his joggers from a drug dealer?"

"Ha, really?" Wendy responded.

"Yes, he's still unsure what they were laced with, but he's been tripping ever since," Benny delivered with a broad smile. The three of them laughed with a level of abandon I'd never seen in my family. They were almost pissing themselves.

"OK, I've got one," said Will through the laughter. "So we now suspect some of the Abnormals are thieves. Well, I've figured out the type of shoes those thieving Abnormals should all be wearing."

"Tell us," smiled Wendy.

"Sneakers!" beamed Will.

And those bastards were off again with their damned hysteria. With each rising shrill of laughter, I was silently screaming on the inside. I'd had more than enough.

What happened next was largely out of my control. I took off one of the trainers I was wearing and threw it as hard as I could at Benny's head. It connected hard on one of his cheekbones with a loud whack that echoed like a warning signal around the little flat. Benny turned around and stared at me in disbelief, as though I was an unpredictable wild animal who may attack again at any moment. He was spot on.

"Sorry, I thought I heard someone ask for a sneaker. I know feet and shoes matter more than people in this demented household, so I'll communicate through my shoes from now on. Did you understand the hidden message behind what I was saying then? You may need to analyze the data to figure that one out!" I shouted.

I had officially lost the plot. It's hardly surprising in hindsight, but I blush when I recall that scene.

However, things never turn out as one expects. Benny, Will, and Wendy glanced at each other, looked at my wayward trainer, and then back at each other. Then they resumed their hysterical laughter in their exclusive club. Rather than starting a fight as my subconscious had clearly intended, I was nothing but a source of light entertainment in the game they were playing. It was more fuel for my anger.

"I'm so glad my pain is funny to you three monsters!" I hissed.

Benny stopped laughing and eventually the children followed his lead.

"What's the problem, Bell? The three of us are only having a laugh," Benny reasoned as though I were the bad guy.

"The three of you! Everything revolves around the three of you, doesn't it? But what about me? Do you even remember me? Hello! Can you see me?" I shouted. "I'm your wife, I'm your mother. Nice to meet you by the way. And yet you treat me as an inconsequential stranger. Well, I've had enough!"

It was a welcome release to unload some of my stress despite the fact I expected no remorse from my robotic tormentors.

"Whoa!" responded Benny, looking surprised. "Hang on one pretty minute. Aren't you the one who accused us of being crazy? Didn't you tell us we are wasting our time here? How did you expect us to react when you attacked our important work without even understanding it?"

Benny's confidence had returned since the three of them had rebonded as a family, and with it came his innate ability to out-reason anyone. He'd been famous for it when he used to work with corporate executives who were used to getting things all their way. One of the big wigs at Google used to affectionately refer to him as "The Equalizer" for good reason. It was unlucky for me that he'd regathered this superpower at the very moment I was falling apart. The ramifications were monumental.

"I did say those things. But, for god's sake, my position in this family doesn't depend on me believing foot-watching is important work," I responded.

"Doesn't it?" Benny retorted with the stern look of a parent addressing a wayward child. "Oh, so what you're saying is that our values don't need to align with yours. Is that it, Bell?"

"No, we aren't talking about values," I answered. "We're talking about watching peoples' sodding feet walking past on the street. They are very different things."

It was too little, too late. Benny had already caught me within his web of words.

"But honey, you're making judgments about something you don't understand," Benny continued like a master chess player. "Your words don't align with the way Will, Wendy, and I view our work and the world in general. Would you like to understand what we are doing? Or would you prefer to judge your family without the facts?"

Despite sensing I was screwed, I quietened down to think hard in that moment. I'd witnessed what had happened to both the children during Benny's recruitment process, so I knew what would happen to me if I said yes. I weighed up the options in my mind. On the one hand, my husband, son, and daughter were sitting in front of me as a happy and loving family unit, asking me to join the family again after a long time apart. And on the other hand, three obsessive foot-watchers were sitting at that minuscule window trying to recruit me into their pointless Peeping Tom operation. What would you have done?

"OK then, I'd like to understand a little more," I finally responded like a lemming charging off a deadly cliff.

"Come over here and grab a chair," said the leader of the foot-watchers.

CHAPTER 13

"Just watch the passing feet for a little while, honey," instructed Benny as the four of us stared awkwardly out the little window. "And we'll fill you in with more information along the way."

It all sounded so simple, so innocent. The way Benny spoke about it, we could have been doing something as normal as learning to fish as a family. In hindsight, we were learning to fish—it was what we were fishing for that was the problem.

If anyone had been unfortunate enough to gaze down into our tiny window that day, they would have witnessed an entire family of four standing on chairs staring through a minuscule window at the outside world. A psychiatrist would have had a field day. At first, I was angry with myself for joining their freak show. I stared out that damned window as instructed but all I could see were shoes on feet passing by. I wasn't struck by the epiphanies the other three had experienced. I felt like an idiot. But then, I decided to accept the idea of watching the passing feet for a few short moments as I was so tired after all the drama. If I could watch TV, I reasoned, I could watch a foot show. So I stopped watching the individual feet walking past the window, and I allowed my focus to zoom out to take in the whole scene. I think the technical term is: I zombified.

That's when it happened. I relaxed into the foot-watching. And as I relaxed, I started to become hypnotized by the rhythm of the passing feet. Those feet could have been a pendulum in Benny's hand for all I knew, but I didn't care anymore. It was like falling into the most wonderful deep and restful sleep after a long and stressful bout of insomnia. It was a blissful experience. No longer aware of what I was doing, I heard a voice whispering to me. It sounded like it was dancing in through the window from the street above.

"Honey, do you see what we see? It's beautiful, isn't it?" whispered Benny standing right beside me.

I nodded.

"When I first allowed the rhythm in, I was in awe like you are now. But there's more to it than relaxing into the flow," Benny whispered. "There are thriving complex patterns out there, patterns that reveal hidden truths—truths that are far more important than most people can imagine."

Again, I nodded as though I was under a spell.

"You may recall I told you there's an army out there. Well, I wasn't joking," Benny continued. "Wendy, Will, and I have developed a system to identify the difference between normal and abnormal foot movements, and in doing so we are gradually uncovering who's in the army."

Benny stopped talking for a moment. Maybe he was trying to assess if I was buying into whatever he was peddling. Crazy as it sounds, I was. I nodded on cue.

"Once we've finished the important job of identifying who's in the army, we'll focus on uncovering exactly what they are all doing," Benny explained. "Suffice it to say, we believe whatever they are engaged in is a big deal that affects the safety of all Londoners, including us. Do you understand why our work is so important now? All of our lives depend on our winning this game, I mean, solving this mystery."

Benny may as well have directed the question "Am I worthy?" to his father. Even amid the chaos of our lives, it was obvious that was the subtext to everything he was doing. But I was his wife, and I needed to give him the right answer regardless of how hypnotized I was at the time.

"I do understand, honey. Thank you for explaining it to me," I responded in an attempt to take the high road, or rather, to avoid being alone on the low road.

From that moment on, I was a member of the team again. I'd be lying if I said it wasn't great. To be reunited with my family was like having my heart and soul reinserted after a long absence. Forgiveness—for each of us—arrived much faster than I'd have imagined only days earlier. Benny and I were talking again, albeit mainly about foot movements, but I didn't care. And Will and Wendy were having fun with each other, and with us. We were soon closer as a family unit than at any time I could remember, even during the good times before the little flat. Yes, we were still living in a dire situation, but we had dug ourselves out of the biggest hole we'd been languishing in: our lack of love for one another.

The one thing I remained uneasy about was Benny's stubborn insistence that the children continue their homeschooling. I didn't agree with him. Like their father, they had become people-fearing cave dwellers who never left the flat. It had been months since they'd last seen daylight. I couldn't believe that living motionless in a dark dungeon was a healthy way for any child to grow up. I tried to reason with Benny, but he was resolutely in favor of them staying at home.

"Honey, surely it won't affect our work if the kids were to attend school," I implored. "After all, school only takes up a few hours a day on weekdays. They can still do their other work in the mornings and evenings. Most of the key foot movements are in the morning and evening anyway."

"But that would mess up our analysis of the lunchtime foot movements," Benny responded with a shake of his head, "If we're going to solve for the rest of the Abnormals in time, we absolutely need that data. Sorry darling, it's out of my hands."

And so Will and Wendy were to be educated by the passing feet. It was far from ideal, but that's the case for so much of our story, so much of most people's stories. I accepted the situation for the greater good of our family remaining together, but I did wonder what Benny's reference to "in time" meant.

My joining the team got Benny thinking about team movements, and not the digestive variety. It was as plain as day that I was the only one in the team who enjoyed leaving the flat, and actually walking. In contrast, the other three had become inert and weak in the preceding few months of standing motionlessness at the window. I suppose it's the same whenever a new team member joins any highly functioning team. The manager needs to assess the new arrival's strengths to ascertain what they can contribute that the rest of the team can't. And in my case, it was obvious I could address the team's mobility challenges. So it was decided that I would become the team's eyes and ears on the street, the source of all data that was unavailable from the limited gaze of the flat's window.

Everyone was excited. Benny, Wendy, and Will believed my role in the team could become a game changer since they were in desperate need of more data.

"Honey, you couldn't have joined us at a better time," enthused Benny. "The data gaps are emerging faster than we can plug them, so we need new surveillance, new perspectives to stay ahead."

"It's wonderful to be in a team with you three," I responded.

Benny looked at me more like he used to from that moment onward. Being ignored by your family is a brutal experience, so to be reunited with a family who was celebrating all I could bring to the table was a godsend.

So everything was back on track, albeit the world's most unusual track. Unbeknownst to us at the time, we were building a nest within the eye of a monstrous storm. However, ignorance is bliss, and we were due to experience a little more of that joyfully ignorant time together.

CHAPTER 14

You'll no doubt want to understand whether I believed there was indeed an army of Abnormals planning something sinister before our eyes. Well, first consider the alternative. If, in fact, everyone walking past our window was perfectly normal then that meant my husband was totally insane, and my children and I weren't too far behind. It would have been a tough pill to swallow. Putting the alternative aside, my eyes were wide open from the moment I joined the team. While I was prepared to willingly suspend my disbelief on behalf of my love for my family, there was also something deep inside me searching for the truth. I guess that means I wasn't a true believer when I was brought into the fray, but that soon changed.

One day, only a few days after my joining the team, Will became excited by some data analysis he'd been working on.

"Guys, we've been focusing on the wrong Abnormal!" Will cried out. "The answers are all here in the data."

Benny glanced over Will's shoulder so he could see the data Will was referring to.

"It's here, Dad," said Will as he pointed at a line in his spreadsheet. "You can see Red High Heels' movements are as abnormal as the rest of them, but the problem is they are too highly correlated with Blue Joggers' movements. It wasn't obvious using the shorter-term data, but now we have more data to work with, check out what happens to the correlation coefficient."

"Whoa, I see," joined Benny. "Well done you, that's huge. And how do you know Red High Heels' movements depend on Blue Joggers as her key determinant, rather than the other way around?"

I was beginning to understand their statistics speak, but only just. I knew we could never socialize with normal people ever again.

"Good question," answered Will beaming with confidence, "and the answer is, drumroll please . . . because Red High Heels always appears before Blue Joggers. My model takes human biases into account, and if there's a recurring pattern of one input consistently leading another, the data shows it's extremely likely the leading input is the follower. You see humans who are trying to manipulate other humans will almost always try to distract them before the real action starts. And that means creating the illusion you are the leader when in fact you are the follower."

Benny again perused Will's work and nodded.

"Clever, Will. Your work on this is remarkably similar to the software I've been working on that uncovers biases to reveal true human beliefs. I can't believe you came up with this by yourself," Benny enthused.

"I've been watching the master at work," smiled Will.

Benny put his hand on Will's shoulder, and the two of them connected in a beautiful father-son moment.

"So if you're right, Blue Joggers is the second most important Abnormal, and Red High Heels could be a red herring to throw us off the scent. These people are impressive, aren't they?" asked Benny, shaking his head.

"Very," agreed Will.

"OK, this information changes everything," responded Benny with managerial authority. "What I propose is a two-step evidence-gathering process to test Will's thesis. Step one: we use Will's longer-term data to predict Red High Heels' movements using nothing but Blue Joggers' movements to guide us. If Will's data is right, we should be able to predict her movements with at least 90 percent accuracy."

"Ninety point five percent accuracy," added Will.

"Indeed," Benny continued. "And step two: we gather more data about Blue Joggers, much more data than we have access to from our limited vantage point in the flat. That means it's almost time for Bell's inaugural street data-gathering mission."

Pardon my French, but shit got real in that moment. My heart raced at the mention of my mission. There was no time to dwell on my impending career as a street-stalker though, as the team swiftly prepared for step one in Benny's plan. The efficient machine my family had become was quite something to behold.

Will started trawling through all the data they'd collected on Blue Joggers; Wendy watched the video footage she had of both Blue Joggers and Red High Heels walking past the flat; and Benny started computing the movements and timings both Blue Joggers and Red High Heels needed to show us to prove Will's theory correct.

In a matter of minutes, Benny concluded that if Red High Heels walked past our house at quarter to four that afternoon, and Blue Joggers crossed the road walking away from our flat at a quarter past four, then that part of our puzzle was solved. If that happened, we could confidently say Blue Joggers was directing Red High Heels movements, although the reason would remain unknown.

The excitement in the air was palpable, and the high fiving was running out of control. It was a wonderful Basil-worth family bonding moment to treasure.

A question bubbled up into my mind amid the excitement. It had been niggling at me from the moment I'd joined the foot-watchers, but it was the first time I was confident enough to ask about it.

"Hey guys, I'm concerned we may be missing something here," I said, aware of the growing gravity of each and every word I was using.

Everyone stopped what they were doing and stared at me with expressions that made it clear it had better be important.

"We are basing all these theories on the type of shoes each of these people are wearing," I continued, "but no one wears the same shoes every single day. What happens if these Abnormals decide to wear different shoes on different days?"

It wasn't exactly worthy of a Nobel Prize, but I was proud to have potentially saved us a lot of wasted time.

"Mom!" Wendy exclaimed while shaking her head. "As if we're that stupid. We've been videoing each foot owner for months, and we've been analyzing the footage with some basic software called Movement Matching, which identifies people based upon the way they move. We just named each of them after the first pair of shoes they were identified in to keep it simple."

With Wendy's feedback, I no longer felt remotely intelligent. In fact, I felt like a right dunce as my son gave me a sympathetic look that translated into: "Oh bless, she thought she was helping." I resolved then and there to show all of them just how valuable I could be. I'd be the best damned street-stalker ever to have lived, and I'd supply them with more data than they could dream of.

CHAPTER 15

We were all in position at the window ready for Red High Heels' expected afternoon arrival well ahead of time like a sophisticated army unit engaged in a top-secret, undercover mission. Benny peered through a pair of binoculars at the window while communicating with military hand gestures, Will crunched some Abnormals' data, and Wendy positioned her laptop and iPhone so she could video the street at multiple angles. I was only observing, but I knew my time in the sun was approaching.

"Dad, there's something we should look out for when Red High Heels arrives," contributed Wendy. "The video footage shows she has carried the same shopping bag on five separate occasions. Wouldn't you use a handbag to carry your regular items?"

"Good point. Well done, Wend," responded Benny. "This information raises the possibility she's more than a red herring and may have a courier role to play as well. Let's investigate that theory once we have the relevant street data."

Whenever I heard anyone refer to gathering street data, I understood they were discussing my impending role. I'm not going to lie, when I started picturing myself walking the streets as a data gatherer, I became quite excited. There was something seductive about the idea of following others around when they didn't know they were being followed. Who cares if the invisible woman comes to dinner, I thought, as long as she only shares her findings with the rest of her kind. And in that moment, I officially became a believer in whatever the hell it was we were doing. My head and heart both agreed we were indeed doing important work—and I trusted them both.

While the others prepared for Red High Heels' impending arrival, I googled "how to follow a person without being watched." To my surprise, I found a huge number of articles on the subject. I wondered how many people in the world were out there tailing people on the streets at that very moment. Maybe the entire human population was doing nothing but following one another in ever decreasing circles. As I read through multiple articles on the subject, I made copious notes to ensure the important information sank in. I've still got the list I made that day—here it is:

> 1. Dress appropriately—avoid red and black as it attracts attention. Go with neutral colors like gray and green. Hooded jackets/jumpers are particularly effective at hiding your face when required.

2. Always wear some type of disguise and carry another more extreme disguise with you. Sunglasses and caps are a great starting point, while wigs are worth carrying with you.

3. Carry an empty bag with you at all times—people tend to recognize others based upon what they're carrying rather than what they're wearing, so by dumping an empty bag you can convince most people you are a different person.

4. Once you have spotted your target, walk ahead of them for a while, then gradually drop back behind them by walking at a leisurely pace. Once you are behind them, keep them within sight.

5. If your target stops, keep walking, and find an excuse to enter a shop or stop for another reason up ahead until they are in front of you again.

6. If you are seen by your target, remain calm and keep walking. Once you find a suitable place to abort the mission, step out of view. Even if you are hiding, always pretend you are reading a book or talking on your mobile phone. Always assume your target will find you and prepare for that scenario in advance.

7. If your target finds you and approaches you, create a diversion. For example, pretend to answer your phone and walk off in a hurry in response to an apparent request from the caller. Avoid engaging with your target at all costs.

I memorized my list and put it in my pocket. Little was I to know there was a lot more to learn about following someone unnoticed. Google made it sound so simple.

"Mom!" called out Wendy. "Get in position! We are approaching the sixty seconds countdown to Red High Heels' expected arrival."

I joined Wendy at her technology hub. I was amazed by how refined her surveillance system was using nothing but hers and Will's basic laptops and mobiles. Even though we were below street level, Wendy had set up cameras that allowed her to watch what was happening from all directions on the street above. She'd obviously learned all this on the job as I couldn't remember her showing any remote interest in technology before, apart from texting on her mobile phone.

"Which camera should we be watching?" I whispered.

"Camera two is likely to give us the best picture," Wendy responded. "Will's laptop is connected to it, so you'll get the best view by watching from over there."

I tiptoed over to Will, who was watching his laptop intently.

"Any sign of her?" I whispered.

Will shook his head, but I could tell he was still viewing me as more of a liability than an asset when it came to the real work.

Benny started to count down out loud.

"Ten, nine, eight, seven, six, five, four, three, two, one . . . " Benny ended with an emphatic thumbs-up.

"And we have her!" called out Will. "She's on camera two now. She's around twenty yards away approaching from the south."

Benny joined us at Will's laptop.

"Who's that with her?" Benny asked as he pointed at a tall man walking beside Red High Heels. "Wend?"

"Hang on. It's Black Business Shoes!" Wendy responded with surprise.

"What on earth are they doing together?" asked Benny.

"No idea," responded Will. "But I note Red High Heels is carrying a normal handbag with her today."

"Yes, interesting," responded Benny.

I watched Red High Heels and Black Business Shoes walk past us. They were nothing more or less than the owners of four feet who were making their way up our street like any other humans going about their daily business. And yet, to us, the foot-watchers, their movements had important meaning. They had become players in a game we didn't understand but needed to win. And it was only by winning the game that we could prove we were once again worthy of a normal place in human society. I was struck by the contrast of perspectives, and for a brief moment I wondered if the four of us had lost the plot entirely.

Once Red High Heels and Black Business Shoes were out of sight, Benny initiated an unusually affectionate group hug.

"Well done, team. We're now halfway to proving Will's theory correct. You're all legends," he said with genuine warmth.

All my doubts once again evaporated. All I can say is I trusted my husband again at that point, and being united as a family meant everything to me. Besides, it was beyond compelling to watch Benny count down Red High Heels' arrival to the second. That was proof enough for me that we were on the right path. I'd remind myself of it many times thereafter.

"Guys," continued Benny, "we have around half an hour before Blue Joggers' expected arrival. Let's use that time to analyze the data on Black Business Shoes. I want some working theories as to where he fits in."

"Roger," responded Wendy.

Will and Wendy again launched into their respective work with finesse well beyond their years. It was clear Benny's homeschooling strategy wasn't harming their progress. I continued my stalking research online, and in short order it was nearly quarter past four.

"Any progress on Black Business Shoes?" asked Benny.

"Negative," answered Will. "We don't have enough data on him to draw any firm conclusions, and the data we do have is confusing."

"Confusing how?" asked Benny.

"Well, he has been seen with both Normals and Abnormals, and his movements are remarkably irregular," responded Will.

"OK, let's keep him on close watch, team. He sounds like trouble," concluded Benny with gravity.

"Dad! Look at camera one!" called out Wendy all of a sudden.

"Shit. Blue Joggers is a minute early," responded Benny after checking the camera. "And he seems to be in a hurry today. Wend, please connect with camera three for a clearer visual."

"Got it," responded Wendy.

We all crowded around Wendy's laptop to watch Blue Joggers' approach. All I could see was a shortish person wearing a hoodie walking fast toward the camera. I tried to gauge what he looked like beyond his blue joggers, but he was nondescript in every way. I was immediately reminded of my googled advice about how to remain unseen on the streets.

"Five, four, three, two, one," Benny counted down again, "and . . ."

Nothing happened. Blue Joggers kept walking past our flat, but he didn't cross the road as we expected and needed. My heart sank for Will, for Benny, for all of us. I knew how important it was for us to be right on this. The mood in the flat nosedived as the team digested our failed mission and defunct theory.

Benny patted Will on the shoulder in a heartwarming gesture despite his obvious disappointment.

"It's OK, team. Most theories take multiple tests to be proven correct," said Benny calmly. "We'll get there."

"Dad, my motion detection software shows Blue Joggers was walking 18 percent faster than his previous approach-speed average," contributed Wendy. "That's strange, wouldn't you say?"

"It is indeed," answered Benny in deep thought.

CHAPTER 16

After a few days of collectively licking our wounds, Benny called a team meeting.

"Guys, although we didn't prove our theory about Red High Heels correct, it's become apparent that we desperately need more data if we are to make progress. So Bell, we'd like to ask you to head out for your first data-gathering mission," said Benny as though I were a soldier being called onto the battlefield.

"What, now?" I asked aware my voice squeaked like a scared schoolgirl.

"No, tomorrow," Benny answered.

"Sure, I'd love to," I responded with excitement.

"Tremendous," Benny said. "While we were initially focused on learning more about Red High Heels and Blue Joggers, for this mission we'd like you to learn more about Black Business Shoes. His role is a true mystery at this point, and we think it's better you start with a less-than-critical mission."

"Understood. So what sort of data would you like gathered?" I asked, knowing full well that the subtext of Benny's comment was: "We think you're an idiot, so we're not trusting you with the serious work just yet, honeybun." I'd show them.

"We'd like to know where Black Business Shoes goes, when he goes there, and anything else you notice that strikes you as important," Benny explained. "Go with the flow and let him reveal his secrets to you. But please remember everything. Write it down if you need to, take photos, record videos, whatever you need to do to capture the data. The more details, the better. And please assume *everything* is important!"

"Assume everything is important" could have been the anthem for Benny's life at that point. I wasn't convinced it worked as my anthem though.

"OK, that all makes sense," I responded. "One more question. How will I recognize Black Business Shoes?"

"Mom!" called out Wendy, once again as if I'd asked everyone how to suck eggs. "We'll tell you who he is. We'll watch him walk past on our cameras, and then we'll signal to you when you can safely leave the flat without being seen."

"Oh, of course, that works for me," I responded, scared to ask any more stupid questions. I excused myself and went to bed early that night knowing everything was about to change for me.

The next day rolled around, and I rose early to prepare myself for my mission. I dressed in jeans and a gray jumper with a hood. I had a cap and sunglasses at the ready, and I carried a bag that only contained a fanny pack homing my more extreme disguise, which was an old Dolly Parton wig I'd used for fancy dress on a number of occasions. The outer bag was simply a shell ready to be dropped if needed. I was as prepared as any Google-trained street-stalker could be, so I joined the rest of the team at their stations, which I suspected they had manned all night.

"Morning, Wend. Any developments this morning?" I asked.

"Not yet," answered Wendy flatly. "Will thinks there's a decent chance Black Business Shoes walks past with someone else at around eight o'clock, so in around an hour."

"Five past eight is my best guess," called out Will.

"With someone else?" I asked.

"Yes, all the data we have on Black Business Shoes was gathered when he was in the company of others, which is unusual. He was sometimes accompanied by Abnormals, sometimes Normals, and sometimes Unknowns. That's why he's so interesting," explained Wendy.

"I see," was all I could say.

I sat quietly during the rest of the countdown to Black Business Shoes' impending arrival as I was conscious not to say anything else less than useful. In desperate need of a diversion, I gazed outward at the passing feet and started to relax. By then, the rhythm of the passing feet always improved my mood.

"We have a visual on Black Business Shoes!" Wendy called out.

I sat upright as though my name had been called out in assembly at school.

"He's approaching fifty yards from the north," continued Wendy. "At his current walking speed he'll be in front of the flat in forty-five seconds. Mom, that means you should be ready to leave the front door in one minute on the dot."

With a silent nod, I positioned myself at the front door and waited. It reminded me of playing hide-and-seek as a child although I wasn't sure if I was the hider or the seeker. I watched the timer on my mobile countdown to zero.

When my time for action arrived, I slowly opened our front door and emerged into the daylight as a nondescript woman going about her all-so-normal business. I glanced around, but, of course, I couldn't see anyone since our flat was a level below the street.

Aware Black Business Shoes could be getting away from me, I lunged toward the rickety steps ahead of our front door. However, as I pushed off the first step something tightened around my neck, and the next second I was lying flat on my back at the foot of the stairs. It was terrifying! My racing mind wondered if Black Business Shoes had somehow preempted my tailing mission and had lassoed me to stop me in my tracks. However, then the awful truth hit me. In my haste, I had clumsily allowed the bag strap, which was hanging around my neck, to become caught up in the stair railing. As I'd stepped upward on the step, the entangled bag strap had yanked me back down to earth. I had no one to blame but my stupid self.

Upon realizing my mistake, my first reaction was to check if Benny, Will, or Wendy had witnessed my embarrassing error. I prayed they hadn't, but then I remembered Wendy's bloody cameras could see every angle. I was mortified.

I regathered myself and decided to rectify the mission. Quite frankly, the idea of reentering the flat with no news beyond the fact I'd tripped myself up on the steps was too much to bear. So I climbed the stairs as fast as I could and headed in the direction Black Business Shoes had been walking. There were a number of people walking up ahead at around the spot where I thought Black Business Shoes should be by then. I broke into a run to catch up with them.

As I neared the group of prime suspects, I slowed down to a fast walk and searched around for a pair of black business shoes. However, every single man in the vicinity was wearing the same damned, black business shoes. Why are men so boring with their shoe choices anyway?

What would Benny do in this situation? I asked myself. And one word descended upon me as though from above: data. Of course. He'd gather data that he could use to identify the right black-business-shoe owner. So I glanced around at all the black-business-shoe owners nearby of whom there were four. There was a man of around sixty carrying a newspaper while walking with a thoughtful expression; a man of around twenty-five with slicked back hair walking fast as he gazed at his mobile phone; a man of around thirty-five talking with a stressed tone on his phone; and a man of around fifty carrying nothing and walking in a carefree manner.

What did I know about Black Business Shoes? I pondered. I recollected everything I had gleaned about him from the foot-watchers. The first data point was he was social: almost all the sightings to date had been of him with another person. And the second data point was he had been spotted with Red High Heels, whom I suspected was a younger woman. That suggested to me that Black Business Shoes was most probably a younger man, although I'm not sure now why I concluded that. Without further thought, I excluded the sixty- and fifty-year-old men on the spot.

The next thing I needed was a data point to steer me toward one of the two remaining contenders. So I approached the thirty-five-year-old, and attempted to listen into his phone conversation.

"For god's sake, why would Miriam say that?" I could hear him asking whoever he was talking to. "The members of the public aren't idiots. Maybe she's forgotten that after all this time in her ivory tower." He was genuinely angry, or at least a talented actor.

My gut instinct screamed out to me this was Black Business Shoes in all his glory. He was anxious like a man would be who was at the center of some serious shit, and his phone conversation sounded too rehearsed to be real. So I locked onto my target. My first street-stalking mission had officially begun. I was exhilarated.

CHAPTER 17

After following my target for a couple of streets, my online research suggested it was time to overtake him, so I sped up like the diligent street-stalking student I was. As I overtook him with as much casual randomness as I could muster, I couldn't help but glance at my target out of the corner of my eye. Yes, it was a rookie error. He was no longer talking on his mobile and had moved on to listening to music on a set of cordless head-phones. He was deep in thought, and my overtaking maneuver appeared to have gone unnoticed, so I walked on.

As I moved ahead of my target it struck me how useful it would have been to have a rear vision mirror as I didn't have any way to view what was happening behind me. I didn't need Google's best stalking tips to explain that turning around to check would give the game away. So I decided to walk up to the street corner ahead where I'd pretend to do up my shoelace while recalibrating my target's movements. I was fast adapting to this street-stalking business.

Having positioned myself at the street corner, I knelt down to tend to my laces and glanced around, but Black

Business Shoes wasn't in sight! I couldn't believe it. I prolonged my shoe lace charade, and perused the entire street without finding him. Instantly, my street-stalking adventure transformed from a fun, first outing into a stressful disaster as the reality sunk in that Black Business Shoes had escaped on my watch. I jumped up and quickly retraced my steps to check all the nearby side-street exits. However, if he had escaped up one of them it was likely he was long gone by then. I was heartbroken.

As I trudged back toward the flat, I thought through all the excuses I'd relay to Benny, Will, and Wendy upon my return. I could already picture their condescending looks when they learned I'd made schoolgirl errors just as they'd expected. But it wasn't my fault, I'd argue. Black Business Shoes surely had help to have escaped my clutches so efficiently. And if he had help, then he wasn't the right target to focus on for my first data-gathering mission anyway, I would continue. We would be better off focusing on targets who were unaware of what we were doing, I would conclude. The three of them would no doubt listen to all my excuses while nodding and appearing to feel sorry for me.

However, by the time I arrived home, I'd reached the painful conclusion that my best chance of redemption was to be honest, and drumroll . . . to ask for help. All my life I have struggled to ask for help as I've always thought it should be me helping others. But after the disaster that was my first data-gathering mission it was as plain as the nose on my face that I needed help.

When I walked into the little flat, I found Benny, Will, and Wendy still hard at work in the living room. No one looked up when I walked in. I knew why.

"Guys, I royally fucked up," I started with genuine humility. "My data-gathering mission was a fiasco and I've got nothing, absolutely nothing to show for it. All I can say is I'm sorry. Please forgive me, and please help me to become better at this. I know I can do it with your help."

It had been incredibly hard for me to say, but I'd done it. The only problem was my confession hadn't inspired the type of response I'd hoped for. In fact, the other three were still working away and didn't respond in any way. I wondered if I had become invisible.

"Oh, so it's to be the silent treatment then?" I asked as the blood in my veins warmed.

"Sorry, honey," Benny finally responded. "There's no need to ask for forgiveness. Yes, it wasn't a raging success as a data-gathering mission but we did learn something important."

"Really?" I asked shocked.

"Yes. When you tripped yourself up on the steps you made quite a racket," Benny explained. "Black Business Shoes heard the noise and became interested by what was going on. He was so interested that he did an about face so he could watch your little show unfold. He even laughed."

"Really?" I asked with 49 percent interest and 51 percent mortification.

"And when you finally climbed the stairs," Benny continued without emotion, "Black Business Shoes walked back in the opposite direction, so he was clearly influenced by your movements. The incident proves beyond doubt that he knows far more about our role than we thought he did."

When I heard the words "the opposite direction" I wondered if I should fire myself from all future missions then and there. My self-esteem had officially left the building. And with that information, the mystery of who on earth it was I'd been following remained firmly unsolved. All I knew was there was a black-shoed man out there with a perverse sense of humor.

"How exactly is that information useful to us?" I asked.

"Because it was first time an Abnormal has revealed they know who we are," Benny responded. "That in itself confirms Black Business Shoes is an important Abnormal, and one we need to be particularly careful of. And it 100 percent proves we are playing a part in the bigger game I've been banging on about. I'm not crazy, none of us are. I knew our safety was at risk but, Bell, this is scary stuff. Our family is in grave danger."

Fear rose uncontrollably in my chest when Benny told me this. I remember checking we weren't being watched in case there may be Abnormals hiding in the flat while he spoke. Fear has a way of playing with your mind.

"Honey, one more thing," continued Benny. "The answer is yes."

"To what?" I asked.

"To your request for help with the data-gathering work," Benny smiled. "You handled the situation exactly how we hoped you would. You were honest, humble, and open to learning. Well done. Your critical training will be a key priority from now on."

It was a relief, and I could breathe again. But the way Benny referred to my training as critical concerned me. I had always considered "critical" to mean a medical emergency.

CHAPTER 18

Although my self-confidence was at a low point at this stage in our story, I was optimistic it would improve as soon as I could prove myself worthy of the team's respect. The big carrot. I was thinking rather like my husband, wasn't I? That's the nature of marriage: We pick up our partner's character traits whether we want to or not. However, being desperate to prove my self-worth to my family and the world at large definitely hadn't been on the top of my "to do" list when I'd married Benny.

"Come over here, honey!" called out Benny as he navigated to a YouTube clip on his laptop. "Your training is about to start."

Oh great, I thought, here comes some more meaningless statistics I don't understand. Numbers weren't of remote interest to me when I'd been at school and remained less than enlightening then. Still, I sat down in front of the laptop like the obedient wife I was.

Benny pressed play, and a video of an orchestra accompanied by a choir started playing. It was music that I immediately recognized as being from *The Phantom of the Opera*.

"You want me to listen to some classical music?" I asked with surprise.

"Yes. I want you to watch this video. Watch closely, there will be a quiz at the end," responded my cryptic husband.

So I watched the few-minute video. It was your typical classical musical performance with a main singer, a backing choir, an orchestra conductor, and an extensive orchestra. At the end of the video, Benny was standing next to a big piece of paper, which he'd attached to the wall, pen in hand. I couldn't shake the nagging feeling I was married to a twat.

"So, here's a simple question for you, honey," Benny started. "I want you to recall all the people you saw in the video."

"All the people? OK, you strange man," I responded. "Well, there was the orchestra for starters."

"Hang on, the orchestra is not a person. Please recall each individual you saw, not each group," Benny requested.

I wanted to recall what my husband had been like in better days, but I played his game.

"OK, OK. There was a violinist, a cellist, and a flautist," I answered with more confidence.

"Is that all?" Benny asked.

"No, there were loads more people, but they were the most memorable," I responded.

"Interesting. And beyond those three people in the orchestra, who else do you recall?" continued my Spanish inquisitor.

"There was the choir," I recalled.

"Remember, individuals only," Benny reiterated.

All I could remember was being annoyed.

"OK, gestapo. Well, there was that bigger lady at the back of the choir whose eyes popped out of her head when she hit the higher notes," I responded.

"Excellent. Anyone else?" Benny asked.

"Yes. The choir had a lead singer standing out the front," I answered proud to have noticed him.

"Describe the lead singer for me please," Benny requested.

I racked my brain, but I couldn't remember a single detail about the lead singer.

"I can't," I confessed. "All I remember is that he was standing out in the front of the choir and singing loudly."

"It's OK, Bell, you're doing well," Benny stated. "I have one more question for you, and it's an important one. If you were to suspect one person in the video of being involved in an undercover criminal organization, who would you guess it was?"

Benny was loving this. I wasn't. I sensed there was a punchline coming, which would make me feel stupid once again.

"It's most likely to be one of the orchestra players. I'd say the violinist," I concluded.

"Why an orchestra player? And why him?" Benny asked.

"The orchestra players were more hidden than the rest because they were playing music in a large group," I reasoned. "If I was a terrorist trying to hide in the video, I'd choose to be in the orchestra. And the violin player is my top pick as a potential terrorist because there was something about his face that came across as shifty."

Benny was quiet for a moment to contemplate my answers. The big reveal was fast approaching. He pulled the top off his pen. I held my breath.

"That's great, Bell," he eventually responded. "It gives us a lot to work with. Let's use your biases, which match up with the biases of the vast majority of the human population, to identify the three key lessons from the video that will allow you to remain hidden whenever you want to. All the answers are here."

"Go on then," I said, running out of patience.

"Lesson number one: You couldn't recall any details about the people on the stage apart from the orchestra's shifty-eyed violin player and the eye-popping singer. That's interesting considering the vast majority of the video's time was focused on the people at the front of the stage such as the lead singer and the orchestra conductor. Why do you think you didn't notice them as much?" Benny asked with gravity.

"Because they looked like they should be there?" I asked, ready be wrong.

"Almost," Benny responded. "The real reason you didn't notice the main players was because they were front and center on a stage you knew was being watched by thousands of people. And when we believe someone is being watched by many others, most of us assume those people are high up in the human hierarchy. It's a complex human bias called the halo effect based on the power of social proof. It explains why people like the orchestra conductor and the lead singer are ideally positioned to hide in plain sight. The more people who are watching them, the more hidden they become."

"Hang on. You're telling me the people who are most on display are actually the most hidden?" I asked, perplexed.

"Exactly—for the simple reason that most of us assume a person in the spotlight on a stage has all the attributes we imagine a person in the spotlight on a stage should have. But the instructive point is it's all in our heads. We create a persona for those people in the spotlight on their behalf, but the persona we create has zero correlation with the truth of who those people are. I'm sure you can see where I'm going with this. Being an orchestra player and wearing neutral clothes are the wrong strategies when you want to hide. The best thing you can do is be front and center on the stage of your life—be yourself and own it. And remember, the louder you are, the more watched you are, the more hidden you really are, thanks to deep-set human biases," Benny concluded.

I nodded. I was strangely uplifted by Benny's first lesson. Being myself and owning it sounded like exactly what I should be doing.

"Lesson number two:" Benny continued, "When you did become suspicious of someone in the video, the violin player, it was solely because you thought he was shifty. The reality is the violin player is a musician who was in the depths of a complex performance and thus wasn't consciously controlling his facial expressions. However, that didn't stop you, and probably most other viewers, from judging the poor fellow based upon his facial expression in that single moment the camera focused on his face. Humans judge incredibly quickly based upon minuscule inputs like that. The implications are enormous if you don't want to be noticed. You see, it's all in your face. Do you follow me? If you want to remain hidden, you must develop excellent control of what your face is doing at all times. And that means you must understand what your face is doing when you are experiencing different emotions. Easier said than done, I'm sure you'll say. Well, there's only one way to learn what your face is doing on autopilot in different situations. You must watch your face in the mirror as you experience a range of emotions. As you notice facial expressions that aren't helpful, you must train and empower yourself to take control of your face in a more productive way."

Throughout my life, my face has always given me away. As Benny was lecturing me, I had a flashback to sitting in a religious studies class at school when I was around twelve. I was bored, so I was exchanging notes with a friend sitting next to me. We were struggling to hold back our giggling because our notes were filled with silly little jokes.

My friend had just written: "We went to a zoo on the weekend. It was rubbish because there was only one animal at the zoo: a dog."

"Really? How strange," I responded.

"Yes, it was a *shit-zou*," my friend wrote back.

I smiled at the memory. At the time, I couldn't control my laughter, and the teacher turned toward me in a fury.

"Belinda Harry, are you finding this passage of the Bible funny?" he snarled at me.

"No, sir," I answered with a broad smile on my face that betrayed me. It cost me a detention and has been a failing of mine ever since.

"That's a great piece of advice," I admitted to Benny. "I know my face gives me away at the best of times."

"It does indeed," agreed Benny. "In fact, it's the main reason we didn't invite you to join us earlier on. Your face openly told us we had a snowball's chance in hell of convincing you."

I laughed. He was right.

"And finally, lesson number three: When you talked about all the people you remembered in the video, you didn't mention anyone in the largest group of people present, the audience. It was as if you hadn't seen them at all," Benny said with a smile.

"That's because I couldn't see them," I countered. "The video only focused upon the people on stage."

Benny silently replayed various parts of the video that, in fact, showed the camera had focused upon the audience members on numerous occasions.

"OK, scratch that. I have no idea why I didn't notice them," I responded.

"I'll tell you why. It's because your subconscious instructed you not to focus on the people in the audience. And it did that for one simple reason: your subconscious decided they were similar to you. It then concluded that if they're similar to you, they must be all right," Benny answered.

"But why on earth would my subconscious decide those random audience members are similar to me? I don't even know them. Is my subconscious stupid?" I asked perplexed.

"Not at all, darling. It's because you and the audience were both watching the same musical performance. You were laughing together, clapping together, and thinking similar thoughts together. For a species as simple as we humans are, those basic shared actions go a long way toward creating a deeper bond between you and everyone in the audience. And when we have a deeper bond with someone, we tend to trust them from the get-go. I'm sure you can see how this can help you. If you want to quickly navigate below someone's caution radar, you just have to become an audience member with them in whatever context works, even if that means pretending you enjoy watching the same sport as them. Why do you think so many men pretend to enjoy watching football together? Lesson concluded," Benny said with his most charming smile.

For all my husband's eccentricities, it was hard to do anything but respect him for his immense brainpower. I can't remember learning as much from a classical music performance before, and I'm certain I won't ever again.

"Thank you, honey. I understand what I have to do," I responded. Benny had just saved my career as a street-stalker.

CHAPTER 19

There are certain moments in life when you just know what you have to do, and that orchestra video lesson was one of them for me. The instant Benny advised me to be myself and own it, pictures of a better me popped into my head from the land of what could be. I walked around the kitchen in the little flat and imagined it with me running a thriving baking business in it. It was a better look for both me and the little flat, so I decided then and there it was time to relaunch my baking business. It was time to thrive again.

When I explained my plan to the team it was warmly received.

"Great idea, Mom. That's a much better disguise," responded Will, ignorant that it was in fact the opposite of a disguise.

"Yes, you learned the lessons well," agreed Benny with more understanding.

It was time for a little less conversation, a little more action. If the kitchen and I were to become friends, I needed to cleanse it of its sordid past. The flat's no doubt desperate occupants of

yesteryear had left a vast array of items they no longer wanted throughout the kitchen. Everything carried a story of waste
and pain. I found a can opener that was so rusty, the turning
mechanism was locked in an unusable position. I understood
its predicament. I filled three rubbish bags with all the items
that made me cringe. The energy in the flat lifted immediately.

Next, I gave the kitchen the clean of its life as the flat
hadn't been cleaned since our first attempt at wiping away
the built-up scunge when we arrived. But the scunge had
continued to thrive since then and needed to be extermi-
nated once and for all. I disinfected everything in sight, and
then I did it twice more for good measure. As I scrubbed
away with all my strength, I also scrubbed at all our bad
memories since we'd arrived in the little flat. And I scrubbed
away everyone else's bad memories who had at one time also
released pain in the flat.

As I cleaned, Benny, Will, and Wendy were again in the
depths of their data-analysis work.

"So let's play with how their hierarchy works," I heard
Benny say to the kids. "My best guess is Black Business Shoes
is higher up than both Blue Joggers and Red High Heels."

"Hang on, Dad," Wendy responded. "If Black Business
Shoes is higher up the hierarchy, why do we often see him
with Normals? I don't think we can say much about him
with confidence at a time when our list of suspected high-
risk Abnormals is ballooning. We have bigger fish to fry."

It was becoming hard to imagine any of them ever leaving the flat again. I left them to it as the best thing I could

do was focus on myself. The good news from my perspective was that I was busy once again and my family was implicitly supporting what I was doing, even if they failed to notice it. I had repossessed my previously idle hands from the devil and what a difference it made.

My next priority was to acquire some baking supplies with which to work my magic. I had hidden a small stash of cash I'd saved in better days inside an old pair of trainers ever since the idea of escaping had reared its head. I decided then and there to invest those funds into the necessary ingredients for relaunching my baking operation. Closing off my one and only escape route was a scary idea, but I needed to wear my big girl pants from then on. So I retrieved the cash and went shopping.

My first stop was the local Tesco. I bought a food mixer along with a few baking and cake trays, as well as the basic ingredients I needed to create my most popular baked products. It was surreal to be shopping again like a normal person.

"After you, love," said an elderly gentleman at the checkout. I wasn't sure if he was talking to me at first as I had been invisible for such a long time.

"Thank you so much," I said as I stepped forward.

If I was going to successfully relaunch my baking business, I was going to have to pull out all the stops. So I walked over to a little baking supplies business in London Bridge I frequented during better days. It sold a number of hard-to-access ingredients from around the world that had become game changers for me over the years. Rarities like blueberry essence, coffee emulsion, and vodka-pickled mangos were to be found on each and every shelf. I needed my superpowers like never before, so I loaded up my shopping cart with the good stuff. I was in baking heaven.

"I remember you," said the friendly lady in the shop, "but you look different to when I last saw you. Have you been on a diet?"

I wanted to tell her I had been serving hard time in prison and the prison food wasn't the tastiest.

"Yes, that's it. Thanks for noticing," I answered with a forced smile, remembering Benny's advice on facial control. I made a mental note to start training my face from that moment onward.

"There's something else different about you," the shop lady continued. "Are you recently single?"

"No, just older and thinner," I smiled. Controlling my face was more challenging in that moment.

I left the shop and returned home inspired to bake. I unpacked everything I'd purchased and strategically set up the kitchen for action. As I surveyed the minuscule amount of space I had to worth in, I reminded myself the kitchen didn't define the baker—it was only ingredients and love that mattered. I had everything I needed to make my baking business fly again.

I started baking that very afternoon and I didn't stop. It was like getting back on a bike after a long break. Everything came rushing back to me. I focused on baking the five products that had always been my top sellers of the past: luxury cookies, cheese and bacon muffins, cheesecake, brownies, and macaroons. I put a sample of each of them into some small white cardboard boxes I had picked up at the supplies store. By the time I finished work that evening, I had twenty sample boxes of my baking talent ready for action. It was my very own Elvis Comeback Special. I even did a few Elvis-inspired hip swivels to celebrate. I was alive again.

The next morning, I rose early. I was ready to walk the streets as a real person going about her business who may just happen to come across some valuable data, rather than the other way around. The pressure was off as anything I discovered would be a bonus. Of course, Benny, Will, and Wendy didn't see it quite the same way.

"Honey, we've analyzed the profiling data we've collected to compute where you are likely to find the key Abnormals in the local area today. They've handed us far more information than they realize care of data such as the shopping bags and tube tickets they carry, and even the speed and ease of their walking motions. Here's the list. We're really hoping you can come back with more data on Blue Joggers as his movements are increasingly worrying us. He is a top priority at this point," explained Benny.

As I read through the long and detailed list of Blue Joggers' suspected movements, it was obvious none of them aligned with the café run I'd planned for my sample-box deliveries. It was a test of which pathway I wanted more.

"OK, that's fine. I'll do what I can," I told Benny as I nonchalantly put the list inside my pocket.

Before leaving the flat, I spent half an hour doing facial control training in the bathroom. I watched my face in the mirror as I relived both good and bad memories. I had plenty of the latter to work with from recent months. It was painfully obvious that whenever I thought of The Connection Game my face looked like a soggy thumb that had been underwater for too long. It was my blind spot. I clearly had a lot more work to do, but I reminded myself Rome wasn't built in a day. And the good news was I was starting to like my face again, like an old friend I hadn't seen for ages.

With my sample boxes in hand, I left the flat with a joyful spring in my step. I calculated I had time to visit the first three local cafés on my list before I needed to focus on Blue Joggers' predicted movements. Off I went into the intoxicating freedom of the outside world.

CHAPTER 20

My plan was to hand out my sample boxes to a selection of local cafés and restaurants to market my baking talents. It was how I'd built up my baking business when I launched it the first time. It had only taken one marketing trip to the local cafés near where we lived at the time to create more business than I could handle—so it was a winning strategy for me. However, my waning self-confidence reminded me it had originally worked in a different part of London, in a different era, and when I was a different person. With a deep breath, I reminded myself the real reason it had been so successful at the time and would be again: I'd provided the cafés with food of such a high quality they couldn't say no. I was ready to dazzle them again.

I quickly found the first café on my marketing run, The Milkman, and entered. My best chance was to speak with the owner or the manager as serving staff generally had other priorities.

"Excuse me," I said to the young girl serving behind the counter, "I'm hoping to speak with the owner or manager please."

"He's sitting over there," she said pointing at a man drinking coffee in the corner. "His name is Bert."

So I walked over to this Bert, suddenly feeling nervous.

"Morning. I hear you own this café," I said with a smile.

"Guilty as charged," answered Bert who was only around twenty-two and relishing being young and arrogant.

"Nice to meet you. My name is Bell. I run a local baking business and want to drop in these samples for you in case you'd be interested in working together," I explained.

Bert glanced at my sample box, then back at me.

"Thanks, but we aren't allowed to receive food from un-licensed operators," he said with a distracted air.

In my haste to get my products out there I'd forgotten to renew my food production license. It was a blow. But the question suddenly struck me, how did this Bert know I was unlicensed? As I pondered the situation, I noticed he was wearing a pair of blue joggers. The hairs on the back of my neck stood on end and my heart started racing. *Could this be Blue Joggers?* I wondered. Rather than remaining cool, my face contorted of its own accord into an expression that could only translate into "What the fuck?" I did all I could to regather control, but Bert noticed my facial foible. He smirked without trying to hide it.

"Is that right?" I asked on high alert. "May I ask why you think I'm unlicensed? I don't believe we've met before."

"I don't think so either," Bert said with an unnecessary follow-up smirk. "I assumed you were unlicensed because we are asked to take free baking samples by around twenty chancers a day. And I can't remember the last time one of them was licensed. Are you licensed then?"

"Yes. I mean, not right now, but I'll renew my license straight away," I responded. If this was Blue Joggers, I wasn't doing a great job of owning my life on center stage. I was most definitely an orchestra player.

"OK, good luck with that. Please don't come back when you are licensed unless you have at least ten thousand followers on your Instagram page. It's the minimum we expect from all our suppliers," Bert concluded with a wink.

Are winks socially acceptable behavior these days? Bert and I clearly disagreed on the subject. With a final glance at his blue joggers, I gladly retreated from Bert and The Milkman none the wiser whether he was a potential Abnormal or a definite asshole.

Unperturbed, I tried the next two cafés on my list. However, I was greeted by the same negative response to my lack of license and Instagram following. I was shocked by how much the world had changed since the last time I had done this. Social media had insidiously crept into all parts of society to change life as I knew it. Long gone was the era when showing up with the best products and a winning smile was enough. It's now all about who can post the most messages onto their social media pages, and my marketing strategy had become useless as a result. Life can be so humbling. I decided to shift my focus back to Blue Joggers' suspected movements. It was my best chance at salvaging an otherwise disappointing day.

Rather than carrying the weight of my twenty redundant sample packs around for the rest of the day, I handed seventeen of them out to homeless people I passed en route to the first expected Blue Joggers sighting location. I kept three sample packs with me as part of my strategy to own my role on center stage, even if it was nothing but an act. Despite the fact I'd wasted most of my launch budget, it warmed my heart to see those homeless peoples' faces light up when they understood I was giving them free food. One lady named Deidre was particularly memorable.

"That was the greatest muffin I've ever tasted," she said after taking a big bite. "I'll remember it until my dying day. Bless you, darling."

Inspired by Deidre's words, I decided that when I was next riding high in the game of life, I would focus on helping the homeless. What we'd experienced in the little flat was still a far better life than what most of them endure on a daily basis.

"And I'll remember you to my dying day," I responded. "Thanks for appreciating my muffins and giving me some much-needed joy."

I pulled out Benny's list of Blue Joggers' expected sightings. The first one was due at quarter past ten in front of the British Museum. God only knows how Benny, Will, and Wendy were predicting Blue Joggers' movements in any part of London apart from our street, but they had been adamant. After a brisk walk through some quiet back streets, I reached the front of the British Museum at ten o'clock on the dot. I sat down on the steps leading up to the museum and waited.

After Will's recent miscalculation about Blue Joggers' movements, I half expected this prediction to follow along the same lines. I surreptitiously surveyed all the people in front of the museum. There was a large group of international students congregating around the bottom of the steps, and a few families dotted around the courtyard. It was the sort of place where standing and watching was the norm rather than the exception, so it was the perfect place for me to wait alongside everyone else who was waiting for someone. There were many people in the vicinity wearing blue joggers, but no one who seemed suspicious. Despite my identification error with Black Business Shoes, I remained confident I would recognize Blue Joggers if he showed up. Benny's lessons about how to remain unseen had given me the advantage. I knew I needed to be on the lookout for someone who looked like they should be there, possibly someone in the limelight.

Quarter part ten arrived, and I was still searching for my target. The seconds slowed as I waited. I still suspected he wasn't going to show up at all. And then a small dark-skinned boy walked past me down the stairs carrying a courier bag. He was walking with noteworthy purpose. What an ideal disguise I thought to myself as I looked down at his feet. There he was. Blue Joggers had finally arrived, and he was on time.

CHAPTER 21

I jumped to my feet and jogged down the steps. Then I remembered I'd left my backpack with the remaining sample boxes on the steps. After my previous street-stalking mistakes, I wasn't prepared to accept anything less than success this time. So I ran back up the steps, grabbed my backpack, and resumed my pursuit of Blue Joggers. The good news was I could still see him—he was heading right on the footpath in front of the museum. However, he was walking remarkably quickly and the distance between us was growing.

All my street-stalking training momentarily went out the window. I ran, yes ran, after him, like a policewoman chasing a criminal. I don't think he saw me, but if he had, the game would have been up in the most inglorious of ways. By the time I was firmly on his tail, he was turning onto Bloomsbury Street. With relief, I recognized this part of London from my time at UCL. It was comforting to know Blue Joggers didn't have a home ground advantage over me.

As I rounded the corner onto Bloomsbury Street, I was about a hundred yards behind him. From what I had seen of him on the steps all I could confirm was that he was a dark-skinned boy of around twelve years old who was carrying a courier bag. The only thing I'd noticed about his facial expression was that he was particularly focused on every step he was taking, like a courier who was running late. At a distance, it was easy to forget he was anything more than a pair of shoes I was following, but I reminded myself he was also a young boy going about his day. If he was indeed caught up in some bad business as Benny was so certain he was, it may not have been of his own accord.

Before I could explore that thought further, I noticed Blue Joggers had stopped outside a townhouse up ahead. He was gazing up at the top floor window and waving at someone from the street. Rather than attempting the walk-past maneuver, which had been such a disaster for me previously, I pretended to answer a phone call and stopped walking. I put my hand on the fence lining the street where I stood and talked into my mobile.

"Hey, great to hear from you, Angie," I enthused into the ether. "It's been a while. How's life?"

I awaited an imaginary response and then continued my charade.

"Oh, that's great. I knew you'd make a wonderful nurse—you're such a caring and loving person. I remember playing doctors and nurses with you when we were kids. You always wanted to be a nurse and I now understand why."

I paused for a moment while the illusion of my sister considered her response.

"You're right, Ange. It has been ages since we were in touch, and it's all my fault. I would have called but the truth is I've been in trouble, little sis. I didn't want to burden you with our problems."

I heard the beep of an intercom up ahead. Blue Joggers pushed open the front door leading into the flat above. I stopped talking and gazed up at the window Blue Joggers had been waving at. A curtain moved ever so slightly, but nothing else happened. Without a better plan at the ready, I decided to wait where I was. Besides, I was finding it strangely therapeutic to pretend I was chatting with Angie. What strange creatures we humans are. What a strange human I am.

"What sort of trouble? Well, that's a difficult question to answer, Ange," I continued. "It all began with our money being stolen in an online fraud, but it's evolved into something different, something I don't recognize. Like Mr. Nincompoop on that train when we were kids, I don't know where this train is going. What do you think I should do, Ange?"

Before the next imagined response, Blue Joggers re-emerged onto the street. He glanced around so I kept holding the phone to my ear as though I was still talking. I noticed he was no longer carrying the courier bag, and was moving with less urgency as he walked away from the townhouse in the direction of UCL.

"Well, it's been wonderful to hear your voice. I love you too, sis. Let's speak again soon," I concluded as I resumed my mission a little lighter.

As Blue Joggers wandered along the street, he was particularly interested in the people around him. He was walking along the right-hand side of the street adjacent to UCL's main campus. It still held an important place in my heart, and I wondered what the university-version of myself would think of my current street-stalking activities. Before I could further that thought, without warning Blue Joggers veered off the street into the UCL campus. That's unusual, I surmised, as there can't be too many twelve-year-olds who spend time wandering around university campuses. I sped up, driven by my growing interest in where Blue Joggers was heading next.

Blue Joggers walked through the campus while glancing around in all directions. It suggested to me he hadn't been there before. I was getting the hang of this data-gathering gig. As he neared the café and restaurant area, he sped up and walked into the front door of Kaleidoscope, the bar I used to frequent when I was a student there. *What a strange coincidence*, I thought to myself.

Emboldened by my initial success in following Blue Joggers, I entered Kaleidoscope to discover it had evolved into more of a café than a bar since I'd last visited. I couldn't think of a better café disguise than being a coffee drinker, so I sat down at a table near the front door, which allowed me to easily view all the other customers in the café. However, our blue-shoed friend was nowhere to be seen. My heart sank. The only people in the café were a group of university students chattering away about exams, and an older Asian fellow with the air of a mature-aged student who was drinking a coffee alone. Had I been played again?

A waiter, who could only be a fresher, bounced over.

"I used to go to UCL back in the day," I explained to him as he took my coffee order.

"Wow, that's cool," he answered with feigned interest. "What was it like here in the sixties?"

I willingly lost control of my facial expression and gave him my best "Are you fucking kidding me?" look, but he remained oblivious and walked away. I made a mental note to invest in a decent facial moisturizing cream.

By the time my coffee arrived, I had come to terms with the fact Blue Joggers must have left the café. Maybe he'd somehow seen me and had done a runner. One more point to the bad guys. But then, I saw him standing behind the counter talking with an older man. I couldn't see the man or his shoes clearly, but I noticed the two of them were deeply engaged in conversation. Even from where I was sitting, it was clear they weren't discussing the weather.

It occurred to me that when Benny, Will, and Wendy asked me for their data fix when I returned home, I would have little of substance to give them. All I had discovered thus far were inconsequential glimpses of Blue Joggers walking around as a courier. Knowing how my family could make me feel unworthy inspired me to take action. Before returning home, I was determined to learn who Blue Joggers was talking with and what they were discussing. I hatched a plan to pay for my coffee with my ears wide open while Blue Joggers and the older man were talking nearby. It was my best chance of getting close enough to listen into what they were discussing. So I made my way to the serving counter.

"How was everything?" asked the waiter.

"Great, thanks," I answered, trying to listen in to Blue Joggers' conversation.

"By the way, I meant to ask if you attended Woodstock? What an amazing experience that would have been," continued my pimple-faced tormentor.

"I'm afraid not," I answered fighting every instinct to tell him I wasn't even born then.

"Because I'm studying English literature and we're reading this fascinating book that brings together a bunch of funny but real Woodstock stories. For example, did you know there was only one toilet for every 833 people who attended that magical day? The average toilet wait time was over two hours. I would have just found a tree!" he said, chuckling.

What were the chances I'd meet the world's chattiest waiter the moment I needed silence? I thanked him and excused myself. As I was about to leave, I noticed out of the corner of my eye that Blue Joggers was also leaving the café through the front door. He was accompanied by the man he was talking with. It was game on again.

CHAPTER 22

Blue Joggers and his companion remained in animated conversation as they walked together. I couldn't recall ever seeing a twelve-year-old in such an engaged conversation with an adult before, particularly an adult wearing brown suede shoes. I recalled everything Benny had mentioned about Brown Suede potentially being a high ranking Abnormal. My curiosity took on a life of its own as I stepped wherever their footsteps led me.

The two of them continued walking through the UCL campus into Gordon Square, a green courtyard area across the road from the campus, which provided sunbathing space for students on rare sunny days. They continued their stroll along the footpath that circumvented the grounds.

The gap between us narrowed as they slowed to a more leisurely pace in the gardens. By then, I was only ten yards or so behind them so I could hear a little of what they were saying.

"Yes, that's the beauty of mathematics," said the older man who had a strong Russian accent. "It allows you to leverage your learnings in other subjects."

"And not just science," responded Blue Joggers. "I'm finding connections with pretty much everything else I'm working on."

When he used the word "connections" my interest got the better of me, and I inadvertently found myself walking only a few yards behind them. And then it happened. The Russian man stopped walking and turned around to face me.

"Hello," he said, addressing me directly.

"Hi," I responded as nonchalantly as I could.

"What can we do for you?" he asked.

"Pardon me?" I feigned.

"We noticed you watching us back in the café," he explained calmly. "Then we left the café and you started following us. And here we are. I'll ask you again: can we help you with something?"

Google's advice had been to avoid your target at all costs, so I contemplated legging it. But then I recalled Benny's lessons about remaining incognito and decided to go for broke. If I was a leading player on the stage of my life, I would be safe.

"Yes, maybe you can help me. I'm setting up a baking business and I wanted to talk with you about partnering together at your café. I'm hoping to impress you with a sample box of my most popular baked products," I said as I yanked one of my sample boxes out from my backpack like a magician pulling a rabbit, which had fallen asleep, out of a hat.

"Sorry, there's been a mistake. I don't own that café. I was just a visitor," he explained quietly.

"So what were you doing out the back of the café then?" I asked, aware it was none of my business.

The Russian man stepped closer to me as though he was looking at me through a magnifying glass. Blue Joggers watched on with surprise.

"Who are you? Really," he asked.

It was a big question that I wasn't ready to answer, then or now.

"Listen, I thought you were someone else. This is all just a mix up. I better get going," I said as I turned to leave.

The Russian man put his hand on my shoulder and restrained me. I was terrified.

"The next time I ask you a question I want an honest answer," he whispered into my ear.

I'll never forget those words. They meant so much and yet so little to me at the time. I pushed his hand off my shoulder like an unwelcome insect and ran for my life. As I made my escape, he called something out to me, but I couldn't hear what he was saying. Luckily, I was in great shape for all the street-walking I had been doing, so I was able to run fast. With the wind in my sails, I ran through Gordon Square, across UCL, and then back onto Bloomsbury Street. I kept checking over my shoulder but neither of them was in sight.

Once fear gets inside you, it's hard to shake it. Walking it off was my one and only coping strategy, so I relished the long journey back to the little flat. My mind was racing as I contemplated what I would say to the other three. Despite being discovered by my targets, I'd certainly gathered some valuable data to feed the monsters. I could tell them where Blue Joggers went, and who he spent his time with. And I could tell them all about the Russian man whom I strongly suspected was Brown Suede. It was a haul to be proud of. But Benny, Will, and Wendy weren't the type of people to thank me for my efforts and leave it at that. Each and every piece of information I served them with would no doubt be followed up by more questions, trickier questions. By the time I arrived home, I was nervous.

CHAPTER 23

When I walked into the living room, Benny, Will, and Wendy were still engaged in the day's mission. There were graphs attached to all the walls that showed the correlations and probabilities of various Abnormal interactions. The three of them turned around expectantly.

"Honey!" called out Benny. "You've been out for ages. How was your outing?"

"I've lived a few lives since leaving home this morning," I answered.

"Come over here," Benny said with unusual warmth. "Rather than you telling us what happened, we want to ask you a few questions to check we are on the right track."

"OK, that works for me," I responded, somewhat relieved I didn't have to rehash every single event.

"First question, Mom:" started Will, "Did Blue Joggers meet an older man in the Kaleidoscope café at UCL?"

"Yes, he did. How on earth did you know that?" I asked.

"Next question: Was the older man he met wearing brown suede shoes?" Will continued.

"He was indeed!" I exclaimed.

"Those two were easy, honey," interjected Benny. "It's the next question that matters."

"OK, shoot," I said ready to be impressed.

"Was the man wearing brown suede shoes French?" Benny asked with a confident smile.

"French? No, he was Russian," I responded, surprised for the wrong reasons.

"Russian? No, he can't be. Are you sure you know the difference between a French and a Russian accent?" Benny asked with urgency.

"Of course, I do. They are completely different accents. He was most definitely Russian," I responded.

Benny walked over to check some of the charts hanging on the wall.

"Mom, can you describe the Russian man please?" asked Wendy with interest.

"Sure. He was about your dad's height, a little overweight, balding, and I'd guess at least fifty years old," I answered.

"Houston, we have a problem," responded Will.

"What's the problem?" I asked.

"Honey, our data tells us you ran into Brown Suede today, but he's a Frenchman of around forty-five years old. The data never lies," added Benny with gravity.

"So are you suggesting I am mistaken?" I asked.

"Not mistaken, honey, but maybe your vantage point didn't allow you unrestricted access to the data," continued Benny.

"My vantage point?" I responded with anger. "My vantage point was talking with the guy face-to-face. I had access to the data!"

"It can't be," responded Benny shaking his head.

As I mentioned earlier, when Benny and I fought, the situation always became perilous fast. And after the adrenalin-charged day I'd had on the streets, I was ready to fight back with everything I had.

"I'll tell you what can't be—" I responded, "it can't be that I'm married to a man who doesn't listen to a bloody word I say, a man who devalues my viewpoint without a second thought, a man who thinks he knows everything about everything. Well, hear this. If you want me to work with you on this crusade into the depths of your crazy mind, you better start respecting me and listening to what I say!"

With that, I retreated into our bedroom for some space. I lay down on our bed and cried my eyes out. The one and only reason I had been so enthusiastic to be a part of the team was to regain some respect in my family's eyes, but Benny and the kids were still talking to me as though I were a young child. I wondered if there was any point even trying anymore. It was obvious I couldn't influence what they thought of me.

Eventually, when my tears ran dry, I returned to the living room. I was surprised to discover Benny was in the kitchen cooking dinner. My words must have had an impact as he only ever cooked when he was genuinely sorry for his uncaring behavior.

"You're right, Bell," Benny admitted. "I should have listened to you. The data has become overwhelming to say the least. I obviously can't see the wood for the trees right now."

"I can see you are struggling to keep it together, but let's remember we're on the same team, please," I responded.

"I will, I promise. From now on, I'll consider your street reports to be data of a similarly high quality to every other piece of data we collect," he stated. It wasn't exactly a line from *Romeo and Juliet*, but it was a big thing for Benny to say. In his language, it was the equivalent of "I love you." You may laugh, and you'd be entitled to, but no one can judge a relationship from outside a relationship—there's so much more at play than meets the eye. And our relationship was hanging together by the thinnest of threads, so all I could do was respect the thread.

After we ate the almost inedible pasta dinner Benny cooked that evening, we sat down to watch a film. Watching TV was most unusual in our household as everyone was so focused on their work, even in the evenings. So it was with excitement that we noticed a conspiracy film called *Take Shelter* was about to start. As you can imagine, our household was particularly interested in anything with a conspiracy theory at the heart of it.

So we all sat down to watch the film, which was about a man who lives underground as he prepares for arrival of the Apocalypse that he, and only he, believes is imminent. As the story progressed his wife and friends increasingly questioned the state of his mental health, but he insisted they were all wrong as he fought to hang onto his dark view of the future. As we watched his mental health deteriorate on screen, I glanced around at Benny, Will, and Wendy. They all looked perturbed and uncomfortable. I understood exactly where they were coming from as I was experiencing the same feelings. I stood up and turned the TV off.

"Remind you of anyone?" I asked.

At first, no one answered.

"It's us," Wendy eventually contributed. "We are real life underground freaks waiting for bad stuff to happen in the world. No, willing bad stuff to happen."

No one could have summarized our lives more succinctly.

"We're not quite as bad as that guy, are we?" asked Will.

"When was the last time any of you were outside in the daylight?" I asked.

Benny looked down at his feet.

"When was the last time the two of you went to school?" I asked Will and Wendy.

They both turned to look away.

"When was the last time we did anything as a family beyond staring at passing, sodding feet?" I asked with more venom.

No one answered.

"When was the last time we had a shred of sanity in our lives?" I concluded.

"We hear you, Bell," Benny finally responded. "Maybe we are on the wrong track here. Your mission today disproved our main theory, so maybe we need a break from this project to regain some clarity."

I would have preferred if Benny had addressed the elephant in the room: his mental health. But at least he understood we were in deep trouble as a family. Watching that film had been the wake-up call we all needed. While it was progress of sorts, I could see Benny's eyes didn't look right—they reminded me of Jack Nicholson's eyes in *The Shining*.

CHAPTER 24

Recognizing ourselves as the freaks we had become was the truth that set us free, at least for a while. It was time for change. So, after much debate, we decided to give normal life a go again. Benny even agreed the kids should return to school so they could learn from others. I was overjoyed because in my heart of hearts I'd stopped believing we were doing important work through our foot-watching, or stalking, or whatever you want to call it. I no longer believed there was a group of bad people walking the streets around us who were plotting to end the world. The turning point for me had been overhearing Blue Joggers' conversation with the Russian. Rather than plotting terrible things, the Russian man had simply been mentoring a young boy in his studies. He was trying to help a kid get ahead—it was hardly scary stuff. We were the scary stuff. What a realization!

When I say Benny agreed to resume a normal life, he wasn't exactly over the moon about it. He acted as though he'd let the world down, let us down, let his father down in every way possible. He carried himself like a broken man. It took a few weeks of constant encouragement from the rest of us before he eventually applied for a job. It was a positive step, but when the day of his interview arrived, we weren't optimistic he would be successful. He awoke that morning lethargic and unresponsive like an out-of-work zombie.

"Benny, would you like me to cook you breakfast?" I asked with as much positive energy as I had in me.

"No," he answered.

"Would you like me to walk you to the tube?" I offered.

"No point," he grunted.

When a man wants to believe the world is ending, there's not much you can do to convince him otherwise. So I gave up trying to inspire him, and prepared myself for a long road ahead in finding Benny a job. We would have to hope for an extremely charitable and open-minded employer who could see beyond the rough surface Benny was showing the world. But our experience suggested those were few and far between.

When Benny arrived home from the interview his face remained downcast, confirming our fears had manifested themselves.

"You all right, honey?" I asked.

"They offered me the job," Benny answered without emotion.

I was dancing on the inside. We needed good news as much as anyone I've ever met.

"Well done you, what wonderful news!" I enthused.

"It's news," Benny responded.

"Did they ask you any curly questions?" I asked.

"Not really," Benny stated. "The interviewer mentioned they'd heard of my reputation a while back, but they hadn't heard of me for a long while. They asked what I've been up to of late, and I mentioned I've been laying low since winning that game show. They left it at that."

So Benny started working again, the kids returned to school, and I resumed building my baking business from home. Step by step, we all got on with our lives in the outside world. It was hard at first as we weren't used to being around other people, talking normal talk, or doing anything normal humans did. We were like aliens coexisting with the human race during those first few weeks. It was so strange. I remember Wendy being particularly upset about life in the outside world one evening.

"Mom, I don't understand the girls at my school," she started.

"What happened?" I asked.

"Well, today two of the mean girls started picking on me," she explained. "One of them told me she felt sorry for me for being so quiet and boring. And the other said she knew dead people with more life in them."

"Sorry to hear that, Wend. How did you respond?" I asked.

"I told them they shouldn't waste their time feeling sorry for me because I don't think about them at all," Wendy said. "I explained that because they are so average in every way, they don't have anything about them to inspire any interest from me, or anyone else with any sense."

I couldn't help but chuckle out loud. Wendy is very much her father's daughter.

"And what did they say?" I asked.

"Nothing. One of them had tears welling in her eyes, and the other one looked at me as though I was the one picking on her. Then they both stormed off. What I don't understand is why they were upset with me when they were the ones attacking me. Shouldn't it be the other way around?" Wendy asked, perplexed.

"Well," I responded, "the truth hurts, particularly for those of us who haven't admitted it to ourselves as yet. I'd say those two girls were better at bullying others than receiving feedback on their own existence. You'll meet many people like them throughout your life. And you know what the good news is?"

"What's that?" she asked.

"People who attempt to bully you genuinely don't matter, just as you said to those girls," I explained. "You'll only remember those who have shown you love and kindness along the way, and the rest will fade into nothingness when you're ready to let it go."

"Do you think we'll remember Dad then?" Wendy asked.

What a question.

"Your dad loves you in his own way," I responded. "You'll understand that when you're older. And besides, you and your dad have a lot more time to figure each other out."

There were many more incidents like Wendy's bullying story as we reacquainted ourselves with the long list of human flaws. While our household had been a long way from being emotionally healthy, we had become a high-performing team, a team like the world had never seen before. All our operational kinks had been ironed out. So our perspective on life in the outside world revealed as much about us as it did about the human race.

As a few more weeks ticked by, our lives gradually became more normal. No, let's say functional. Let's face it, we were never going to be truly normal. But there's something about being busy that lubricates the movement of time and helps us forget the less-than-adequate parts of our lives. We even started getting used to living in the little flat, and I never thought I'd say that.

The other significant development was Benny had stopped dragging his feet to work, which I was particularly grateful for. His new job was with an airport management company in a role focused upon improving security through unique technology solutions. His company's objective was to lower the risk of terrorist attacks within the global air travel sector. While it wasn't quite as abnormal as monitoring suspicious foot movements from below street level, he couldn't have been more qualified for the job. And once he got his teeth stuck into the work, the old Benny started to return. He was most welcome.

"Honey, did you realize that most airport security areas are nothing more than a smokescreen designed to scare terrorists out of taking action?" Benny asked with excitement one evening. "The truth is there's very little real risk-reduction action going on behind this charade."

"That's shocking. Why hasn't the technology evolved to deliver genuine safety improvements at airports?" I asked knowing my husband well.

"I know, right!" Benny enthused. "Peoples' lives depend on getting this right, it's not a pony race. At least I'm on it now. There's so much to be done, so I'll be working longer hours for a while."

I relaxed once I heard those words as they informed me we were on track for redemption. We could finally put the foot-watching behind us. Benny's talents were unstoppable once he was passionate about something, particularly if that something involved reducing the risk of bad stuff happening to others. As with all unstoppable forces, all we had to do was get out of its way and allow it to run its course. Or so I thought.

CHAPTER 25

Once I renewed my food production license, my baking business quickly boomed as it had before we moved into the little flat. While the local clientele wasn't quite as happy to pay ten pounds per cookie as the Harrods' customers had been, I developed solid relationships with a few of the local cafés who wanted to sell high quality, locally baked goods. And after learning my lesson about how important social media had become, I started an Instagram account showcasing a photographic portfolio of my best baking. At first, I thought the whole Instagram thing was a waste of time, but slowly my online following grew and soon I was receiving more orders than I could cater for.

The kitchen in the little flat soon became too small for my needs, so I had to rent out space in an industrial kitchen a few blocks away. It was only a couple of hundred yards from the little flat, so it was convenient. However, it meant my free-spirited, street walking time all but disappeared as I became busier with my baking. In its stead, I walked the short distance from the flat to the kitchen about five times a day. I also sometimes delivered my orders locally on foot, but increasingly I needed help from couriers to meet my growing list of delivery deadlines. Whenever a courier arrived to pick up a delivery, I watched out for the little boy previously known as Blue Joggers. I wondered if we might randomly meet each other again one day. I hoped his maths studies were going well and would have liked to tell him as much. However, he didn't show up, and as time went on, I thought about him less and less. Time has a way of burying all that came before.

Whenever I had a surplus of baked goods beyond my clients' requirements, I made a point of walking the streets to hand them out to the many homeless folk living locally. It was something I knew I had to do ever since I'd first experienced the joy of giving food away on my ill-fated, street-stalking mission. And it was the most uplifting thing I'd done since we arrived in the little flat.

It was when I was handing out food to the homeless that I reconnected with Deidre, a jubilant lady in her sixties who could generally be found begging just around the corner in Clapton Square. Deidre had been a successful musician in a former life and was passionate about the healing power of music. She positioned a number of homemade drums in a circle around her in the well-worn corner of the park where she resided. When I say homemade, her drums were just old cardboard boxes she'd found in her travels that she placed upside down without any further adjustment. It was simple but it worked. If she sensed an audience may be interested, she banged her beloved boxes with nothing but her hands in tune to well-known songs. Something happened between Deidre's hands and those boxes that's hard to describe—the music she created through her box drumming was genuinely beautiful and far more sophisticated than seemed possible. And her talents didn't go unnoticed. When I met her, Deidre was already a minor local celebrity. Many locals went out of their way to visit Deidre's corner of the park—to start their day with morning coffees in hand—for a dose of Deidre's unique brand of magic.

I scheduled my visits to see Deidre at times when she was sitting quietly by herself rather than entertaining groups. Those were the special moments when we were able to chat and get to know each other. I'd go so far as to say Deidre was the closest thing I had to a friend in those days, and she seemed to see something in me she liked.

"Bell, your baking talents are beyond comparison! I'm not worthy of such posh nosh," Deidre said to me one afternoon after I'd delivered some of my scones with homemade raspberry jam.

"I'm glad you like them, and yes, you are so worthy of it. In fact, I can't think of anyone more worthy," I responded.

Deidre bowed her head graciously.

"So how is Hackney's most famous street musician today?" I asked.

"I'm thriving, thanks. Just look at where I live," Deidre responded as she swept her hand in a royal motion like a queen in her palace. "I'm the luckiest person on this beautiful planet."

"Deidre, how do you stay so positive?" I asked in all seriousness. I wanted whatever she was having.

"Well, it's a magic trick, so I can't tell you how I really do it," Deidre smiled.

"Now I'm even more curious. I promise to keep it between you and me and the trees," I pleaded.

"OK, I'll tell you, but only because it's you," Deidre responded. "Here's how it works. Just imagine today is the last day of your life and start appreciating every little gift it delivers you."

Deidre awaited my response with interest.

"That's it?" I asked.

"That's it," Deidre nodded. "That way of thinking will lead to more and more beautiful gifts arriving in your life. Some of them will already be in your life but just haven't been introduced as yet. All you have to say is 'hi and welcome' when you notice them, and they'll get on with making your life better. It's easy."

When Deidre explained her philosophy, Benny's handsome face appeared in my mind. *Had I been appreciating all the gifts Benny brought into my life?* I wondered.

"What a beautiful way of viewing life. It sounds so simple when you put it like that," I said.

"It is, Bell. I promise," Deidre responded. "Look at me, I'm certainly no genius. I'm just a woman who's decided to be happy. And what would make me happy in this moment would be to play you a little ditty."

Deidre started playing her cardboard drums ever so softly. At first, I couldn't tell which song it was, but I eventually recognized she was playing a slowed down version of "Yellow Submarine." I grinned as that song had long been a favorite of mine when I was a little girl watching trains pass by from atop the garden wall. Angie and I used to sing it to our imaginary friend Mr. Nincompoop, speeding past below us, as a way of cheering him up for being so lost. As the song progressed, Deidre gradually increased the volume of her drumming. I was mesmerized.

Then, without warning, I found myself involuntarily singing along to Deidre's beautiful song. Her energy was so warm and welcoming that I even stood up and started singing along far more loudly than I should have been. I have no idea what I was thinking as I'm at best a shower singer. When I reached the words "As we live a life of ease / every one of us has all we need," it was as though Deidre's soul was inspiring mine to be as thankful as hers.

Some passersby noticed our performance and came over to watch. They had the good grace to pretend to be entertained, and at the end of our impromptu performance they were generous with their contributions to Deidre's collection box. An elderly gentleman said to us, "You're a wonderful band. Where can I buy your albums?" Deidre and I laughed and explained we weren't a band, just two friends in the park. He thanked us and wandered off.

"Sorry for my voice. I'm not used to singing in public," I smiled.

"You have a beautiful voice, Bell. Always remember that," responded Deidre with unusual seriousness.

I left the park that day lighter. If Deidre could choose happiness, I could do the same. After all, happiness was a normal thing to want, and I was doing my best impression of living a normal life again.

CHAPTER 26

It's fair to say life delivered us a dose of happiness as soon as we chose to accept it. Well, at least for a while. Benny and I were both loving our jobs, the kids were enjoying going to school, and our social life once again had a pulse. And I'd started appreciating my all-so-complex husband more for the beautiful genius he was, beneath the surface where the rest of the world couldn't see. I hadn't completely forgotten about his days as the leader of the foot-watchers, but the memories were starting to fade.

After a few months of this vastly improved existence, I returned home one evening after a long day of baking in the industrial kitchen. Benny was playing video games with Wendy and Will in the living room. They were talking and laughing and having fun. It was the portrait of a happy family, and it warmed my heart to see. Redemption had officially arrived for the Basilworths after a long wait, and it was most welcome.

"How was your day, honey?" Benny asked once the game ended.

"Excellent, thanks. Two local restaurants placed large cheesecake orders today. At this rate, I'll be able to retire early!" I smiled.

"I struggle to picture Hackney's most successful entrepreneur putting her feet up when the calls for her famous cheesecake are growing louder," Benny grinned. "Your retirement would upset too many sweet-toothed people."

"Hello successful kettle, I'm the overachieving pot. It's nice to meet you," I said holding my hand out to shake Benny's.

"I'm charmed, successful kettle. We certainly have something in common beyond our abilities to boil water efficiently and whistle," Benny said as he took my hand while he whistled out of tune.

Will and Wendy roared with laughter. They loved it when Benny and I joked around with one another like normal human parents. We were doing that more and more by then.

"Hey Dad, let's get back to the video games," Will said with typical teenager finesse at redirecting the scene toward himself.

I took a deep breath.

"Before you do that, guys, I have a question that affects all of us," I said to the three of them. It was the perfect moment to broach a delicate subject.

"Shoot, oh-she-who-must-be-obeyed," responded Benny with his increasingly regular smile.

"We received a letter from the housing office the other day," I explained.

"Not the 'do you like windows' guy again! What does he want? To close off our last remaining light source now we've survived the almost-complete darkness?" asked Benny.

"Not exactly," I responded quietly. "The housing office is giving us the option of extending our stay in this flat if we agree to start paying rent now that we are earning income again. Otherwise, they are giving us four-weeks' notice to move out and move on."

I was so excited to deliver this news. It was the beginning of the next chapter for the Basilworth family, which was no small feat after all we'd been through.

"What does everyone think we should do?" I asked.

Knowing what I know now, we should have run for our lives without a second thought. However, Benny, Wendy, and Will paused to consider the two alternatives. The fact it wasn't a no brainer is shocking in hindsight, but that's what a run of living a somewhat normal existence for a few months can do—your defenses are down in the very moment they're needed the most.

"I vote we stay," responded Will. "Against the odds, we've gotten used to this funny little place, and it has helped us to view life from different perspectives."

Well, I nearly fell off my chair. I never believed I would hear those words come out of Will's mouth.

"I vote we stay too," added Wendy. "I like the neighborhood more than I thought I would. People are far less snobby here than in Pimlico."

A shiver ran down my spine. I'd been certain Wendy would by overjoyed at the idea of moving on. The ratios were once again conspiring against me, although Benny could still split the vote. We all stared at him as he considered his answer. I could see he was calculating all the competing angles in his mind, just like the way he handled Connection Game questions. I prayed common sense would factor into his calculation.

"I agree with the kids," Benny responded after a long pause. "We should stay here. It may not have always been easy, but we're now thriving here. And besides, we're well-positioned for what is coming in this little flat under the stairs."

My heart sank! I'd been outvoted and wrong-footed by my family. At the time I didn't understand what "well-positioned for what is coming" meant. Once again, my husband was a few steps ahead of the rest of us. He was always playing the long game, while the rest of us were being carried along for the ride.

So the decision was made to start paying rent in order to stay in the little flat. The prisoners had been offered freedom but chose to remain inside the prison. This decision may well prove to be the most inexplicable in our entire story once you've heard everything. However, all I can say is life can be confusing with its ups and downs. Sometimes we think a short term up-cycle will continue in the ascent, whereas in reality, it's just a smokescreen designed to throw us off the scent of an upcoming downturn.

CHAPTER 27

Despite my uneasiness about our decision to remain in the flat, I decided to appreciate my life in all its inexplicable glory, just as Deidre had taught me. So I embraced our decision to stay. But if the flat was to become our longer-term home, it needed a makeover. I'd had more-than-enough of paint flaking off the walls and little things breaking on a daily basis. One day, when I was walking along the entrance corridor the ceiling lamp actually fell on my head. The flat was clearly calling out for help. So I painted and decorated the flat over the ensuing few weeks. They say you can't dress up a pig, but I did a pretty good job. By the time I'd finished, the little flat could almost have passed as a loving home. Almost. The one thing I couldn't fix was the lack of daylight entering through that tiny sliver of a window.

One sunny day around that time, I chose to do all my baking deliveries myself rather than enlisting the help of couriers. When you live in the darkness, you gain a newfound respect for sunlight, so I wasn't going to let that rare beautiful day pass me by. There was a spring in my step that day as I hit the streets of Hackney for a walk just like I used to before I restarted my baking business. I was becoming adept at finding things to be grateful about in my life, and what a difference it made.

My first delivery stop was one of my main customers, a café a few blocks away called Premonitions. I got on well with the owner, a lady called Annabel, and her customers had quickly developed somewhat of an obsession for my cheese and bacon muffins. After only a few weeks, I was supplying her with over fifty muffins a day, so she was keeping me busy.

"Morning, what a glorious day!" I beamed at Annabel who was looking at her phone behind the counter when I walked in.

"Morning, Bell. It is indeed. Aren't we lucky to see the sun?" Annabel smiled back.

"We are. Good things come to those who wait," I responded.

"Agreed. Hey, by the way, you should be proud of yourself," Annabel continued.

"Oh yes. Why's that?" I inquired.

"We're getting requests for more and more of your products," Annabel answered. "It's great news for both of us as my food sales are going through the roof. In fact, you are single-handedly responsible for all the growth in my business this year."

"I'm so happy to hear that, Annabel. You deserve to be successful," I enthused.

Nothing made me happier than receiving positive feedback from my baking clients. I'd go so far as to say as my business grew, so did my self-worth.

"A couple of customers even asked if you could leave your business cards here, so they can order directly from you," Annabel continued. "One Russian gentleman explained it is very important he contacts you soon."

The hairs on the back of my neck stood to attention in unison.

"Yes, he was insistent that you listen to what he has to say. I assumed he was referring to an upcoming baking order," Annabel explained. "He's a regular here, so he's well versed in the joy your muffins provide."

"Oh, thanks, Annabel," I responded. "I appreciate the positive feedback. I'd better get going as I have a busy morning ahead."

I left Annabel's café in a fluster. Could it be a coincidence that a local Russian man wanted to talk with me? Benny would no doubt say there were hundreds of thousands of Russians living in London, so the probabilities didn't suggest anything suspicious was going on, but my gut instinct told me otherwise. Remembering his urgent warning when I last saw him, I wondered why the Russian man wanted to talk with me.

As I continued my deliveries that day, I sensed I was being watched by a sinister presence. Maybe it was the talk of Russian men, or maybe I had spent too long living in the darkness, but everyone I passed seemed abnormal. Worse than that, despite enjoying the resumption of our lives as seminormal humans, something deep inside me regressed straight back to my role as the street eyes of the foot-watchers.

I would forgive you for falling off your chair at this point. Normally, I was the most sensible one in the family, but the truth is I was ready to resume my family's weird obsession with searching for dangerous people without a second thought. Well, it took me by surprise as well. After all, it was me who had pushed Benny, Will, and Wendy back into the outside world to resume their normal lives. But my inner street-stalker came back to life with a vengeance and without an invitation that day. Truth be told, I was exhilarated by the notion I was being watched. You may be inclined to judge me for becoming what I'd been trying my best to avoid, but you'd be judging yourself as well. Because that's the nature of thoughts. We end up becoming whatever we think most about, good or bad. So I was guilty of nothing more or less than becoming my most dominant thoughts. And there they were that day, emerging from their hiding spot in the shadows of my mind. I was a foot-watcher who was back in the game whether I liked it or not.

Once I'd finished my deliveries, I continued walking the streets of Hackney on the lookout for Abnormals. You see, along with my passion for street-stalking, my belief in the existence of the Abnormals simultaneously bubbled its way back to the surface despite my better judgment. It's hard to explain. Maybe, despite my protestations, I needed to believe we were a part of something bigger after all we'd been through. Maybe, despite appearances to the contrary, I was happier when I thought there were bad people around us from whom we were trying to save others. Maybe, despite telling myself I was worthy, I believed if I helped save others, my life would be worthy in a way it could never be if I was pretending to live a seminormal life. Maybe Benny's father had been my father too.

I walked for hours. However, beyond my gut instinct insisting I was close to danger, I didn't actually see anything suspicious, just lots of people going about their daily business, ignorant they were being watched by a redeployed soldier from the foot-watchers.

And then it happened. As I rounded the corner onto our street, I saw a smallish boy in a hoodie carrying a courier bag who reminded me of someone I once knew. He was walking around seventy-five yards ahead of me. My heart skipped a beat. *Could it be Blue Joggers?* I wondered. Without a second thought, I locked onto my target and started following him as though my life depended on it. From my vantage point, he looked a lot like Blue Joggers, but I reminded myself there were many young people from diverse backgrounds living in Hackney, so it was a longshot. The distance between us was increasing so I sped up. He walked right past our flat, but he didn't turn his head toward our window. It was a data point that I noted. He continued to the end of the street, turned right, and disappeared out of sight.

I broke into a jog to bridge the invisibility between us. As I rounded the corner, I saw the boy I suspected was Blue

Joggers entering a townhouse shaded by a silver birch tree lining the street. I surveyed the windows of the three-floor townhouse, and noticed a curtain move on the second floor. Bingo, I thought, all we needed to do was to find out who lived on the second floor, and we'd have something concrete to work with. I stopped walking and jotted down the townhouse address in my phone: 4 Halidon Crescent. There were a few people approaching from the other direction, so I pretended to answer a phone call from Angie. I was basing all my moves on muscle memories from a few months earlier.

"Hey sis, what's up?" I beamed into my mute phone.

I paused for Ange's imagined hello.

"Oh that's great! It's so wonderful to hear your voice. So how's Great Ormond Street's most famous nurse enjoying her job?"

The silence echoed through my phone.

"Of course, you are! I'm sure you're making sick children feel better with your warm smile alone. And I can just imagine the way you light up the hospital wards with your light-hearted banter and bad jokes," I smiled into the ether.

I paused and then chuckled as the inevitable bad joke made its way from Make-Believe Land.

"That's so you, Ange. How are Michael and Jasper doing? Will you please send them our love?"

I paused. I knew the name of Angie's husband and son, but I knew next to nothing about them at that point in our lives. All the closeness between Angie and me had come to nothing for the simple reason I'd let her go when our lives went off track. But why didn't I reconnect with her when things had improved? It's a hard question to answer. I wonder if I was ever content playing happy families. I was thankful it was a pretend phone conversation that I could end whenever I wanted.

"What are we most grateful for in our lives, Ange? Oh, you remind me of my friend Deidre whom you'd love. Well, we're grateful for being together as a family, fighting the good fight as a family, and staying safe as a family. It's comforting to be united together in a disconnected world."

Even now, I can see how revealing my imaginary conversation with Angie was. Yes, maybe I needed more than the semblance of normality.

"Great to chat, sis. Speak soon," I concluded as I resumed my wait for Blue Joggers.

I waited for another ten minutes, but Blue Joggers or whoever he was didn't reappear from the townhouse. I asked myself if maybe he was simply returning home to his family like a normal person. However, despite his best efforts to convince me otherwise I was certain he was about as normal as we were. I walked past the townhouse he'd entered and gazed up at the second floor, but I didn't see anyone there. I marched home full of surprising news for Benny and the kids.

CHAPTER 28

When I arrived home, Benny and the kids were watching The Connection Game. It was a strange coincidence that they'd chosen to watch that damned TV program again on the very day I'd reconnected with my inner street-stalker. But I don't believe in coincidence anymore.

"Hey guys, can we talk?" I asked the three of them with urgency.

"Mom, can't it wait until after the game?" asked Will as he high-fived Wendy for getting an answer right. "We're nailing it."

"Sorry, it can't wait," I implored.

Reluctantly, Benny led Wendy and Will over to the kitchen table. Benny knew it was rare for me to interrupt anything. On this occasion, he'd clearly noticed the seriousness of my tone.

"What's happened, Bell?" Benny asked.

"Guys, there's no easy way to say this," I began. "We were on the right path with our foot-watching work after all. I found out today that the Russian man is looking for me."

A heavy silence descended as the three of them contemplated my terrible admission.

"Mom! We've let go of all that. And besides, as we told you last time, we were looking for a Frenchman, not a Russian. A Russian man wanting to talk with you is hardly newsworthy," Will said, rolling his eyes skyward.

"There's more," I continued. "Just after discovering the Russian man was looking for me, I came across Blue Joggers walking the streets of Hackney. It was definitely him. I followed him to a townhouse *just around the corner* and awaited his return to the street. But he didn't leave the townhouse, which suggests to me it may be his home."

Benny thought long and hard about what I was saying.

"Honey, I'm a little surprised you are so worked up about this," he eventually responded. "You made it abundantly clear you thought we were on the wrong path with our work. Remember what you said after we watched that film? You basically told us we'd all become ghoulish freaks who'd lost our minds."

"I'm not sure I used those words," I responded.

"And anyway, there was the not insignificant problem that all our recent data was conflicted," Benny explained. "We couldn't prove any of our hypotheses, so we were well and truly stuck at square one. That's the real reason we moved on with our lives. And I never thought I'd admit this, but it's almost working for us."

"I know, Benny, *almost*. I'm confused and I don't have the answers. All I know is that something inside me came back to life along with the reemergence of the Russian man and Blue Joggers in my life. Call it an epiphany, but I'm certain we were on the right track despite the data conflict," I confessed.

It's hard for me to admit now that it was me who had said those things. (If the kids are reading this, I am so sorry. I accept responsibility for all that followed.)

"You were right to tell us, Mom," responded Wendy with kindness. "We are a family and if one of us has a strong belief, we all need to take it seriously."

"Wend's right, honey," said Benny with his charming smile of old. "We are here for you, just as you were there for us when we hurtled blindly down this path. What do you need from us?"

"Thanks, Benny," I said with relief. "All I want is for you to explain to me in simple terms exactly what our data challenge was. What was the obstacle that stopped our work making any sense?"

"That's a big question," contributed Will.

"Is it?" asked Benny with growing intensity. "I'm not sure it is, nor should it be if we did our work properly. It's actually very simple. Data is like a sky that can range from clear and blue to cloudy and stormy. Our sky full of data started out perfectly blue, but it became more and more cloudy as we gathered more data on the Abnormals. Each and every step we took added to the expanding cloud cover."

"So what caused the change of weather?" I asked.

"OK, I'll get to the point," Benny responded. "As you know, based upon our intricate data analysis of their independent movements and interactions with one another, we had clearly categorized all the foot owners we were monitoring into three separate groups: Normals, Abnormals, and Unknowns. The data suggested the Abnormals were of particular interest as they were outliers on multiple data points, while there was also an unusually high correlation in the type of outlying data points we gathered for each of them. That confirmed they were somehow connected as a group. Given the highly suspicious nature of the Abnormals' movements, the large size of the group, and their obvious attempts at concealment, our strongest working theory was that they were working together on an illegal project which poses considerable risk to all Londoners."

"Yes, I knew that much," I responded.

"Right, of course. As you may also remember, we'd identified a number of Abnormals who we believed were leading or controlling the other Abnormals," Benny continued. "We called them key Abnormals. We initially thought this group included Brown Suede, Red High Heels, Blue Joggers, and Black Business Shoes, but as the clouds emerged, we weren't so sure by the end. Our thesis suggested that by being able to explain the key Abnormals' relationships and movements, we should be able to uncover what the wider group of Abnormals were doing, and when it was due to happen."

"Understood," I responded.

"However, every single time we tested a theory about any of those four key Abnormals, our data let us down and the cloud cover expanded. Nothing they did fit within the thesis we were modeling, but without them nothing made sense. So, in essence, the whole project became redundant because the rest of the Abnormals' movements were explicable only by looking at the movements of those four key Abnormals," concluded Benny.

"I see," I responded. "It's almost as if those four key Abnormals have been playing some sort of game with us. So the challenge is to somehow figure out the game's rules that we haven't been privy too."

Benny stopped and stared at me, first with surprise, and then with love.

"Yes, exactly," he nodded. "What a brilliant way of summarizing the challenge. That's it. We don't know the rules of the game."

"Got it. So my next question is: may I please have a look at the data you compiled on the four key Abnormals?" I asked.

"Mom, you won't understand it. It's too hard to explain," grumbled Will with annoyance.

Benny shook his head at Will.

"Of course, you can. We'd welcome your opinion on it, darling," added Benny with more softness than I expected.

"Thank you for listening to me, Benny. I appreciate your support more than you know," I responded as I put my arm around his shoulder.

"Ditto squared," smiled Benny.

It was a special moment that I recognized as such, thanks to Deidre's lesson about appreciating life. I was as highly valued by my family as I could remember being since we'd arrived in the little flat. My opinion was being listened to, respected, and supported, and I was determined to make my rising status count. You'll no doubt be wondering if my need for having a bigger role in my family was the real reason I was so keen to poke a stick at the misty world of the Abnormals after we'd happily moved on. Maybe you'd be right to ask that, but as with everything in our story, there's much more to it.

Benny opened his laptop and showed me the many files of data they'd collected on each of the three groups. He talked proudly about each foot-owner like a parent talking about their children. He knew so much more about those feet than he knew about most humans in his life. He could tell me all about their movements, their habits, even their passions. When he mentioned Red High Heels, he knew all about her love of Mr. Zimmy dresses and expensive high-heeled shoes, as well as her tendency to walk 20 percent faster in the evenings. As his eyes lit up, it was clear I had awoken in Benny what I had awoken in myself—Pandora's box was officially open for one more peek.

Much to my baking clients' disappointment, I canceled all baking deliveries the following day and focused on understanding the data. Benny, Wendy, and Will reluctantly attended to life in the real world while I got on with the important work. The tables had turned, and I relished every moment.

As I delved deeper into the data, I soon discovered that numbers without stories were meaningless to me. They only came alive when a story gave them the breath of life. So I quickly became adept at creating stories that brought the data to life. It was like searching for a pair of perfectly fitting shoes for the passing feet. And as I searched for those shoes, I discovered a talent for storytelling residing deep inside of me. It was high time it was called upon. While the other three excelled at maths and spreadsheets, they were dyslexic when it came to piecing words together to create meaning out of their data analysis. I'd finally found my unique niche in the team, and it was a much better match than street-stalking.

The story the data was telling me was changing fast. Initially, I'd been stumped by the same challenge as Benny and the kids. There were only four key Abnormals, but their movements almost always preempted the movements of each and every Abnormal. However, this didn't make sense to me as a story. I couldn't shake the nagging feeling that the key Abnormals were playing by different rules to the other Abnormals. So I decided to let go of Benny's overriding assumption that Blue Joggers, Red High Heels, Brown Suede, and Black Business Shoes were the leaders of the Abnormals. That theory only made sense if the data reconciled, but it didn't. Instead, I started viewing those four as a separate group entirely. I named them the Inexplicables, and the moment I did everything started making more sense.

What I knew of the story of the Inexplicables was that the four of them were working together, and they were aware of our existence. They were also aware there were Abnormals walking among them and seemed to be aware of most of their identities. More than that, the reason they appeared to Benny, Will, and Wendy to be the leaders of the Abnormals was that, like us, they were watching the Abnormals from street level. Yes, they were another group of street-stalkers. It meant we weren't the only Peeping Toms in town. It was a strangely comforting thought. So, rather than leading the Abnormals, it was actually the other way around for these four. They were in fact utilizing the valuable street-stalking advice that you won't be noticed if you remain a few steps ahead of your target. I was starting to believe they were a group of professionals who knew far more about street-stalking than any of us.

While my story of the Inexplicables was becoming clearer, it lacked an explanation. Why on earth were these four individuals watching us watching them, while at the same time watching the other people we were also watching? I suspected the Inexplicables' motivation was connected with our own motivation, but that part of my story needed more work. How they were doing what they were doing was clearly dependent upon creating a mask to hide their true identity, but from whom I wasn't sure. It had to be either us or the Abnormals. I hoped it was the Abnormals as that meant we were all fighting the same fight together. It was an easier pill to swallow within the perverse world we found ourselves in.

My story was a breakthrough, and patches of blue were emerging from behind the clouds within our sky full of data. I was overjoyed. But before I told the others, I needed more clarity about the Inexplicables' interest in us. I was closer than I expected.

CHAPTER 29

Why would someone become a Peeping Tom of a Peeping Tom? That was the question I asked myself as I tried to piece together the Inexplicables' relationship to us.

Despite Benny and Will's insistence he was French, I remained confident the Russian man was Brown Suede. But his role remained a mystery as did his relationship with the other Inexplicables. I wondered if by ignoring the Russian man's invitation to talk I was looking a gift horse in the mouth. I needed more data on him and he wanted to tell me something, so it was a two-way street in the making. The more I pondered the challenge, the more urgent a meeting with the Russian man seemed. If I only knew who he really was, I was sure I'd be a step closer to the truth.

The next day, I texted Annabel to let her know I could drop in some muffins the following morning if she had her usual demand. She quickly confirmed the order, and I got to work in the kitchen.

Benny arrived home that evening to find me up to my ears in eggs, flour, and butter.

"Hey honey, have you returned to life in the normal lane then?" Benny inquired with a tinge of disappointment.

"Not quite," I replied. "I need to run a little further down this rabbit hole before I'm ready for normal. I'm baking my entry ticket."

"I love it," Benny smiled. "As the resident master of rabbit-hole investigations, I understand your plight. So what's the plan?"

"I'm going to gather some data on the Russian man as he's the only one raising his head above the parapet," I answered.

"Oh, the mysterious Russian man again. OK, on one condition though. Promise me you'll remain in public places. We suspect these people are involved in something huge, but we don't know how much danger we're in," Benny warned.

"OK, Mom," I smiled, loving the fact I was the one taking action, and Benny was the one worrying.

"I'm serious, Bell," Benny responded.

"I've been taught by the best, honey. I'm owning my position at the front and center of the stage. I'll be fine," I insisted.

The next morning, I left the little flat armed with nothing more than a basket full of freshly baked muffins and a curiosity I needed to scratch. As I made my way to Premonitions, my heart was running faster than usual. I half expected the Russian man to creep up behind me as I walked to the café, but he didn't appear.

When I arrived at the café, Annabel was busy serving customers. I waved at her and sat down at a corner table.

Premonitions always attracted an eclectic crowd, and that day was no different. There was a large boisterous family sitting nearby who was discussing a disagreement they had with their neighbors.

"I said good morning to her yesterday, and she ignored me!" exclaimed the father. "Can you believe it! What sort of person ignores another like that?"

"All because she doesn't like good music," contributed one of his daughters. "A little bit of happy music may be all she needs to wipe that sourpuss frown off her face."

The rest of her family laughed.

"Yes, anything to cheer up her stuffy-bummed impression of a Tyrannosaurus rex in a dinosaur-sized bad mood," added the smiley mother.

They roared with laughter as a group. It was wonderful the way they laughed with abandon. And the more they laughed, the more they laughed. I couldn't help but join in.

The smiley mother turned to me, rolled her eyes, and said, "What can you do?" Even now I can picture her generous face. She was the type of normal I aspired to be, and still do. Maybe one day.

"I hear you," I smiled back. "I know a few grumpy dinosaurs as well. They are at their best when they're extinct."

The family roared with laughter again. Everyone else in the café turned around to understand what the commotion was about. But no one looked at me or anyone in the joyful family as they were more interested in learning what we were laughing about. I was wonderfully hidden behind the cloak of group laughter. Benny's advice about being hidden as the member of any type of audience was once again spot on. When the laughter stopped and the family left, I sat alone, naked and exposed. I missed their joyful energy more than I had any right to.

Annabel had finished dealing with customers at that point and called me over.

"Morning honey, I'm so glad you are supplying again! The business suffered during your hiatus," Annabel said.

"Thanks, me too," I said as I handed her the basket filled with muffins.

"They smell wonderful! Shall we sneak a cheeky couple ourselves?" asked Annabel.

"Great idea," I responded. She pulled out two of the muffins, which we both took satisfyingly large bites out of in quick succession.

"Life is worth living again," Annabel oozed.

"It is," I responded. "Hey, by the way, do you know how I can track down that Russian gentleman you mentioned was interested in chatting? I'm expanding my client base, so I'd like to talk with him."

"I sure do, but please remember to keep supplying us with your muffins when you grow your business to the next level," Annabel said with concern.

"I promise I will," I smiled.

"Great. Your friendly Russian pops in at around nine thirty most mornings to pick up a takeaway coffee. You're in luck—he should be here in around ten minutes," Annabel responded as she checked the clock on the wall.

"OK, good to know. I have to make tracks this morning but maybe I'll see him next time," I said.

I'd intended to talk with the Russian man in person and in public, so you'll no doubt wonder why I said that. Truth be told, as my inner street-stalker thrived, I was more comfortable watching people from a distance than participating in conversation with them. You see, foot owners are so much more predictable from at least fifty yards away than up close and personal.

So I left the café and positioned myself across the road inside a music store. From my vantage point I could see everyone who entered and exited Premonitions while I pretended to peruse the old record collection in front of me. Nine thirty came and went with no sign of the Russian man. I wondered if I was on another wild-goose chase. And then he sauntered up the road with the same calm energy I remembered. He walked into the café.

While I watched and waited, the shop assistant in the record store tried to get my attention.

"That's a classic album," he called out from the front of the shop. I looked down at the record I was holding. It was *Song to a Seagull* by Joni Mitchell.

"Everyone raves about *Blue* and *The Hissing of Summer Lawns* but in my humble opinion it's her best record. Shall I play it for you?" he continued.

"Thanks, but I'm looking for something else," I called back. He cowered like a hurt animal, but I had to focus.

A few minutes later the Russian man left the café with a takeaway coffee in hand, and brown suede shoes on his infamous feet. "Hello again, Brown Suede," I whispered under my breath. He walked back in the direction from whence he had arrived. I left the record store without another word and walked around a hundred yards behind him. He was a much slower walker than Blue Joggers, so I had to ensure I didn't unwittingly catch up with him.

When I noticed he was approaching the same silver-birch-tree-lined townhouse Blue Joggers had entered, my body tensed up like a tennis player awaiting to return a big serve. If Brown Suede entered that house it had to mean something monumental. And I was in luck. He stopped outside the front of the same townhouse, pressed the buzzer, and waited. It had to mean he didn't live there but was somehow connected with the people inside. I was about to start my pretend phone call routine, but I changed my mind and kept walking slowly forward.

The door opened a couple of minutes later. Two people held the door open for Brown Suede to enter the house, and then they walked past him out onto the street. I recognized Red High Heels straight away, and she was accompanied by a tall man wearing black business shoes. Bingo! I had proof that the four Inexplicables were working together from one location. It was a significant development for my story-weaving. I wanted to run over and high-five them. However, I had a serious problem to contend with: I was getting too close to my targets. I was only twenty yards away as Red High Heels and Black Business Shoes connected their infamous shoes with the less than worthy street. I panicked and decided to evade contact at any cost, so I turned to cross the road.

As I checked for traffic in either direction, out of the corner of my eye I noticed Red High Heels glance quickly in my direction. It was fast, it was subtle, but it definitely happened. I'd been seen by an Inexplicable in an inexplicable world—I felt naked. Part of me wanted to run over and say hello to her as these were the only people who could explain to me the purpose of our role in the game, my obsession, and my family's obsession. But in reality, I couldn't trust them as I still didn't know why the hell they were doing what they were doing. So I crossed the road and sped up.

CHAPTER 30

I walked in the opposite direction from home as my gut instinct instructed me that with the Inexplicables knowing where I lived, I'd be safest anywhere but there. I kept glancing over my shoulder, but I couldn't see anyone following me.

Then my phone rang from an unknown mobile number. Curiosity got the better of me.

"Hello," I answered.

"Hello, Belinda," said a voice with a thick accent. Somehow the Russian man had gotten my phone number. I froze where I was standing.

"What do you want?" I asked.

"I just want to talk with you," he answered calmly.

"Tell me what you want to say now," I implored.

"All I can say is you are on the wrong path," he responded. "I can explain more in person."

"No, thank you," I said as I hung up.

I was annoyed. How dare Brown Suede, or the Russian man, or whoever the hell he was, tell me I was on the wrong track without explaining what he meant. I kept walking, propelled forward by annoyance rather than fear. If an Inexplicable wanted me, they could come and get me.

As I continued walking, my annoyance migrated away from Brown Suede toward myself. I'd left home with the explicit intention of talking with Brown Suede, and then, like a moron I'd hung up on him when he phoned me. I'd once again botched up my daily mission. I was disappointed with myself. The only consolation was there was no way Benny and the kids could know about my latest mistake.

I noticed I was standing across the road from Clapton Square where Deidre lived. The idea of seeing Deidre's smiling face filled me with joy in a less-than-joyful moment, so I crossed the road, and walked across the park to Deidre's corner. I found her sitting quietly by herself gazing wistfully at the trees.

"Hello, stranger!" I said as I sat down by her side.

"Bell! It's lovely to see you," Deidre beamed back.

"Right back at you. I need my dose of Deidre today," I smiled.

"You look tired, Bell. Is everything all right?" she asked.

"I don't know. I'm not sure if I'm moving forward or backward in my life right now. To be honest, I feel stupid," I admitted.

"I know the feeling," Deidre said with empathetic eyes. "All I know is the times in my life when I've felt like I was moving backward were the times I was actually moving forward. You see, we aren't privy to the big picture until much later on."

"Yes, what a wise observation," I responded. "If only the answers were clearer in the moment. I just want to *know* I'm on the right pathway rather than wasting my time."

Deidre nodded and accepted my confusion in all its haziness.

"How are you always so present, so clear, so relaxed?" I asked. "You make being Deidre look so easy."

"Ha! Let me assure you, it's not always easy being Deidre," she smiled.

"Has something happened?" I asked.

"Not really, but take today for example," Deidre responded. "I performed a rendition of *500 Miles* for a large crowd this morning. They were generous with their contributions, and I was on track for a hot lunch as my reward. I could almost taste Fabio's famous lasagna from the little Italian café across the road. But then, half an hour later, my situation changed. Two of the local young guys noticed my contribution box was particularly flush and stole it from under my nose."

"What? That's terrible, Deidre! What can I do to help? Shall I call the police? Do you want me to find them for you so they can be brought to justice? I know a thing or two about tracking people down. What did they look like?" As I asked Deidre those questions, it suddenly occurred to me that I was a lot more stressed about Deidre's theft than she was. She observed me becoming quite worked up about it without saying a word.

"It's OK, thanks, Bell," Deidre eventually responded. "Because after a wee bit of reflection I was happy those boys stole my money."

"Pardon me?" I said in shock.

"Think about life as a young person on the streets of Hackney," Deidre said. "Believe me, it's hard. My money may well make the difference between an average day and a great day for those two boys."

As Deidre spoke, my mind wandered to the memory of the day our savings were stolen and we were so ingloriously dethroned from our lives. My heart raced just as it had when the awful truth had become apparent that day.

"But then, I changed my mind with the help of some more time," Deidre continued. "I decided it's more likely those two boys will be overwhelmed by guilt for what they did. I'm a weak and vulnerable elderly lady, and they stole from me. It was hardly a heroic thing to do. Whether it be today, or sometime in the future, they're going to have to come to terms with their actions. Hopefully that realization will lead to positive changes in their lives. So I expect they won't be stealing from anyone else thanks to what happened today. Once I understood that my money has paid for positive changes for the world, I became overjoyed they'd taken it."

As Deidre spoke, I considered myself unworthy to be in her presence. I was confused about what her story could teach me about our story. We certainly weren't celebrating our losses with similar grace and poise.

"You are a force of nature, Deidre," I responded quietly. "I can't even comprehend how someone can be so full of love, kindness, and forgiveness."

"Thanks, Bell, but it wasn't always the case for me," she stated. "This way of reframing situations to make my day better started as a survival strategy. You see, when you live on the streets, you're exposed to these types of stories on a daily basis. After many years of being stressed and hurt and distraught I learned I had only one option: to somehow find peace amid the chaos. And that brings me to your question about clarity."

"Please enlighten me," I said.

"The real reason I'm able to retell the stories that make up my life in a more positive light is because I'm sitting in Deidre's corner," she smiled.

"Does this part of the park have special powers?" I asked.

"No," Deidre smiled, "but sitting still does. And I don't mean not moving. I mean observing the world from a quiet and safe place where you can take your time to piece it together into a picture that works for you."

"That sounds similar to the way we watch the world from our flat," I jumped in, knowing it was also very different. "But how does that help you achieve clarity?"

"It's the stillness and the distance that provides me with the necessary space to recreate the stories I want in my life," Deidre explained. "And it's the same stillness and distance that allows me to see the extraordinary beauty in this magical world we live in."

Unexpectedly, tears welled up in my eyes. Deidre's words connected with something deep inside of me and they also confused me. Was I on the same page? I wondered. Or was foot-watching or street-stalking or human-judging actually the exact opposite of Deidre's beautiful philosophy? Was I willing bad stuff to happen to avoid dealing with some hard truths in my life?

Before heading home that day, I bought Deidre a lasagna and coffee from the Italian café across the road.

"You shouldn't have, Bell," was her graceful response. "I feel so loved."

"You are, Deidre," I stated.

CHAPTER 31

By the time I arrived back at the flat, I was exhausted after an eventful few hours. As I descended the stairs, I noticed our front door was wide open. Something wasn't right. I checked my watch. It was two thirty in the afternoon, which meant Benny was at work and the kids were still at school. Maybe one of them had forgotten to shut the door on the way out. No, they never forgot anything.

After taking a deep breath, I stepped inside the flat. Nothing appeared to be amiss in the corridor, so I walked into the kitchen and living room area. Something had changed, but I couldn't tell what it was at first. The living room was tidier than usual. I wondered if maybe Benny and the kids had decided to clean up before leaving. In hindsight, I clearly wasn't thinking straight. Then, the chilling realization hit me that all our technology had been taken—Benny, Wendy, and Will's laptops, Wendy's video hub connections, everything important was missing.

I quickly checked the rest of the flat. Being as small as it was, it took me all of a few seconds. But there was no one there. Maybe I had just missed the thieving bastards.

I shut the front door and returned to the living room to collapse on the sofa. They had dealt us a serious blow. All our data, all our work was gone. It was the equivalent of chopping the legs off an Olympic sprinter just before the race was about to start. My tears flowed freely. I wasn't sure if it was this latest theft or Deidre's words that were their real inspiration, but the tears wouldn't be held back. It was devastating that in the very moment I had understood how important our foot-watching work was, they'd taken away our ability to do it. When I say they, I had no doubt the Inexplicables were responsible. Yes, we lived in a part of London where theft was a problem, but if you were a thief with even the slightest sense our little flat was the last place you'd want to break into. The only story that made sense of the data was the Inexplicables wanted to stop us in our tracks. And of course, that meant we were on the right track.

When Benny and the kids found out about the theft, all hell broke loose. Deidre's beautiful way of reframing theft was most definitely not the Basilworth way.

"Those bastards!" Benny shouted. "They've taken everything we had, including our data and my software program. In the wrong hands that information could be extremely dangerous. And if they discard it, all my work will be worthless. Worthless! Years of work down the drain."

"Dad, didn't you save everything critical to the cloud?" asked Wendy.

"No, of course not," responded an angry Benny. "The cloud can be hacked—everything can be hacked. And now our lives have been hacked for the second time. Do you understand the type of world we are living in? The dangers are hidden from most people's sight but they are very real." He collapsed in a heap in the corner.

"I can't believe you, of all people, didn't prepare for this in advance!" exclaimed Wendy.

"I didn't say that, Wend. Security is always at the forefront of my mind. There's more to this than you understand," Benny responded without going into more detail.

Wendy rolled her eyes skyward.

"Someone needs to pay for this. You mark my words," added Will with the same look in his eye as when he tormented our verbal abuser on the tube. A shiver ran down my spine.

"Maybe Will, but there's more at stake for us than revenge," responded Benny. "We made a serious mistake when we stopped working on this project. We were clearly on the right path, and we've gone and wasted time, the greatest sin of them all. The Abnormals have no doubt progressed their plans while we've been idly watching from the sidelines, pretending to be bloody Normals. Whatever they are planning next will be on us if we don't stop them. Do you understand? It will be our fault if bad stuff happens because we are the only ones who can do anything about it. Well, we were, before our technology was stolen. This is a disaster."

All our half-baked efforts of pretending to be seminormal members of the human race crumbled in that moment.

"I'm with you, honey," I stated. "My recent work has highlighted we were indeed on the right path, and today's theft has just confirmed that. If there's a silver lining here, it's that our work has been validated. The importance of our work is even more significant than we thought. What we do next is a no brainer. We have to move forward despite what's happened."

You may be wondering if I was a sandwich short of a picnic at this point. Maybe, maybe not.

"Yes, you're right, Bell. Our work is the game changer and must go on," agreed Benny with a warmer smile than I was expecting. "We'll just have to figure out a new way to work. But before we do that, where did you get to with your recent data analysis and street work?"

And the old band was officially back together. I updated the three of them on all my conclusions about the Inexplicables being separate from the Abnormals, how they were working together in a nearby townhouse, and how the Russian man had called me to warn me we were on the wrong track. I was proud of my work as I filled them in.

"I can't believe I hadn't seen it before," Benny responded. "Yes, you're right, darling. Those four Inexplicables, as you call them, have been watching us watching both them and the Abnormals. The data wrong-footed me as I was focused on the least improbable directional relationship. The Inexplicables are definitely a step ahead of the Abnormals, and us for that matter. Thank god, I'm married to a genius."

"Well done, Mom!" exclaimed Wendy. "You nailed it."

If I could have pressed pause on that moment and re-played it forever, I would have. After months of being devalued, I was back on top, and my self-confidence was thriving. We were a team of equals in our battle against whatever it was we were at war with.

CHAPTER 32

While we contemplated our next move, Benny had a surprise in store for us, although it shouldn't have been a surprise to me as his long-term partner.

"Guys, all is not lost. Look at this," Benny said holding up his mobile.

It was a map of the local area around the flat with a small red dot hovering in the middle.

"What's that, Dad?" inquired Wendy.

"A while back I had a tracking device installed in my laptop to prepare for a scenario just like this. The red dot there tells us exactly where our technology has been taken to," Benny explained pointing at his phone.

Will high-fived Benny, Wendy, and me.

"Well done, Dad!" Will exclaimed. "And we are back in the game."

"We can't celebrate yet," responded Benny. "Information like this is a blunt tool without a sharp plan behind it. We need to recalibrate before we do anything."

"Your dad is right," I contributed. "We can't just break in and steal our laptops back. These people know what they're doing. By the way, what's the address of where all our stuff is being held?"

"It's just around the corner at 4 Halidon Crescent," responded Benny.

I pulled out my mobile and checked the note I'd made of the townhouse address Blue Joggers and Brown Suede had both entered.

"What a remarkably small world we live in," I smiled. "4 Halidon Crescent is where I witnessed our friendly local Inexplicables coming and going as a group. So that confirms they stole our stuff. I'd say this suggests they're foes rather than friends."

"Bastards!" seethed Will. "They'll pay for this."

"Guys, one more bit of good news for you," added Benny. "The tracking device inside my laptop is also connected with audio capabilities. As long as the laptop is still in one piece, we can listen in on my phone."

The excitement in the room took on a life of its own at that point. We foot-watchers lived for opportunities to peep on people when they least suspected it. And there was something particularly seductive about the idea of listening in to our enemies through our own laptop. The four of us positioned ourselves around the kitchen table like a hungry pack of wolves. Benny put his phone on the table and pressed "Access Audio." Wendy simultaneously pressed record on her phone so we could play it back later. We couldn't hear much apart from white noise at first, but then a voice faded in as if from beyond the grave.

"Semejstvo obez'an iz igrovogo orientirovano ne na teh ludej," the person stated.

I recognized the voice straight away. It was our brown-suede-shoed comrade, and his tone remained as calm and controlled as ever.

"Mom, you're right, that's Russian," said Will.

I rolled my eyes.

"A ne uveren, cto oni mogut nam pomoc," continued Brown Suede.

"Guys, my phone is translating as we go," commented Wendy. "He's explaining we are focused on the wrong people, so we may not be able to help them. He's implying we are idiots—he called us 'game-show monkeys.'"

"Game-show monkeys? Do they know who we are? Do they know who *I* am?" Benny asked as though we were all the Russian man. "How dare they steal from us and then throw cheap insults in our direction like this. I won't tolerate it."

"Hang on, he's saying something else," interjected Wendy.

"Mozhet byt', oni gotovy k yeshche odnoy igre 'Dayte nam svoi den'gi'," said the Russian man with a little more enthusiasm than usual.

"Oh shit!" whispered Wendy.

It was one of those moments it would have been best to leave alone. Knowing what the Russian man said next would change everything. All we had to do was pretend we couldn't translate his foreign words, and we could have remained blissfully ignorant. But we were drawn in like moths to a flame.

"What did he say?" growled Benny with the venom of an angry alley cat.

"Dad, it really doesn't matter. Please don't ask me," Wendy implored.

"Wend, I need you to tell me. This is important. What did he say?" Benny asked, ready to explode.

"OK, OK. He said: 'Maybe they're ready for another game of "Give Us Your Money"'," Wendy finally answered.

We lost reception at that point, and you could have heard a pin drop in the little flat. We all stared at Benny's mobile while we digested those dreadful words and what they meant.

"I always suspected whoever orchestrated the fraud against us was unusually talented," Benny finally stated.

"So these Inexplicables are the ones who ruined our lives by stealing all our money?" asked Will who was struggling to accept the cold hard facts flying in our direction.

"Yes, dots connected. We are nothing but pawns for these people to move around the chess board as and when they feel like it. Welcome to whatever game we are smack bang in the middle of," responded Benny with a twisted grin.

There was no turning back from whatever was coming next. Benny's passions were ignited by an anger to prove to the world he was right, and the rest of us were suffering the same contagious symptoms. All of our limp-wristed efforts to resume our lives as humans in the outside world were forever lost. Benny's job, the kids' schooling, Deidre's kind vision of the world, and any semblance of normal social interaction with the outside world went flying out that minuscule window with frightening speed. The little flat was to become our last stop as a family, and we had just progressed to the final stages of whatever strange game we were playing. It was fast becoming a winner take all situation.

CHAPTER 33

"Surely we have all we need to confront these bastards," seethed Will as we pondered our next steps as a team. "We know they stole all our money and all our technology. It's clear they are playing some sick game with us. Let's go have a friendly chat with them about it." Will was ready for a fight. His teenage testosterone was bubbling to the surface against his will.

"Hang on, Will. What do we really have on these people?" responded a calmer Benny. "We can't prove they stole our money based on them mentioning a game called 'Give Us Your Money.' That's just us connecting the dots in a way only the Basilworths would understand. And why would we want to show our hand too early anyway? We are obviously players in a much bigger game here. You and I both know that the best way to win any game is to spend your time developing a proactive strategy, rather than reacting to the other players' moves. Remember, the other players want us to make a mistake."

As I listened to Benny, I knew he was right. Our thinking was as aligned as at any time in our relationship, and our differences melted away like distant memories. I smiled on the inside.

"Your dad's right, Will. When has reacting to the bad stuff in the world ever worked for us? We need to get back in front of the game to regain and own the advantage," I added.

"I get it, guys," responded Will. "So what do you think our next move should be then?"

"Well, let's start by fine-tuning our theory about what the Inexplicables want. Once we know that, we'll be positioned to create leverage over them," said Benny with his old smile.

"That's what I've been working on, honey," I responded with excitement.

"Perfect. What are your thoughts?" Benny asked.

"The Inexplicables desperately want to understand what the Abnormals are doing," I answered. "That's why they're always one step ahead of the Abnormals' movements. And that's why they're closely monitoring our analysis of what the Abnormals are doing as well."

"So why do you think they want to know what the Abnormals are doing?" asked Benny.

"That's less clear," I responded, "but my working theory is they are deeply worried about it. Maybe they believe the Abnormals are planning an attack that could affect them or their organization in some way."

"Yes, and that aligns with our own theory about the Abnormals. Good. So is everyone in agreement that we should further our theories about what exactly the Abnormals are planning before we attempt any discussions with the Inexplicables?" asked Benny with bright eyes.

We all nodded.

"All I ask is that we look the Inexplicables in the eye one day to ask them why they ruined us. I just want to understand why," responded Will.

"We will son, once we are positioned to win the game," returned Benny with confidence.

"Dad, one small problem," added Wendy. "How are we going to position ourselves to win the game when all our technology and data have been stolen?"

"I thought you'd never ask," smiled Benny. "Look around at the mind-blowing computer power in the room."

Wendy gave Benny an 'are you mad?' look.

"It's all here, Wend, everything we need," Benny continued as he tapped his brow. "Inside our heads, the four of us are carrying computers far more powerful and adaptable than the ones stolen. And as for collecting data and videos looking forward, we have mobile phones with more than enough capabilities. Plus, we have your mom's recent findings to help guide us in the right direction. Now I think of it, we are much better off than when we had the laptops. We are finally on the right track."

I was roused and aroused. My husband had returned in all his glory. And we were all empowered to do whatever needed to be done to win the game. We got straight down to work.

"Will, how many Abnormals had we identified at last count?" Benny asked.

"Twenty-two. We reached Abnormal classification status for the remaining two suspected Abnormals a few months ago," responded Will.

"OK, so our first step is to write down from memory the names of as many of those twenty-two as possible," Benny said.

And we were off. The Connection Game had morphed into The Abnormals Game before our very eyes, and we weren't skipping a beat.

"White Tennis Shoes, Gray Boat Shoes, and Red Trainers," started Wendy.

"Yellow Low Heels, Brown Boots, and Beige Ballet Pumps," added Will.

"Pink Running Shoes, Black Brogues, and Stripy Walking Shoes," I contributed.

In minutes, we had listed out all twenty-two Abnormals as well as everything we had learned about them to date. Benny wrote the information on large sheets of paper, which he stuck to the walls like an artist brainstorming creative thoughts, and soon we were sitting within our very own case headquarters. The walls vibrated with the rhythm of progress.

"Great work, team," Benny enthused. "The next question is what do all of these Abnormals have in common whether it be a belief, a hatred, a relationship, or an objective? I'll start the bidding with the fact the data suggests they all live in Hackney. That's more likely to be causal, but we can't exclude anything just yet."

"I've got one—we believe they are all originally from places outside the UK based on the video footage," contributed Wendy.

"Yes, well done, Wend," cheered Benny.

"All of them can be connected with at least one other Abnormal," I added.

"Nice one, Bell. Can we learn anything from the way the relationships are distributed by sex, religion, and cultural background, for example?" asked Benny.

"Great question," I jumped in. "If anything, the distributions are remarkable for their lack of patterns. I'd say someone is purposefully controlling those factors."

"OK, so it's likely this is being orchestrated by a global group who are extremely well organized. For them to have a team of twenty-two people on the streets of Hackney suggests this is a major operation. Is there anything else the data can tell us?" asked Benny.

"One thing, Dad," said Wendy. "Some of the Abnormals have been witnessed carrying technological equipment with much more computing power than your standard laptop. A while back we even noticed Beige Ballet Pumps and Gray Boat Shoes were carrying the top-level AERO laptop. That's mighty unusual considering only a few thousand people in the world are prepared to fork out over five thousand pounds for one of the most powerful laptops in the world. Let's just say they don't tend to be used by people engaged in anything remotely normal."

"This is great," responded Benny. "So let's assume they are involved in some sort of software programming that requires serious computer power. If that's the case, the next question is: What type of software can be used by bad people to mess things up on a monumental scale?"

We glanced knowingly at one another as the answer collectively descended upon us. Life is sometimes so humbling.

CHAPTER 34

"Aha!" exclaimed Benny. "So that's our role here, at least partially explained."

"It's always been your belief-revealing software they were after," I agreed with a nod.

"Who's after it though? The Abnormals or the Inexplicables?" asked Will.

"The story that best fits the data is that the Abnormals want the software to use for their own purposes, while the Inexplicables are trying to stop them and are watching our every move to ensure they have the upper hand in the game. The Inexplicables are using us like hired help, or more like servants," I explained.

"That's all well and good, Mom," responded Wendy, "but that doesn't explain why the Inexplicables would steal everything we have to force us into this less-than-ideal position we now consider so normal. Surely, we're of less use to them without our technology."

"Wend's right, there's more to this," added Benny. "But I'm confident we won't understand the full picture until we reach the end of the game, at which point everyone will take their masks off. Then we'll understand everything we're meant to. We need to reside amid this foggy data for just a little while longer."

Never were wiser words said. Looking back, I wonder if Benny knew more than he was letting on—his guidance was always one step ahead of where we were standing.

"One more question:" Will jumped in with, "Why are we so sure it's Dad's true-belief-revealing software the Abnormals are after? I'm not being funny, but that software hasn't exactly sown the seeds of the next Microsoft. I thought it was just another of Dad's side projects that was a brilliant idea at the time, but which has gathered dust ever since."

"Geez, thanks a lot, Will," answered Benny with more hurt buried than Will could possibly understand at the time. "In defense of that particular software project, and most of the side projects I've been involved in over the years, my issue has always been that no one has understood the potential I created. Whenever I've tried to explain the opportunity to people who could use it to their advantage, all I've ever received were blank stares. I guess the cumulative impact of all those non-responses affects a man over time. So I stopped believing that my software—all my software—was of value to others."

It was a huge admission for Benny. I was proud of him. I took his hand in mine and held it tight.

"Dad, your work is awesome," said Wendy as she put a hand on Benny's shoulder. "Even if the rest of the world can't keep up with you, we're proud of you."

I'm not sure if the kids noticed, but tears welled up in Benny's eyes. Those were the words he'd been so desperate to hear all his life from his father, but he'd been barking up the wrong tree. The words were to be delivered to him by his daughter in the most unexpected of situations. Thank god for Wendy. It was a Deidre-worthy moment.

"Yes, well done, Dad," added Will. "But how are these Abnormals even aware of the existence of your software? If no one would listen in the past, why have you suddenly got a captive audience among the world's bad guys?"

It was the right question to ask even if it did shatter the beautiful moment preceding it.

"My best guess is that someone witnessed me talking about my software on The Connection Game," answered Benny. "Maybe they wouldn't have thought too much of the idea had I not won the game so emphatically. It was possibly the combination of the idea and the context that has led to all this."

Normally, when Benny provided an explanation to an otherwise inexplicable situation, I had at least one aha moment as the truth was revealed in all its glory. However, on this occasion it didn't happen. I couldn't imagine the chain of events playing out as Benny described. With the benefit of hindsight, it showed he was human just like the rest of us.

"I hear you, Dad," continued Will, "but take another step back. What's the big deal about a software program that can be used to reveal peoples' true beliefs? Isn't that the simple idea Google monetizes on a daily basis? It's hardly rocket science."

We all paused to reflect on that one. By then, Will had developed a real knack for throwing valuable new perspectives into the ring, even if it was at his father's expense.

"Google is a useful comparison," responded Benny with more fortitude than I expected. "Their software is built to predict which products have the greatest chance of being sold to each and every sheep—I mean human—using their platform. However, as with all aspects of the capitalist economy, it's a one-dimensional approach based only on financial returns. Consider the potential of a software program that reveals what people really believe in all areas of their life. For example, imagine you are leading a terrorist organization and you are desperate to find like-minded people to join your ranks. How are you going to find and recruit people who share your beliefs about punishing people who don't share your beliefs, the importance of violence, and what happens in the afterlife? Sure, you may meet a few like-minded people through your existing networks, but what if you could instantly gain access to millions of people who genuinely share your beliefs? Your potential power growth would be enormous."

"Aha, I get it. The bogeyman becomes much scarier when he hangs out with all the other bogeymen," said Will with less sarcasm than it sounded.

I was envious of Will's aha moment as mine continued to elude me—something wasn't adding up in my mind. But there was no time to dwell on it as we had urgent team work to get on with.

"Guys, this is a great start!" enthused Benny. "We now have the Abnormals' likely motive. We know who is involved and where they live. We are so close. However, the one thing we can't answer is what exactly the Abnormals are planning to do. Once we figure that out, we'll be ready to stop them in their tracks."

"I've got an idea, honey," I contributed.

"Great stuff, we're all ears," responded Benny.

"We fight fire with fire," I said, pausing to let it sink in. I'd learned a thing or two about rallying my family from watching my husband at work.

"Go on," said Benny.

"OK. If we're right, your software is the fire here, and it's already burning. But it's not out of our reach just yet. If we're going to figure out what the Abnormals are up to, we need to take back control of the software so we can use it to our advantage. It's our secret weapon and, by the way, it's sitting in the room with us right now," I concluded.

"Mom, in case you hadn't noticed our laptops have been stolen along with all Dad's work," responded Will with a shake of his head.

"Yes, I had," I said avoiding the temptation to roll my eyes like a teenager, "but we can rise up regardless. Over the past few months, with the benefit of your father's most welcome salary, we've not only been gradually repaying our debt, we've also managed to save a few pounds for a rainy day. Newsflash: The downpour has well and truly begun. So I propose we use our savings to buy a laptop with enough power to recreate your dad's software for our own purposes. As someone wise once said: All we need is in our heads. Well, in this case, in your father's head."

"You never cease to amaze me, my magical wife," Benny smiled as he took hold of my hand.

"Thanks, honey," I responded with joyful tears welling in my eyes. "Remember, we need to own our place at the center of the stage of our lives if we're to remain hidden. It's time for Mr. Benny Basilworth to reveal the full extent of his unique superpowers for the whole world to see."

"You're right, darling," Benny said quietly. "I can customize a new version of the true-belief-revealing software to help us uncover what the Abnormals are working on. I should have seen it myself. I think I've experienced one knock-back too many to see the wood for the trees."

"Well, the wood and the trees are both on our side now, honey, and it is time for you to show them what you can do," I said to my emotionally fragile husband.

So the Basilworth family's fight against the Abnormals was officially back in business. We went out that very afternoon to buy a new laptop, and shortly thereafter Benny started working on his customized software. The difference between the first and second version was that his family helped him on the second version. The end product was far superior, if I do say so myself. We were able to test it out almost immediately.

CHAPTER 35

In a matter of days, we'd created a software program that sorted through a vast array of information to allow us to digitally follow people living in our neighborhood who ticked a list of boxes based upon their personal beliefs and actions. It accessed the information from a vast array of not-always-legal sources including energy consumption maps, software company client lists, and credit card statements. (Please don't judge us—we were just doing what we needed to do.) We included things on the list like accessing the Internet during unusual hours, using unusually large amounts of broadband capacity, and the use of more-powerful-than-normal Internet security walls. The list went on and was a thing of beauty to a data analyst. Benny described it as a "digital Michelangelo." And guess how many people ticked each and every one of the boxes in our local vicinity? Twenty-two. Yes, that's exactly the same as the number of people on our list of Abnormals. What a relief it was! It was further confirmation we were on the right track.

Wendy started playing the song "Twenty-Two" to celebrate. The four of us jumped erratically around the flat in a rather embarrassing display of our passion for solving complex puzzles. It was as though the Basilworths had been collectively told we were worthy of our place in the game, the world, whatever you want to call it. Thank god, no one could see us—dance skills were not high on our list of competencies.

Benny resumed his activities of digitally monitoring the Abnormals, while Will, Wendy, and I stepped up our physical surveillance efforts. That meant Will and Wendy watched the street from our tiny window, and I continued my street missions under the guise of my baking business. In hindsight, something had shifted inside me: I no longer baked for the joy it once gave me. That's hard for me to admit. By then, I was viewing every single batch of muffins or cookies as nothing but a tactical tool to help me access more data about the Abnormals and the Inexplicables.

Benny and I were getting on well. It's fair to say fighting the good fight against a common enemy was better than visiting a marriage counselor for us. It allowed us to focus on fixing everyone apart from ourselves, which played to our strengths as a couple.

"We're a team to be reckoned with, aren't we, honey?" Benny asked me when I was baking ahead of a data-gathering mission one afternoon.

"We are indeed, Mr. Basilworth. It's as though we were destined to do this," I smiled.

"I certainly can't imagine anyone else living our lives," Benny laughed.

"At least no one on planet Earth," I agreed.

"Maybe we should colonize our own planet when the game is over," Benny suggested in all seriousness.

"Ha! What do you think we'll be remembered for when the game has ended?" I asked in a rare moment of self-reflection.

Benny thought for a while.

"You mark my words, Bell. People will be thanking the Basilworths for what we've done for far longer than my lifetime. People will remember us as the people who saved their lives, and our legacy will be enduring," Benny stated.

"I hope you're right, honey," I responded. "We're the only ones on the front line so some recognition seems fair. I'd better get on with baking my way toward our legacy then."

What did I understand about legacy at that point in our story? I talked about it as though it actually meant something.

While hiding behind the mask of my baking business was often effective, it wasn't foolproof. I was still working closely with Annabel's Premonitions café where muffin demand was booming. Annabel was highly intelligent, and one day she saw through my mask. I had just arrived at her café with my daily deliveries when I noticed an Abnormal queueing ahead of me. She was a thin older lady with a cold face, and we knew her as Slippers because she often wore her slippers outside. Benny added her to the Abnormals list a few months earlier when her evening foot movements became highly suspicious. At first, he wondered if she was attending an evening class with other elderly folk, but his research confirmed she was an outlier on too many data points to be considered normal. I stepped closer so I could hear her talking when she ordered her coffee.

"I'll take a flat white, please," Slippers said to Annabel without fanfare.

"Nice choice. There's nothing like a flat white to un-flatten your day," responded Annabel with her customary warmth.

While they were talking, Slippers' handbag opened a little. It was a data-gathering opportunity if I ever saw one. So I stepped forward to gain a better view of what was inside her handbag. Unfortunately, the moment I glanced inside, Annabel caught my eye and her face transformed from friendly café owner to suspicious citizen in an instant.

"Morning, Bell," she said when she'd finished attending to Slippers. "Thanks for the delivery."

Annabel was never short with me up until then, but she dialed down the friendliness toward me from then on. She obviously concluded that I was an undercover thief targeting little old ladies when they were paying for their coffee. If only she'd known the truth, she'd have been a lot more scared of the little old ladies themselves.

When I left Premonitions, I walked the streets for longer than I needed to. I had to walk off a nagging feeling that what lay beneath my mask was just as ugly as the Abnormals themselves. I started walking toward Deidre for a dose of her positivity to divert me from my negative thoughts, but

I changed my mind and resumed my homeward journey. If Annabel could see beneath my mask, I was sure Deidre would be able to as well. And as hard as it is for me to admit now, I wasn't in the mood for any of Deidre's holier-than-thou ideas, which would no doubt have brought everything I was doing into question. There was no time for that as we had urgent work to get on with.

When I returned home, Will and Wendy were staring out the tiny window with an overwhelming level of intensity, even by Basilworth standards. In the brief moment they turned to say hello to me, it was as though I'd witnessed two ghosts who weren't yet aware they were residing in the afterlife.

Benny was also in the depths of his work. He was growing more and more excited about what the software was revealing about the Abnormals.

"Guys, this is much bigger than any of us hypothesized!" he exclaimed. "These twenty-two Abnormals are just the tip of the iceberg. I've connected my software with all the UK's major telecommunications networks thanks to a little illegal hacking. And I now have proof that each and every Abnormal is regularly communicating with at least one seriously dangerous terrorist organization on a weekly or even daily basis. But the most significant fact is that they're communicating with different terrorist groups to one another, and yet they're all working together here in Hackney. Do you know what that means?"

"It means the shit is about to hit the fan on a global scale," answered Will calmly.

"Exactly!" smiled Benny who was loving our work despite the extreme level of danger, or maybe because of it. "These people are helping bring together most of the world's bad guys so they can work together right here. It's clear why the Inexplicables are so focused on following their movements. If they don't stop them, we're all in deep shit."

When Benny explained the seriousness of the situation, they were just words to me by then—more data points to be digested and computed for the best possible strategic response.

"Do you know exactly what the Abnormals are planning yet?" I asked without emotion.

"I'm close, honey, really close. I have a few theories, but I should have something more concrete in a day or two," responded Benny. Of course, Benny was right. We were circling around the truth at that point. Or rather, it was circling around us.

CHAPTER 36

The knowledge that there were indeed bad guys planning something sinister just outside our window empowered our collective paranoia to take on a life of its own. Benny typed on his laptop in a frenzy throughout the night and day, while Will, Wendy, and I burned the candle at both ends with our street-monitoring activities. Normal human functions like eating and sleeping were ignored because our work was far more important than all of it. The little flat began to stink of human scunge, and we started to look different. We became thinner and paler, particularly Benny—his eyes were glassy and less than human.

I was still the only one leaving the flat, but I was no longer leaving for the pleasure of some freedom and fresh air. In fact, if I could have stayed inside all day with the others, I would have jumped at the opportunity. The outside world was so full of human problems and so foreign compared to the comfortable watching station we had set up under the stairs. Beyond the comforts the little flat afforded us, we'd all grown accustomed to—no addicted to—silently judging the human race from a place where we couldn't be judged ourselves. We were living on another planet while we watched Earth from afar, and we didn't like what we saw. The human race was becoming uglier and scarier to us by the day.

Benny was loving every moment of our isolation. It was as though his entire life had been destined to end up exactly where he was, and the less normal we became, the happier he became. And his enthusiasm for his software work was becoming manic. One afternoon, he galloped into the living room to report his progress.

"Guys, I've cracked it!" he shrieked with his eyes popping out of his head. "Thank god for the three cardinal rules of data analysis: The data never lies, the data never lies, the data never lies. The only mistakes I've ever made were when I trusted myself, not the data. The data is the king who should always be respected. Long live the king!"

"OK, what have you got?" I asked. I was tired and didn't have a lot of bandwidth to listen to Benny's increasingly incoherent ramblings.

"Where to start? Why don't we pretend we're playing a round of The Connection Game, and I'll let you enjoy piecing the puzzle together. It seems only fitting, don't you think? I'll provide you with five words or expressions, and I want you to link them all together into the correct story to win the game," explained Benny.

Will rolled his eyes and I joined him. I was teetering on the edge between ardent foot-watcher and tired, resentful wife.

"Bear with me guys, I promise you'll enjoy this," implored Benny with mild awareness of our discomfort. "OK, your clues to connect are: words are things, island mentality, leaving the party first, people power, and digital kerplunk."

The only connection I was making was between the words "what a twat" and "my husband."

"I've got it!" responded Will within a matter of seconds. He celebrated with a limp air punch.

"Please tell us your answer, oh wise one," said Benny.

"The Abnormals are targeting the UK Government. Their plan is to take out the weakest parts of the government's technology system as a means of taking control of the entire government. The catalyst for their action is the recent Brexit decision, which has diverted the government's attention away from domestic security at a time when the local population is solely focused upon local issues. The country is more vulnerable right now as a result. The Abnormals believe the UK public will eventually support them in their leadership role if they use words that align with the public's beliefs and values. They are aiming to provide the UK population with the government of their dreams but at face value only. It's a full-on mutiny aimed at furthering their own causes at the UK's expense," Will concluded matter-of-factly.

You could have heard a pin drop as Will's words sunk in.

"You are my son in every possible way," Benny responded as he jumped up and hugged Will.

"What? He's *right*?" I asked as the monumental meaning of Will's words sank in.

"Of course, he is, darling. I told you our work was much bigger than watching a few random feet walking past the window," Benny stated as he pointed at the flat's window like a celebrated orchestra conductor acknowledging the string section's contribution. "The answer was there as soon as I trusted the data. It jumped out like the solution to a previously unsolvable algebraic formula residing within a uniquely average textbook."

The gravity of Benny's conclusions hung heavy in the air.

I wouldn't have been able to even make up such a dramatic story at the beginning of our journey, but by then I was ready to believe every word. No, I needed to believe every word. And—please don't judge me for this—I was secretly overjoyed to learn about the immense scale of the bad shit going on outside our window. It gave our strange lives and all our sacrifices meaning, finally. Does that make any sort of sense?

"So what's next?" I asked, unsure if I was ready for what was coming.

"Let's confront the Inexplicables," interjected Will. "Or maybe we should rename them the *Explicables* now we know why they're so interested in the Abnormals. We even know what the Abnormals are planning. We have all the leverage we need to talk with them."

"Not quite, Will," responded Benny. "We know the Abnormals' why and how, but we don't know their when. It's the final piece of the jigsaw puzzle we need to win the game."

"Do you have a plan in mind, honey?" I asked.

"Funnily enough, I do. But you may not like it," Benny beamed.

"Let me guess. It involves me risking my life on the streets in the name of the greater good?" I asked.

"Close," Benny admitted. "I suspect the Abnormals are circling in on the government's data center network. They've been doing all they can through the cloud up until now, but before they launch their attack, they'll need to take control of the government's most powerful data center, located in the Docklands, to ensure they have the upper hand. If they gain control of that single data center, they're on track to control the government. My modeling suggests they'll be scoping out the data center at least a few days before the attack."

"That makes sense. So no prizes for guessing what you want me to do," I said like the good soldier I was.

"You, my darling, have become our incredibly effective eyes and ears on the ground. You supply us with everything a laptop can't," responded Benny. "So we need your feet on the ground in the Docklands area around the government's data center, on the lookout for abnormal Abnormal behavior."

"Sure, I can do that," I responded, ignoring the fear that was arising within me.

CHAPTER 37

Before leaving the flat to travel across to the Docklands, I did some facial training in the bathroom. I'd been working on it regularly ever since Benny's lesson, and I was making gradual progress. It was remarkable how my face used to give away my feelings, but I was taking control back from the hands of helplessness. However, as I gazed deep into my eyes, I could see it wasn't coming without a cost. Something which previously burned bright behind my eyes was becoming dimmer, and it wasn't just my IQ. But there was no time to dwell on what I'd lost. The main thing was I was as ready for whatever was coming as I'd ever be.

"Good luck, honey!" Benny shouted as I left the flat. "Please be extra careful knowing what you know."

"Roger," I responded as I marched out of the flat into the battlefield.

You may think it strange that I was the only one in the family taking any real risks at that point. The other three remained stationary within the comparative safety of the little flat while I navigated the highly risky and unpredictable world of the Abnormals and Inexplicables. At the time I didn't care, but I sure do now. If Benny were here today, I'd call him on it. He'd no doubt have a good excuse centered around it being our optimal data-gathering strategy, but I'd explain to him it may have not been his optimal relationship-building strategy with his wife. I'm sure he'd have shrugged his shoulders and turned his gaze back to the important data.

I walked to Hackney Central overland station and waited for a train. The first one that arrived was overcrowded, so I stood back and waited for the next one. I was always amused by how many Londoners would push their bodies like sardines into the first train they could access when there was always another train only three minutes away. Our cities make us crazy. I was missing the flat already.

By the time I arrived at Canary Wharf in the Docklands almost an hour later, it was raining cats and dogs. I'd been so focused on my street-stalking strategies that I'd forgotten to bring an umbrella, a cardinal sin in London. So I searched for a café in the vicinity of the government's data center to wait out the rain. Upon googling it, I found a café called The Short End, which was perfectly located as it was near the Docklands Light Railway station and across the road from the government's data center. I ran through the rain and was there within a few minutes.

The Short End was a lovely little café with the ambiance of being inside a warm and welcoming home. It was wonderfully clean and smelled of delicious roasted coffee. It was evocative of an earlier stage in my life when I frequented cafés to enjoy coffee in all its glory. I ordered a latte and sat down on a sofa in the corner. For a moment, I wanted to forget about what our lives had become, and to pretend I was normal. Yes, we were saving the world; and yes, we were saving ourselves; and yes, being normal was the equivalent of putting your head in the sand, but being normal was a hell of a lot easier than what we were putting ourselves through. As I gazed around at the carefree souls enjoying their morning coffees, I was deeply envious of normal.

An old lady sat down next to me on the sofa.

"I hope you don't mind if I sit here?" she asked.

"Not at all. It's a lovely place to sit," I responded.

"It's one of my favorite cafés," added the old lady. "I love sitting here and watching the world go by."

She made watching others sound so therapeutic. If only she knew how far it could be taken in the wrong hands.

"Yes, and what a fascinating world we live in," I responded. "People are changing and not for the better."

"Are they?" asked the old lady with surprise.

"Definitely. The digital revolution has infected humanity's soul and is allowing our dark side to flourish in ways beyond what was possible in the past," I said.

"When I was younger, people said the same about the sexual revolution, then they said the same about television, and so on," she responded. "Good and evil will always coexist, but I'm not so sure anything has fundamentally changed. We just remember the past with rose-tinted glasses."

Panic suddenly arose inside me as the old lady spoke. I'm not sure why. As far as I could tell she wasn't an Abnormal, but she knew far too much about the coexistence of good and evil for my liking. My panic wouldn't be tamed, so much to her surprise I excused myself abruptly and walked straight out of the café.

The rain had almost stopped so I made my way to the government's data center over the road. It was a large, nondescript, box-shaped building surrounded by high and foreboding barbed wire fencing. It didn't exactly present as the key asset a terrorist group aiming to take control of the entire government would want to target, but Benny was always right with this stuff—I'd learned that time and time again. One guard was patrolling the perimeter. The idea that just one man was defending the security of the entire government made me uneasy. And to add insult to injury, he was only around five foot four with a jockey's physique. If he was going to successfully defend the country, it was going to have to be against an army of Oompa-Loompas.

I walked around the block surrounding the data center as part of my initial reconnaissance of the area. There was no one in sight in any direction. It was one of those parts of London that can be as uninhabited as a ghost town. However, I suspected stuff was happening behind closed doors: bad stuff.

Conscious that Benny and the kids would demand valuable data from me when I returned home, I kept walking in circles around that damned data center. On the second loop, the only person I came across was the old lady from the café.

"Hello again," she said. "I hope I didn't upset you somehow. That was the last thing I wanted to do."

"Not at all. Sorry, I'm just going through some challenges right now," I explained truthfully.

"I understand," smiled the old lady. "We all do. That's the beauty of life."

As we parted for a second time, I walked away a little lighter. I was glad I had a chance to apologize to the old lady for my rudeness. Then I remembered Benny's words: the data never lies. Well, the data had spoken and there was nothing to see. We were obviously too early, or we were wrong again. I headed home relieved my mission for the day had come to an end. My passion for street-stalking was starting to wane along with my energy levels.

CHAPTER 38

After my time away from the little flat, I returned home to discover chaos was reigning even more supreme. Benny was running around like a headless chicken and his ramblings were getting worse.

"The data indicates the game is gathering pace. When the end is in sight like this, we must remain extra vigilant. Stay focused!" was all I could decipher from him as I entered the living room.

Will and Wendy were both in their bedrooms. They hadn't left their posts at the window for many preceding days, so I wondered what was going on. I knocked on Wendy's door and entered.

"Hey, Wend. Are you OK?" I asked.

"I'm not sure," she responded.

"What's going on?" I asked.

"I can't watch the feet anymore, Mom. All I can see these days is the same generic foot-owner walking past over and over and over again. It's as though they're doing nothing but walking past our window. I think I'm losing my mind and I'm scared," Wendy explained.

"You just need some rest, darling," I responded.

"It's more than that. Dad's scaring me, Mom. He's talking like a crazy person. Is he all right?" she asked.

"I don't think he is, Wend. He needs help, we all need help," I admitted.

"But we're so close," Wendy said.

"Close to what though?" I asked.

I left Wendy to get some rest and returned to the living room where Benny was typing furiously on his laptop, which was creaking under the pressure.

"Benny, can we talk?" I asked.

He stopped what he was doing and jerked his head toward me. He reminded me of a dog I once saw that had rabies. Its owners unfortunately had to put it down.

"Sure. How did today's mission go?" Benny asked with excitement.

I gave him a full and honest account of my outing to the Docklands.

"OK, so you believe there's nothing suspicious going on right now," responded Benny. "But are we ignoring the glaring piece of data that is screaming out to us?"

"What's that?" I asked, prepared for another rant.

"The little old lady," Benny responded.

"What about her? She's around seventy-five years old and did nothing remotely suspicious beyond putting sugar in her coffee. She's hardly scary," I explained.

"That's your judgment. Why don't you ignore your opinion and come back to the data? Statistically, she's the only person likely to be an Abnormal who's monitoring the data center. She was seen in both the café across the road from the data center, and in front of the data center. Hello!" Benny almost shouted.

I avoided the temptation to respond with annoyance as Benny appeared to be talking to the universe rather than with me.

"Or, it's more likely that we're just too early," I responded. "The data really hasn't given us much to work with as yet."

"OK, I hear you. We need more data then!" Benny exclaimed. "But word of warning: If that same old lady is positioned near the data center again tomorrow then we must be on high alert."

"Hang on, Benny. Have you contemplated the incredibly normal scenario in which this particular little old lady enjoys visiting her local café at the same time every day for a coffee, and then walks home past the data center?" I asked.

"Yes, of course, I have," Benny responded. "Trust me on this one, Bell. If she's there again tomorrow, she's our prime target and a danger to humanity. Let's see what happens in the morning."

"Are you all right, Benny?" I asked. "Can we please talk about your mental health now?"

"I'm fine, Bell. There's no time for anything but the game right now. We're so close to uncovering the truth," responded

Benny as he put some headphones into his ears and continued speed typing. I tried to continue talking with him, but
he was already ensconced in his beloved data. It was useless
to try to connect with him. Maybe it always had been.

CHAPTER 39

The next morning, I once again trudged across London to the Docklands. It was a beautiful day so being outside the flat provided a silver lining to my otherwise grim mission of hunting innocent old ladies. I arrived at The Short End café at around the same time as the day before. I ordered a coffee and sat down in the same position on the comfy sofa as my previous visit. The café was quieter than the day before. There were no suspicious old ladies in sight. I breathed a sigh of relief.

I savored my coffee. It was one of those coffees that transports you to the jungles of the Amazon from whence it was born. As I sipped in the enjoyment, I surveyed the café for potential Abnormals. There were two young guys in suits talking stocks nearby, and a mother and daughter sitting on the other side of the café. At least, I assumed they were mother and daughter since their shared the same rather unique ski-jump nose. Nothing appeared abnormal from where I was sitting.

And then she entered. The same old lady I'd been talking with the day before strolled in the front door, waved at the café owner, and shuffled over to the sofa where I was sitting.

"Oh, hello again," she said with a broad smile. "I wasn't sure if I'd see you again, but I'm happy to."

"Morning," I responded, trying to remain upbeat even though I was disappointed, "I'm happy to see you again too. What were the chances?"

"Pretty decent I'd say," she said. "I'm here at this time most mornings. At my age you don't want too many decisions to make each day, so visiting the same café each morning suits me well."

"I understand," I responded. "Even at my age I enjoy a few predictable rituals. There's a comfort in knowing what's coming next in such an unpredictable world."

The old lady gazed at me intently. She had knowing eyes.

"How are you feeling?" she asked with concern.

I couldn't remember the last time someone had asked me that question with genuine interest. Initially, I was tongue-tied as my feelings weren't surveillance-worthy so had long been buried beneath the more important data.

"Oh, you know. I'm doing my best to stay afloat, but aren't we all?" I eventually responded.

"You look tired," said the old lady.

"I am tired. My life is draining right now," I admitted.

"But you are young," responded the old lady. "Why are you carrying so much weight on your shoulders?"

It was a question that demanded the truth, and I was so close to telling her everything for the simple reason she'd asked me. It would have been so liberating to open up and release the pain that had been congregating inside my soul for longer than it was welcome. But I fought to keep the lid on it as I knew I'd lose control if it blew off.

"I'm carrying the weight on behalf of others," was my best attempt at answering the question without really answering it. But the old lady seemed to see through my mistiness.

"I see. The weight is all the heavier when it's not yours by rights to carry. Have you explained this to those you are helping?" she asked.

"I've tried to, but it's been hard to get through," I explained. "And then there are those who don't understand that the weight is being carried for them: the broader human population."

I expected the vagueness of that comment to confuse the old lady, but I couldn't shake her off the truth that hovered in the subtext of my words, calling out to be heard.

"So many of us don't recognize the angels walking among us, making our lives easier in beautiful ways—ways that are hidden from our all-too-busy eyes," she said with a smile.

I felt seen. The old lady understood me.

"How do you make the weight lighter?" I asked.

"This is a positive first step," she responded. "Talking about it always lightens the load. And beyond that, looking after yourself is the key, even if that means passing some of the weight back to those from whence it came. It may actually do them good to take back some of their own baggage for a while."

It was clear I was in the presence of wisdom. I considered her words carefully. Who was I carrying all this weight for?

Was it for my mad husband who was so determined to prove his worth? Was it for the human race who faced dangers beyond its comprehension? Or was it for me? Did I need to prove my worth as a person just as Benny did? These questions hung heavy in the air that day in the café and have stayed with me ever since.

"Thank you," I said, "your words resonate deeply with me."

"Any time," she responded. "You have a beautiful soul that anyone with their eyes open can see."

Tears welled up in my eyes. As those long-lost words of kindness sunk in, a world of emotions stirred beneath my steely exterior.

"You're too kind. What have you got planned today?" I asked in an awkward attempt to change the subject.

"What does any eighty-year-old have planned? Surviving the day would be a bonus," she laughed. I joined her.

"Do you live locally?" I asked.

"Yes, I live in the street to the right of that god-awful building I walk past to get here. It reminds me of a space station from the seventies," she laughed as she pointed toward the government's data center across the road.

QED. I wanted to high-five her. She was as abnormal as a drop of water in the ocean. For once, Benny was wrong, and I was more than happy about it.

"Oh yes? I think I know the one you mean," I feigned. "It's so unusual to find a beautiful building in a city like London these days. In ancient Roman times, creating a visually stunning city environment was as important as ensuring the city's plumbing worked properly. We could use an ancient Roman or two in the city planning department, if you ask me."

"Thank you, you just reminded me: I have a plumber due shortly. I must return home," she said. "It was lovely to see you. I hope to see you again soon. By the way, what's your name?"

"I'm Bell, and you?" I responded.

"I'm Matilda, but not the waltzing kind," she said as she shuffled toward the door. With a departing wave to everyone in the café, she made her way past the data center en route home.

I returned home uplifted. I'd enjoyed my chat with Matilda on so many levels. Just like Deidre, she had listened to me in a way I'd been craving to be listened to. And she'd showed me how beautiful normal could be.

CHAPTER 40

When I returned home, I tried to avoid Benny by walking straight into the bathroom. I nearly made it, but he called me over. The kids were once again nowhere in sight.

"Bell, have you got anything to report?" Benny inquired with the emotional softness of a staff sergeant with learning difficulties.

"Yes, I do in fact," I responded stiffly. "I had a coffee with the old lady I told you about yesterday. She's most definitely a Normal and is absolutely lovely."

"Hallelujah!" he exclaimed. "I told you we were on the right track. So we've got our Abnormal in place at the data center as expected. That means they're getting ready for action in a matter of days."

"No way, Benny," I responded shaking my head. "As I keep telling you, she's as normal as they come."

"On what basis?" he asked.

"On the basis my gut instinct confirmed she's a nice normal person when I had a long chat with her. She asked me how I was doing and listened to my answers as only someone who cares about other people could do. Oh, and she's eighty years old by the way, and she lives close to that café as I suspected. She passes by the data center on her way home from the café every day. Is it a crime to walk to your local café for a bloody coffee?" I inquired with growing velocity.

"No, but how can you be sure you aren't being played?" Benny responded with more control. "You've just served me a bunch of clichés only an Abnormal would provide if they were trying to appear normal. Can't you see it? The data is howling at us that she's an Abnormal, and an impressive one at that."

"What data, Benny?" I asked. "I had a nice chat with an old lady. That's it."

"There's data everywhere, Bell," he responded. "You add these data points up. This little old lady is the one and only person you noticed walking past the government's data center two days in a row. She talked to you as though she knows you on some level, and she provided you with a bunch of details about her life to convince you she's as normal as they come."

I considered Benny's points. I wondered if there could be any truth in his harsh view of Matilda. Surely, I reasoned, there must still be one or two nice old ladies existing in the world who weren't trying to wipe out humanity as we knew it.

"And then there's the clincher," Benny continued. "Each morning this old lady sits in the perfect vantage point across the road from the government's data center, allowing her to monitor the security situation at their key target."

"Hang on, that last point is opinion, not data. You of all people should know the difference," I hissed.

"OK, so let's call that a high probability guess based upon all of the confirmed data points," Benny hit back at me. "You can't see it because she blindsided you with her kindly, old-lady routine. I'm telling you, she's an Abnormal."

"Benny, if that old lady is an Abnormal, then the Abnormals are less of a threat than we thought," I responded. "How many terrorist organizations do you know of who depend upon eighty-year-old ladies to further their cause? I'm telling you there's zero chance she's an Abnormal. What about trusting your eyes and ears on the street as you told me the other day? Or was that just bullshit aimed at getting me to do more of your dirty work, despite my better judgment?"

"Of course, it wasn't, Bell!" he exclaimed. "But in this case, you've been played. There's more at stake here than accepting everything you say as the truth simply because you're my wife. I need to protect you, the kids, and the population of London. If something contradicts the data, it's my job to highlight it. That's all I'm doing."

"OK, so explain to me why the Abnormals would consider working with an eighty-year-old lady to be a remotely sensible idea? Are they that desperate for help?" I asked.

"Her age is exactly why she's so useful to the Abnormals. It's a genius move designed to throw us and the Inexplicables off her scent. Who would suspect a friendly old lady of working for a terrorist group?" Benny asked as he gazed toward the heavens. "I'll tell you. Me! But no one else. We must listen whenever the data speaks to us and it's throwing the answer in our direction right now."

"So what do you propose we do next?" I asked shaking my head.

"We now have everything we need to confront the Inexplicables. We know what the Abnormals are planning, and how they plan to execute. And your confirmation that there's an Abnormal in place at the Docklands data center proves they are planning to execute the attack in the very short term," Benny continued. "It's high time we paid our friends around the corner a little visit."

You'd think I'd have been happy about the idea of finally meeting the Inexplicables as it meant we weren't far off understanding the bizarre game we were a part of. But I wasn't. A sense of dread, which had been residing inside me for some time, was growing at the same rate as Benny's insanity.

"And what do you expect the Inexplicables to do?" I asked. "Do you think they'll high-five us for explaining we know more than they think we know? Or do you think they'll politely ask us who the hell we are, and why we are storming their castle? Then there's the very distinct possibility they'll call the police to deal with the crazed madman before them, who is raving about inexplicable things no one understands, or is even interested in."

Benny's posture dropped. He stood before me heartbroken when I said that. I still regret it to this day.

"Please come with me to see them, darling," Benny pleaded. "You've come this far. Let's just take one more step toward the truth together. You owe yourself that much. You owe the Basilworths that much."

Even in the depths of his madness, Benny knew how to make me do whatever he wanted.

"OK," I finally conceded, "but what about the kids? Don't they deserve an explanation as well?"

"Of course, they do, but they're both asleep in their rooms. They were exhausted by all the work we've been doing," Benny explained. "Let's leave them to recover for a while. We can tell them what happens when we return."

"OK, let's meet these Inexplicables then," I eventually responded.

CHAPTER 41

We walked out of the flat with urgency in our stride as though our lives depended upon what was coming next. Benny believed they did. But I didn't care anymore. I was too tired of living a less-than-normal life to appreciate the ramifications of anything happening around us. You could have told me the Pope was coming around for dinner and I'd have ordered in takeaway.

Benny's ramblings continued as we marched up the street together.

"We're off the see the Inexplicables, the wonderful Inexplicables of Oz," he chanted.

"Benny, do you want the whole world to know you're mad?" I asked.

"Darling, don't you see?" Benny responded, perplexed. "It doesn't matter anymore. Now we have the winning information we're home and hosed. All we need to do is connect the dots for the Inexplicables, and we'll win the game. Why don't you let yourself smile about it?"

With my newfound facial control, I chose anger. I'd never felt less inclined to smile, and I wanted Benny to know it. I'd always wondered what the expression "as mad as a March hare" had meant, and there it was hopping alongside me on a London street. I continued onward in silence while Benny's chanting morphed into a strange whistling of the *Wizard of Oz* song. A young woman passing by gave Benny a look that could only be translated into "Are you fucking insane?" Benny's eyes went wonky on cue, and her question was answered. She glanced at me with an expression full of sympathy as well as shock. I'd become that person people pass by and feel sorry for. (Maybe some of those passersby will hear our story one day, and all will be forgiven.)

When we reached the townhouse, Benny stopped and stared up at the windows above. The curtains were closed and motionless. He checked his mobile.

"It's the second floor we're after according to my laptop tracker," Benny explained with excitement.

He bounded over to the buzzer next to the townhouse's front door and pressed it long and hard. I joined him as he waited at the front door. However, the door didn't open. Nothing happened at all.

Benny pressed the buzzer again, even longer and harder than the first time, and once again, we waited. I started counting in my head to soothe away the awkwardness of the moment. Finally, by the time I'd counted to thirty, we received a response.

"Yes?" said a deep man's voice through the buzzer.

"Benny and Belinda Basilworth here to talk with you and the team, sir," Benny explained to the buzzer.

There was no response, and the door remained firmly shut. Benny stepped forward again.

"It's that time in the game when you need to hear what we have to say. We promise we'll make it worth your while," Benny implored as though the buzzer was a living, breathing game show host.

Once again, nothing happened, so I resumed my counting. By the time I reached eighteen, the door beeped open without another word from the mysterious deep-voiced man from above. Benny lunged forward to push it open.

"Bell, we're in," Benny whispered loudly as though we had somehow broken in ourselves.

I followed him inside. We found a long staircase covered with old red carpet and started climbing. Benny's energy propelled him up two steps at a time, while mine barely made the journey one step at a time. I was so tired of whatever game we were playing.

By the time I reached the top of the stairs, Benny was banging on the door with far too much aggression. We were again forced to wait. I wondered if the person or people behind the door were having second thoughts about letting us in. Who could blame them if they were?

Finally, the door opened. We were greeted by an older man with wavy gray hair and a broad smile. He was most definitely not Brown Suede, Blue Joggers, Black Business

Shoes, or Red High Heels. He wore a pair of elegant house slippers with an ornamental design on the side.

"Oh, hello! Come on in, this way," he beamed as he ushered us in.

Benny nodded and marched in, and I followed slowly behind him. We entered a beautiful, large flat with high ceilings and magnificent furniture. It would have been better matched to being located in Mayfair than Hackney. That was the beauty of London—things always popped up where you least expected. Our host joined us in the main reception room where there was no one else around, at least that we could see.

"Please take a seat," he said as he motioned toward a deep-cushioned sofa behind us.

We sat down, and I waited for Benny's rant to begin. But he sat quietly, and an awkward silence filled the air.

"Now, what can I do for you?" asked our charming host.

"We have the answers," was all Benny could muster up in response.

Our host's facial expression didn't give anything away. I wasn't sure whether he knew who we were, never mind what we were doing there.

"Oh yes?" he responded.

That was all Benny needed as inspiration to unburden himself.

"Don't sound so surprised! Of course, we do. We know who all twenty-two Abnormals are, what they are planning to do, and a rough time frame of when they're planning to do it," Benny began with animation. "You were so right to be worried about them. They are planning something huge!"

Our host looked uncomfortable. I wondered if he was just a normal man minding his own business.

"You see, it was all in the data," continued Benny ignoring the lack of response. "The data never ever lies. So once I fully committed to following the data, the truth was sitting there like a pot of gold just waiting to be discovered."

"The data?" asked our host.

"Yes, the data," responded Benny. "We've got data on the Abnormals coming out of our ears, and we used it to create a picture of the truth."

"Data is known to drive people mad, son. You'd do well to focus on your own well-being," our friendly host said with more seriousness.

If only he hadn't called Benny "son."

"But I've connected all the dots. I have all the answers!" Benny exclaimed. "Can't you see I'm worthy, Father?"

"Pardon me?" answered our host.

"I've done everything you asked and more," Benny ranted. "More than any son could do. Can't you see that?"

"Hang on," responded our host, "what are you talking about? Who do you think I am?"

"Why aren't you proud of me?" Benny demanded with increasing aggression. "Why don't you love me?"

Our host went silent for a moment while Benny's ramblings circulated awkwardly around the room.

"It's been a pleasure, but I think you best leave now," our host finally responded with sadness.

We left none the wiser who that man was. He could have been an uncooperative Inexplicable or a friendly Normal for all we knew. But he was left in no doubt as to Benny's level of sanity. None of us were.

CHAPTER 42

Benny was inconsolable after we left the townhouse. His manic energy instantly turned inward into a deep depression.

"Who do you think he was?" I asked as we walked home.

"An ungrateful Inexplicable," was all Benny could say.

"What does this mean for our plans? Are we at the end of this road?" I asked, praying we were.

"Over my dead body," Benny responded through clenched teeth. "I need a little time to digest what's just happened, but we are still very much in the game. In fact, we're the only ones left with a chance."

When we arrived back at the little flat, the kids were still asleep. I'd had more than enough of the day, so I went to bed early and fell into a deep sleep. I dreamed of walking across endless ice landscapes in the Arctic. Even in my sleep, the icy cold crept deep into my soul.

I awoke early the next morning still tired. Benny wasn't lying in bed next to me. I rose and walked into the living room where he was working away on his laptop. I could tell straight away that he hadn't gone to bed as his hair was disheveled and there was the unmistakable stench of dirty man in the room. Showers were no longer a priority for my mad husband by then.

"Morning," I said in an effort to retain some civility.

"I've figured it out," was Benny's curt response.

"What's that?" I asked.

"I know why the head of the Inexplicables wasn't grateful for my work?" Benny responded.

At around this time, Benny had started referring to our work as his work. Each little step he took was away from his family.

"Oh yes?" I responded, not wanting to hear his crazed answer.

"Yesterday, I thought I'd solved for all the answers, but late last night the data showed me one glaring gap," Benny explained. "If only we'd thought of it before addressing the head of the Inexplicables."

The one exception to Benny taking credit for the whole family's work was when a mistake had been made—then he rolled out the royal "we."

"Tell me," I said.

"The little old lady," Benny responded.

"Matilda? What about her?" I asked with panic arising inside me.

"Yes, we know she's an Abnormal," Benny continued, "but we don't know the exact date of the planned attack. We just have a theoretical time frame based on the fact there's an Abnormal already in place at the data center. That's clearly not good enough for the Inexplicables. And I get it. It's not good enough, full stop. We should have solved for the date by now."

"OK, so what are you proposing?" I asked with trepidation.

"We need an admission from Matilda that she is in fact an Abnormal, as well as the date the attack is scheduled. That's the final piece of the puzzle. Once we have that, we've won the game," Benny said with a crooked smile.

"You want an admission from an eighty-year-old woman that she's working with a terrorist group. Are you mad?" I asked. In hindsight, it was a silly question.

"Darling, the data never lies," Benny stated.

"No, Benny," I responded, "I can't condone this type of behavior. There's no way you're confronting Matilda."

"I'm not confronting her. We are," Benny said calmly.

"What? No way. I refuse," I seethed.

"OK, Bell. I'll give you a choice then," he continued. "You can remain here and have a nap with the kids, in which case, I'll confront Matilda alone—although, it may not be as friendly an encounter for her. Or we can confront her together and try to handle this situation as nicely as possible for all involved."

"What do you mean I can have a *nap* with the kids?" I asked as stress took hold of my body.

"As I told you, they're tired and in need of rest," was all Benny said.

I ran to Wendy's bedroom and threw the door open. She was tucked up in bed in a deep sleep. I put my hand on her shoulder and shook her gently to wake her up. She remained deep asleep. I shook her harder, but I still couldn't wake her up. I ran into Will's room and found him in the same catatonic state.

I returned to the living room in a fury.

"What the hell have you done?" I screamed at Benny.

"The kids' tiredness was making them a hindrance to my work. Like any loving father, I helped them sleep for a while so they could become productive members of the team again," Benny responded as though it was the most natural thing in the world.

"You drugged them? How dare you, you raving lunatic!" I shouted as I punched Benny as hard as I could in the arm. He looked shocked.

"They'll thank me for it when they wake up feeling well rested later today, even if you don't. One of us needs to think about their well-being, don't you think?" he asked.

"Thinking about your kids' well-being doesn't mean drugging them because they no longer believe their father is sane!" I shouted. "I'd say their theory has been well and truly proven correct."

"So what's your decision?" Benny asked, ignoring my attack.

"About what?" I seethed.

"The old lady. Are you going to make her day that little bit better? Or shall I handle it my way?" he asked.

As Benny stood in front of me, it was as though I was meeting a stranger for the first time. He was as insane as a person could be. And, hard as it is for me to admit, my love for him had died. There was nothing left of the man I had married but his name. Even his face had morphed into a ghoulish version of humanity's worst mistakes.

"I'll come with you for Matilda's sake," I eventually responded. "But only on the condition you promise not to harm her."

"We're beyond promises, don't you think, Bell? And besides, this game has become much bigger than tedious promises between a man and his wife," he stated.

Despite my misgivings, we left the little flat together en route for the Docklands. I hoped and prayed that Matilda would vary her routine that morning rather than going to the same café for her usual coffee.

CHAPTER 43

Benny and I caught the train and then the tube to the Docklands. We traveled in silence because I couldn't bring myself to utter a single word to him. I couldn't even look in his direction. However, he was oblivious to my feelings as per usual. He was coming out of his depression and was bizarrely cheerful considering he was traveling to accost an innocent old lady. He resumed his whistling as we sat on a busy tube of commuters, and was soon in the depths of a rendition of "Take Me Home Country Roads." He was that maddening person on the tube who was ignorant of the annoyance he was causing the poor bystanders around him. After a few minutes of his terribly out-of-tune whistling, an older gentleman in a pin-striped suit intervened.

"Excuse me, old chap?" said the man.

"Yes, *old chap*," responded Benny with a crazed look.

"Would you mind ever so slightly not whistling please? You know how it is. It's only a small space with lots of people," he said to Benny with noteworthy warmth, considering the situation.

"Sorry, *old chap*," Benny responded. "But I'm seeing things clearly for the first time in a long time, and whistling is my best chance of traveling incognito. You may have noticed: no one talks to whistlers. Well, apart from you, of course. But you don't count."

"Oh, why's that then?" asked the man with less ease.

"Because you're average in every *possible* way. The data wouldn't be able to identify a single outlier about a man like you because you are content with all this," responded Benny as he waved his hand around as though he was referring to planet Earth from afar. "You're like the vast majority of humans who don't question anything about their very existence. Don't you see? Being average is the mask you wear that allows you to make it through the day. Without it, you are nothing but air."

"Pardon me?" the man asked, clearly not coping well with Benny's brutally honest feedback on the state of his life. Benny resumed whistling even louder.

The man stood up and whispered "What cheek!" under his breath as he stormed off. (Sorry sir, whoever and wherever you are, my husband was out of his mind that day.)

After upsetting many more commuters who had the good sense to give Benny a wide berth, we finally arrived at the Docklands at around eight o'clock in the morning. Benny marched us out of the light rail station toward The Short End café, which he'd located on his phone. How he knew the name of the café was beyond me. Maybe I'd told him after one of my visits, but I couldn't remember doing so. As we walked, I mentally prepared myself to warn Matilda in any way possible not to trust Benny. She was savvy, so hopefully she would read between the lines. I took some comfort from the knowledge she'd be safe as long as she remained inside the café surrounded by others. Keeping her there while Benny was on the hunt was paramount in my mind.

We arrived at the café within a few minutes. As we entered, I glanced around but luckily Matilda wasn't there. I was overjoyed.

"Where did you sit last time you were here?" grunted Benny in my vicinity.

"At that table," I lied as I pointed at a table as far away as possible from the sofa Matilda and I sat on.

Benny ordered coffee for both of us, then we sat down and waited at the table in an awkward silence. Thankfully, Benny had stopped whistling, but he was still scaring me with his unpredictably manic movements. A cordon sanitaire soon emerged around us as all the nearby coffee drinkers coincidentally needed to leave the moment they noticed Benny's eyes were popping out of his head. "Normals!" Benny smirked as they scuttled away to safety.

Every time the café door opened, Benny jerked his head to see who it was, and soon I was doing the same out of fear. I kept praying Matilda had other plans that morning. But she didn't. On cue, she walked into the café at the same time she always did. I mentally cursed old-person predictability. Couldn't she have done something different just this once? Matilda surveyed the café for somewhere to sit and

S.S. Turner

started walking over to her normal position on the sofa. I turned away to hide my face. However, she suddenly swiveled around as though to check something, and she stared directly at Benny and me. I ignored her, but her eyes had locked onto me like an unshakable arrow destined for its target despite the cost. She walked over.

"Bell, I thought it was you!" she exclaimed. "But you've changed seats, so I wasn't sure."

Benny gave me a look.

"Yes, it is me," I responded. "We were having a quiet chat, so the extra space over here suited us."

"Not at all, honey. It's lovely to meet you, Matilda. I'm Bell's husband, Benny. I've heard so much about you. Won't you please join us?" Benny interjected as he quickly pulled out a chair for Matilda.

"Oh hello, Benny. It's nice to meet you too. Um, OK, why not," Matilda responded as she sat down. My heart sank.

Matilda glanced at Benny and me as though she was trying to figure out what was going on. Weren't we all?

"Matilda, what an unusual name you have," said Benny. "I think you're the first Matilda I've ever met."

"I suppose it is unusual. My parents always liked to be different," responded Matilda cautiously as though she was aware there were eggshells in every direction.

"Being different is in itself unusual, don't you think?" continued Benny. "You see, I work with data and the data never lies. Never. And the data generally tells me there are two main groups of humans: those who are average in ev-

264

ery possible way without even realizing what average is, and those who are trying to look different from the average in order to gain an advantage, the Abnormals. It's always been this abnormal group that has fascinated me the most."

"You sound like you know your stuff, Benny," Matilda responded. "What sort of work do you do?"

"You may have heard of me. I won The Connection Game by the largest margin in the show's history," Benny boasted without answering Matilda's question.

"Incredible. Is The Connection Game a TV program?" Matilda asked.

"Yes, you know it is. Your people have no doubt told you all about it. You know very well who I am and why I'm an important player. No need to beat around the bush on my account," Benny responded with a forced wink.

I wished myself anywhere but where I was sitting. Poor Matilda shifted uncomfortably in her seat, and gazed deep into my eyes searching for answers. I didn't have any to offer her beyond fear.

"Who do you think I am, Benny?" Matilda asked, getting straight to the question that mattered.

"Oh, I'm so beyond thinking, Matilda. I know so much more about you than you could possibly imagine," Benny stated.

"Go on, tell me what you know, Benny. When you reach the ripe old age of eighty you're open to hearing pretty much anything," Matilda said with a forced smile.

"This isn't the time or place for telling you what we know. Good try though," Benny responded.

"Why not?" asked Matilda.

"Because we haven't yet won the game. Once we've won the game, I can reveal everything I know to all the main players. In the meantime, all the important data must stay in here," explained Benny, pointing at his head as though it were an inanimate storage facility.

"Bell, are you all right?" Matilda suddenly asked.

"Sorry about all this, Matilda," I responded. "Benny's just a little tired. The best thing would be for you to settle in here with your coffee while we get going. You and I can catch up some other time."

"But we are all getting along so well!" interrupted Benny. "Why would we break up the party? Won't you come around to our place for lunch, Matilda? You can meet our kids, Will and Wendy."

Matilda again glanced at me for guidance. I shook my head even though Benny was watching me. I didn't care anymore.

"When you're eighty years old, you don't receive too many lunch invitations from young people," Matilda responded. "I'd love to join you."

I was floored. Matilda was plainly aware Benny wasn't right in the head, and yet she agreed to come back to the flat with us. I gave her another warning look with all my newfound facial powers, but it was useless. She had made her mind up.

"Great!" responded Benny. "Let's finish up here and then we have a short trip ahead of us across London to the best postcode in town. You'll love our home. The view is to die for."

"All right then," said Matilda as she prepared to leave.

CHAPTER 44

The trip back to Hackney lasted an eternity. I was less inclined to openly communicate with Matilda since she appeared to have an inexplicable ulterior motive that made her deaf to my warnings. She remained upbeat throughout the journey as though it was perfectly normal for her to be joining two younger people she barely knew for lunch at their home.

"Bell, you travel a long way for your coffee in the mornings," Matilda said as we disembarked the train at Hackney overland station. "Why do you travel all the way to the Docklands?"

Her question took me by surprise. I didn't have a suitable prefabricated lie at the ready.

"Oh, I enjoy spending time in different parts of London," I finally responded. "It's such a diverse place. Spending time exploring the city can be as mind-expanding as traveling to another country."

Matilda nodded but I could tell she was doubtful. I recognized a question being asked behind her canny eyes.

It was almost ten o'clock when we arrived back at the flat. Benny jogged down the stairs in excitement. "Here we are!" he exclaimed as he held the door open for Matilda. "Welcome to our palace."

Matilda stepped inside. I'd like to clarify that point to ensure the record is straight. She willingly stepped into the flat of her own accord. We didn't force her to do anything she didn't want to do. (Sorry, I sound like I'm in front of a judge and jury.)

"Will, Wendy!" Benny called out as he entered the corridor. Of course, there was no response—it was no mystery why. "Those two sure do enjoy a lie-in," he lied.

"I remember being like that as a teenager," Matilda contributed. "Wasting time is one of the unique gifts of having a lot of time ahead of you."

"Well said, Matilda," Benny responded. "I'm sure a lady of your years has much wisdom to share. I'm interested in hearing more. Please take a seat."

Matilda sat at the kitchen table as did Benny. I reluctantly joined them.

"So Matilda, tell us a little bit about yourself," Benny inquired.

"There's not much to tell," Matilda responded. "I'm a widow and a grandmother. I enjoy good coffee, interesting conversation, and keeping active despite my years. I'm pretty normal really."

Benny smirked. I wished she hadn't used the word "normal." It was either a silly error or bad luck.

"Are you though?" Benny asked loudly.

"Am I what?" Matilda responded.

"Normal. Because I don't think you're so normal, Matilda," Benny continued. "In fact, the data informs me it's a certainty that you're as *abnormal* as they come."

"There you go again with all these preconceived ideas you have about me. Why am I here Benny?" Matilda asked, suddenly serious.

"OK, fair's fair. It's that time in the game when you need to give us the all-important date your team is working toward to launch the attack," Benny explained. "I'd say please but we're beyond that, don't you think?"

I wanted to run far away.

"Which date would you like Benny? Your riddles aren't making any sense to me," Matilda responded calmly.

"Oh come on, Matilda!" Benny said shaking his head. "There was me thinking you were so much better than this. Let's cut to the chase and avoid all this unnecessary averageness."

"I'd love to Benny, but I'm unsure what exactly you want," Matilda responded with more concern.

"OK, if you insist on being bothersome, we'll allow you to act out the pretense of normality your colleagues no doubt insist upon. By all means, keep your mask on for now. But do remember I gave you this opportunity to reveal yourself in a safe place," Benny said with a demented twitch.

Matilda shifted in her seat.

"I don't like the way you're talking to me, Benny," she stated. "I now understand why Bell has been so upset of late."

"What on earth are you talking about, old lady?" Benny seethed.

"I know all about you, Benny," she continued. "You pressure Bell into doing things she doesn't want to because they are things you want to achieve with your life. But you are strangling the very life out of her. It's too much, Benny. It's time you started taking responsibility for your own life."

I was perplexed as to what was happening. Matilda was clearly in a precarious position, and yet she was throwing caution to the wind by speaking up for me. I was partially in awe of her bravery, and partially annoyed that she was disclosing things I told her in confidence about my husband to my husband. A picture of a complicated woman was emerging before us.

"Bell, do you know what she's talking about?" Benny grunted in my direction.

"I needed someone to talk to and Matilda was helpful yesterday. What she says is true to an extent. Lately, I've been taking all the risks on your behalf out there," I explained as I pointed at the street through the flat's excuse for a window.

"How dare you talk about our relationship with this duplicitous old woman. Can't you see how this could affect our position in the game? We need to be able to trust one another not to share key data points with any outsiders, never mind Abnormals," Benny bemoaned.

"Oh, you leave her alone," interjected Matilda with more force. "Aren't you the big man for telling your wife to silence her voice? Her voice matters, as does mine. Are you a woman-hater, Benny? Is that what you are? I see you."

"What have we brought into our home?" Benny asked. "Here I was thinking you were an Abnormal hiding behind the mask of a Normal. But you're playing a multilayered game, aren't you? You are an Abnormal hiding behind the mask of being too abnormal to be an Abnormal. You're a real piece of work, Matilda."

"Benny, I'm not interested in hearing any more of your ravings," Matilda responded. "But I would like to meet your children, please. Are they safe and well?"

It was a strange request given Benny had drugged them asleep, and no one else knew that apart from me. Matilda was either very good at making educated guesses, or she knew more than she was revealing.

"You're a nosey one, aren't one?" Benny scowled. "Our children are none of your business."

"Bell, please humor me," Matilda pleaded. "Can you round up the kids so I can meet them?"

The more she talked of Will and Wendy, the more panicked I became. It was a mystery as to why this old lady I barely knew was suddenly so interested in my children.

"OK, OK. I'll go wake them up," I said as I rushed off to Wendy's bedroom.

CHAPTER 45

Wendy was still in a deep sleep in her bed. I shook her gently. She moved a little, but she didn't awaken. After some more vigorous shaking, she eventually opened her eyes.

"Hi Wend," I said, "how are you feeling?"

Wendy remained quiet for some time. She was fighting to keep her eyes open as they remained heavy with sleep.

"I feel like I've been dropped from a very high building," Wendy finally responded. "What happened to me?"

"Your father slipped you something to ensure you slept well," I explained.

"What? Dad drugged me?" she asked.

"He doesn't see it like that, but yes," I admitted. "We're all waiting for you in the living room. The old lady I met in the Docklands the other day, Matilda, has popped around for a catch up."

"We have a houseguest? What's going on, Mom?" Wendy asked as she sat up. "We haven't once had a houseguest since we moved here."

273

"Well, your father believes she's an Abnormal and has confronted her about it, but she's denying it. So it's complicated," I explained.

"Oh my god. Complicated doesn't do this situation justice. How do we press stop on this crazy merry-go-round?" Wendy asked with a weak attempt at a smile.

After giving Wendy a hug, I woke Will up. He was also barely coherent.

"Give me some more drugs please, Mom," was Will's response after I explained Matilda's presence to him.

I rejoined Benny and Matilda in the kitchen. They were no longer talking to one another. In half an hour she had reached the same point I had after more than seventeen years of marriage to Benny. Either she was very perceptive, or I was remarkably stupid. Will and Wendy came out of their rooms a few moments later.

"Aha, the sleeping beauties reanimate!" Benny exclaimed. "Wendy and Will, this is Matilda, the wicked witch from the Southeast."

"Hi," was all Wendy could say, and Will managed a short nod.

"Nice to meet you both," responded Matilda as though this was still a friendly family gathering. "I'm so glad you managed to wake up to meet me."

"Enough of the pleasantries," blurted out Benny. "You had your opportunity to play nice, Matilda. All we wanted was a simple date from you, but you've made your decision. It's time for you to confess before a judge and jury."

Matilda remained silent.

"Here's how this will work. I'm the judge, nice to meet you by the way, and these three are the jurors. Sorry, they were the best we could round up at such short notice," explained Benny as he picked up a large rolling pin he'd taken from my baking drawer. "I'll ask you a series of questions. If you give me the right answer, we can all breathe a sigh of relief that an Abnormal has finally done the right thing. But, heaven forbid, if you give me the wrong answer, I'll be forced to correct it. And the best way to correct any data anomaly is to erase it and start again."

As I watched Benny talking, I couldn't believe I had once loved him. I wondered where all the goodness inside him had gone, and where all this hatred had come from. His father clearly had a lot to answer for. No, Benny had a lot to answer for.

"What about the jury, Dad?" Will asked. "Don't we get a say in the decision?"

"The jurors in this court are here to support the judge with whatever he needs doing," Benny explained like a dictator from a small island nation.

"So more like servants then," Will whispered under his breath.

"Don't do this, Benny," Matilda interjected. "You've just confused me with someone else. If you let me go now, I promise I won't breathe a word of this to anyone else. Let's end this now."

"Yada yada yada," Benny responded. "Let the court hearing begin. The first question for the wicked witch of the

Southeast is, drumroll please . . . why did you come home with us today? What were you hoping to achieve or receive by coming here? You weren't expecting that one, were you?"

"I came here because I care about Bell," Matilda responded without skipping a beat. "I wanted to be friends with her, and I knew she was going through some challenges that I thought I could help with. That's what friends do, isn't it?"

"Do you really want us to believe that?" Benny asked. "Go on then, shovel more of your premeditated bullshit in our direction. Why on earth would you want to be friends with Bell, beyond creating a cover for your real work?"

"Can't you see anything?" Matilda responded. "Bell has a heart of gold, and you are slowly killing her with all your constant demands. I wanted to be her friend because I can see the beauty inside her."

Tears welled in my eyes. Matilda was risking her life for me. But I'd become so skeptical since we'd arrived in the little flat. I had let Matilda down in the worst possible way for the simple reason I could no longer tell the difference between good and bad.

"Enough Benny. Let her go now," I hissed.

"Ooh! The defendant has touched a nerve with one of the jurors. Motion denied," Benny said as he whacked the rolling pin on the table.

My heart was breaking. And I was starting to have violent feelings toward my husband, which I never thought possible before that moment. Love can turn to hate so quickly. I searched around for a suitable weapon, but there were no potential weapons in sight beyond a loaf of bread on the kitchen counter. I considered throwing it at Benny as hard as I could.

"Next question. Why did you agree to work for a terrorist organization that intends to cause as much harm as possible to the country in which you live?" Benny asked.

"I love this country. I would never harm it," answered Matilda with tears rolling down her cheeks.

"Pull the other one, it's got bells on," responded Benny. "All terrorist groups train their people in how to cry during questioning. It works particularly well when there are women around who can feel your emotional pain. Well done, you're good at your job."

Matilda wiped her tears away in silence.

"Next question. What did this country do to your terrorist group to deserve being attacked?" Benny continued. "To live for eighty healthy years here was worthy of more thankful behavior, don't you think?"

"You know nothing about my life," Matilda responded out of anger. "I've done more for this country than you'll ever understand, more than you could ever do with your data. You and your stupid data know nothing."

"Wrong answer!" shouted Benny as he raised the rolling pin above his head.

I jumped forward and held Benny's arm back so he couldn't strike Matilda. Wendy joined me, and then Will did too. With much effort, the three of us were able to overpower my increasingly frail husband, and we confiscated the rolling pin before he could harm Matilda.

"Dad, what were you thinking?" asked Will shaking his head.

"I'm protecting this country from terrorists, and you intervened to help the enemy!" responded Benny in a fury. "I hope for your case you aren't prosecuted for obstructing the course of justice. But if you are, so be it."

"You are a freak," sneered Will. "I hate you."

"Are you happy now?" Benny asked Matilda. "Your Academy Award-winning performance as a normal human has thrown a spanner in the works, hasn't it? But can't you see it doesn't matter anymore. I have more than enough information to shut your organization down either way. Your confession was nothing more than cream on top to keep the Inexplicables happy."

"Benny, it's time to let her go," I implored. "Before she presses criminal charges."

"Oh, that's hysterical, isn't it?" said Benny with a forced laugh. "The wicked witch pressing criminal charges against us! What will the charge be? Saving the country from the most significant terrorist attack in modern history? What a bad person I am!"

"You aren't a bad person," contributed Wendy, "but you aren't well in the head, Dad. It's time we get you the help you need."

At that very moment, someone started banging loudly on our front door. I nearly wet myself. And they didn't stop. It was urgent door knocking if I ever heard it. We all froze to the spot in a stunned silence.

CHAPTER 46

"Help me! We're in here!" Matilda called out to the door knockers.

"Quiet!" Benny hissed. "Another word from you and I promise you'll regret it."

Benny ran over to the door and peeped through the keyhole. For such a technology-focused Peeping Tom, it was the ultimate fall from grace. But it worked thanks to the large old-fashioned lock on the door that let air in and out.

"What are *they* doing here?" Benny whispered to himself once he'd seen who was standing on the other side of the door. He lunged backward in horror.

"Guys, this is an emergency!" Benny implored. "I know the three of you are angry with me right now, but please trust me when I tell you we are in extreme danger. My important work has been ignored and devalued for too long for any of us to be safe. All our worst fears have become a reality."

"What do you mean, Dad? Who's at the door?" asked Will, confused.

"There's no time to explain," Benny continued. "Will and Wendy, will you two please take Matilda to our bedroom and lock the door? Stay in there until I knock on the door and tell you it's safe."

The banging at the door was getting louder. The people outside were starting to exert real force on the door with the intent of breaking it open. I was amazed our old rickety door had been able to withstand so much force without collapsing. Everything about the little flat was surprising.

"Benny, please open the door, and let me go. I won't say a word," pleaded Matilda.

"You should be grateful I'm offering to keep you safe from those people," Benny said. "You really don't want to be meeting them, do you wicked witch?"

"I don't know what you're talking about, but I want to walk out of here right now," Matilda responded.

"Bell, can you please stay with me to help me secure the front door?" Benny asked. "I'm sorry for everything, darling. I understand why you are upset with me, I do. But everything I've done has been to make the world a safe place for you and the kids. I know I've forgotten how to be the man you loved. I know I've become nothing more than a player in the game we're playing. Let's just make it to the end of the game and then everything can go back to how it was before all this."

It was a big moment in our rollercoaster ride of a marriage. There are so many conflicting faces within a long-term partnership. As Benny pleaded with me, I saw brief glimpses of the man I once loved. I wanted that man back.

"OK, for old time's sake, Benny. But only on the condition you promise to get medical help as soon as this episode is over," I eventually responded.

"OK, OK, whatever. Kids, now let's move!" Benny commanded.

Wendy held Matilda's shaky hand and escorted her to the main bedroom at the back of the flat. Will reluctantly followed. All Benny and I were left with was each other versus whatever monster was banging down our door.

Benny grabbed a chair and put it under the door handle.

"Now we need wood, a hammer, and nails," Benny said. "I'll break up the coffee table. Darling, can you please find that small hammer we keep in the kitchen, and there are some nails in the third drawer on the left."

By the time I had the hammer and nails ready, our coffee table was in pieces. Benny started hammering pieces of wood all around the door, and soon the door was boarded up ready for the world to end. But the banging was becoming more forceful, and a voice outside the door called out to us: "Everything will be all right! Please open the door and let us explain." It didn't sound like a monster addressing us.

"Benny, who's at the door?" I asked.

"It's the Inexplicables here to stop us, steal from us, and do whatever else they want to do to us. It's an emergency situation," Benny responded.

I stepped over to the keyhole and gazed through it. I could see the older gentleman whose flat we had visited the day before, and the Russian man.

"They don't sound like they want to cause us harm," I said as calmly as I could.

"Bell, trust me. The only possible reason they can be here today is to cause us harm," Benny stressed.

"I'm not so sure about that. Not everyone wants to cause us harm, Benny. Why would they? We are hidden away from the world in every possible way. Who are we a danger to?" I asked, but I was talking to myself.

"I gave you the opportunity to accept me as the winner the other day!" Benny called out at the door. "But you pretended you didn't even know me. You ignored my value as the winning player despite everything I've done for you. You know I'm worth more than that."

Benny crumpled in a heap in front of the door as the insanity took control. His mind was processing too much data, and at a level beyond the design of any human mind. Like all overloaded machines, his engine was burning itself out.

"Can't you say 'Well done!' to me just once? Just fucking once! Would it kill you to tell me you're proud of me? Is that too much to ask for?" Benny pleaded to the door or whoever he thought the door represented. My heart ached for him despite everything. He was broken in every way a man can be.

"Benny, please listen to us. You are misunderstanding who we are," said the voice behind the door. "We aren't here to cause you harm."

"Too late! Just look at the state of our lives. Can you tell me we haven't been harmed? Because that would be inexplicable!" exclaimed Benny with a forced laugh.

"Benny, maybe we should just open the door and talk to them," I suggested calmly.

"We will be forced to break the door down if you don't open it!" called out the voice outside. "Please, open the door."

"Over my dead body!" yelled Benny at the door.

I lunged toward the door and attempted to open the lock, but Benny jumped in front of me and pushed me away. I fell hard on the floor.

"Bell, what are you doing?" Benny asked, shocked. "I thought we were on the same team."

"Opening that door is doing the right thing by you in every possible way!" I implored. "Benny, will you please listen to *me* this time?"

"Sorry, Bell, but the data never ever lies," whispered Benny shaking his head. I could tell he was weakening. The light behind his eyes was dimming.

CHAPTER 47

The banging outside stopped. In its stead, I could hear hurried talking. It sounded like a woman had joined the two men at the door, and they were filling her in. I heard the words "He's becoming a danger to himself."

Then a key entered the front door lock and was turned. The lock opened. All they had to do was kick away the wooden boards Benny had nailed around the door, and they would be able to enter the flat. I still wasn't sure if I should be welcoming them or fighting them, but my gut instinct continued to tell me they were on our side.

"You're not welcome in here you mean-souled bastard!" Benny shrieked at the heavens.

He frantically searched the kitchen for something else to stop them from entering. I breathed a sigh of relief when our kitchen revealed nothing of substance for his next act of violence. But then, he found the two items in that kitchen that, in combination, could cause grievous bodily harm: a large can of WD-40 and a stove lighter. I stood back as Benny lunged toward the door.

"Will and Wendy!" Benny shouted through the flat. "Make sure your door is shut, you hear me?"

There was no response, but I was grateful they were in the safest part of the flat.

Then the kicking of the wooden panels started. One kick, two kicks, three kicks, and then a foot wearing a familiar brown suede shoe reared its ugly head in the center of the space where the panels had been. Of course, it would be a foot—feet had gotten us into this mess, and feet would continue to pile on the pain. I'd had enough of feet by then. But the front door was open, so the foot had an opportunity to do something good with its time. It could enter the flat and stop the madness. On cue, the foot kicked the remaining wooden panels out of the way, and a different foot revealed itself from the other side. It was also wearing a brown shoe, but it wasn't made of suede.

Benny lit his custom-made flame thrower within nanoseconds of the unidentified foot's arrival. He turned the flames onto the space where the door had been, as well as everything beyond it. The brown-shoed foot reacted to the flames and disappeared in a hurry, but the area around the front door was quickly alight. The old cheap timber burned like a tinder box.

"Stand back, Bell!" Benny called out as he continued to direct his flame thrower in the direction where the intruding feet had entered but were no longer in sight.

"Stand back from the door!" I heard a voice call out from the other side of the flames. "We'll try to get through to you so we can get you out."

Those definitely weren't the words of bad guys there to do us harm, but Benny remained resolute that no one was going to enter. He kept directing his flame thrower at the door, and in short order the entire corridor was alight. As I retreated backward into the flat, I could hear the Russian man on his phone outside saying: "Yes, there are five people trapped inside, five. Please get here as soon as possible! The fire is moving fast!"

"Bell, please stand behind me at all times," implored Benny. "I'll stop them. For you, my darling, I'll hold them back."

"But Benny, they're here to help us! They just called the fire brigade for god's sake!" I shouted. My words faded into the noisy flames that were engulfing the front of the little flat.

As the flames edged forward, I stepped backward. It was the dance of life and I wanted to live. Benny, however, remained rooted to his preordained spot defending the gates of hell from all intruders. Like a die-hard meerkat soldier whose life mission was to keep humans out at any cost, Benny kept fighting what he thought was the good fight. But the flames didn't care what Benny's fight was really about. Their only mission was to destroy everything in sight in as little time as possible. And they did a remarkable job of that.

I cowered at the end of the entrance hall as I watched Benny fighting fire with fire. I was determined not to open the door to the main bedroom because the moment I did I knew the kids' time was probably up. So I witnessed my husband's final stand in horror. By then, Benny was acting as though each flame was an Inexplicable or his father or whomever else the data told him it was.

"Keep out! Keep out! Keep out!" was all I could hear Benny screaming as the flames leaped from the walls onto his arms, and his shoulders, and well, everywhere. But he didn't turn to run. He let them engulf him, and he collapsed to the ground. My dear husband had fallen.

CHAPTER 48

There was no time to dwell on what was lost as the fire was determined to take everything from us. As the flames cornered me at the end of the corridor, I was certain my time was up. I prepared to depart this world and started reminiscing about my most unusual life. All the images that descended upon me were from our lives before the little flat when we were a normal family living a happy life. The day we brought Will home from the hospital for the first time was particularly poignant. We had no idea what to do with him, and we laughed whenever he smiled at us. Present-day me smiled back at baby Will from amid the smoky blaze. Not one image of our lives after we arrived in the little flat made its way through the smoke to soothe away my impending doom. Isn't memory clever? It has a way of instantly burying the less-than-perfect parts of our lives.

At the very moment I was ready to say goodbye to this world, water started gushing in through the front door. In my confusion, I wondered if a river had burst its banks into the flat. But then I realized the firefighters had arrived. I breathed a sigh of relief as the flames around me started to subside. Within minutes, all the flames were out. It was just in the nick of time for me.

The firefighters rushed into the flat, stepping over Benny's lifeless body as though it was nothing but a doormat. Two of them approached me. "Where are the others?" they called out through their protective masks. I pointed at the main bedroom door, unable to speak due to smoke inhalation. They rushed into the bedroom, and I was helped out the front door by the next two firefighters. I was so weak I could barely move.

There was a stretcher awaiting me at the front door which I was lifted onto. However, the smoke was still doing bad things to me. I coughed and spluttered uncontrollably and wondered if my time was up regardless. Everything was fuzzy and unreal as though I was looking at the world through broken binoculars. I should have been accustomed to that by then.

Through the fuzziness, I noticed the posh gentleman and the Russian man were watching anxiously in the background. At one point, the Russian man walked over to me. He gazed into my smoky eyes and said: "Everything will be all right now. You did well to make it this far." His words dissipated into nothingness as my almost dead brain struggled to compute their meaning.

Then I remembered the kids were still inside the little flat. I sat up on the stretcher and attempted to call out to them. Once again, words failed me. I must have made a sound like a beached whale trying to communicate with its brethren. A medic tried to encourage me to lie back down, but I was desperate to see Will's and Wendy's faces come out. I had to know they were safe.

Time slowed as I waited, as everyone waited. The posh gentleman was talking in hushed tones on his mobile, and the Russian man was nervously fidgeting. Different people made attempts to calm me down, but eventually they gave up. They saw the look of a desperate mother in my eyes, and no doubt imagined themselves in my position. "Your children should be out in a matter of seconds," said one medic with a kind face.

Finally, there was movement from inside the flat. A firefighter emerged through the front door supporting my beautiful daughter. Wendy was alive! Thank god, she was alive. I'll never forget the joy of seeing her again. She was shaking and covered with soot, but she appeared to be unhurt. I waved at her and she gave me a weak wave back.

And then another firefighter emerged supporting Will, who was also alive. Tears started rushing down my cheeks. Will was even wobblier than Wendy so I couldn't tell if he was all right, but the main thing was he was alive. Somehow, against the odds, the three of us had survived the most abnormal of days.

Then I remembered Matilda and wondered when they would bring her out. But before they did, two medics started carrying my stretcher up the rickety stairs to street level. I waved again at Will and Wendy as I was shipped off into the

UK's wonderfully efficient medical system. Within minutes, I was riding in an ambulance with its siren turned on. And within half an hour, I was lying in a clean-sheeted hospital bed surrounded by white-coated angels. They must have given me something for the pain as I can't remember much about what happened next. I fell into a deep sleep.

CHAPTER 49

When I finally awoke, it took me a while to piece back together where I was and what had happened. At first, I thought I was at home in the little flat and Benny was already up, or more likely hadn't gone to bed. I contemplated how I could add value for the team in the day's activities ahead. But then I remembered I was lying in a hospital bed and Benny was dead. When I said that to myself, *Benny is dead*, it failed to register in my mind. I struggled to imagine him being dead as he had been such a powerful life force. But dead he was.

After much pleading with the medical staff who were helping me, they allowed me to see Will and Wendy. They were both recovering in the same hospital. Will was apparently in a weaker state than Wendy, so Wendy and I were wheelchaired into his room.

"Hello, my two favorite people!" I beamed when I saw them.

"Mom! I've missed you," Wendy smiled as she moved her wheelchair near mine so we could hold each other's hands.

"Hi Mom, hi Wend," Will said from his bed. "I'm glad you are both OK."

Will was a little subdued, but I was so excited to see him.

"How are you doing?" I asked. "Are you feeling better?"

"I'll pull through," Will said. "I've got third degree burns on my arms, but apparently the pain becomes easier to bear over time."

"Oh no, Will! I'm so sorry to hear that," I responded. "What happened?"

Will took a deep breath.

"The fire made it into the bedroom by sneaking underneath the bedroom door," he explained. "And then everything happened so fast. The door burned through in no time, and then the flames ran up the walls. Wend, Matilda, and I were huddled together in the back corner of the bedroom, and our time was clearly running out fast."

"Mom, there's something you need to know about Matilda," interjected Wendy.

"Oh yes?" I said.

"She started saying strange things while the three of us were sitting there," Wendy explained.

"What sort of strange things?" I asked.

"I'm not sure what language she was speaking, but she was clearly fluent," Wendy responded. "She started chanting in this foreign language, and as the fire closed in on us her chants became louder and louder. I wasn't sure if I was more scared of the fire or Matilda at one point."

A shiver ran down my spine.

"Wend's right, Mom," Will continued. "Matilda became downright scary for an old woman. And then she became even crazier."

"What did she do?" I asked, half not wanting to know the answer.

"She stood up and ran toward the flames on the other side of the bedroom. She ran directly into the fire. It was so grim. I ran after her and tried to pull her away, which is how I got these," Will explained showing us the burns all over his arms. My already broken heart split into more pieces.

"Oh darling, how brave you were," I whispered.

"But I couldn't pull her back," Will continued. "She pushed me away as she allowed the flames to run up her legs. The fire soon engulfed her whole body, and a few seconds later, she collapsed in a black heap. She didn't even scream."

"What a terrible end for Matilda," I responded. "I'm sorry you two had to witness it."

"It was horrible, Mom," Wendy stated. "But it was even harder to see Dad's body on the way out."

"Yes, it was. I'm so sorry for your father's passing," I said.

"Me too, although I'm confused by Dad's recent crazy behavior. What happened to him?" Wendy asked.

"We'll never fully understand what was going on in your father's mind the last few weeks. But I think he'd like all of us to forgive him for his behavior, and to remember him as the man he was before we arrived in the little flat, don't you?" I surmised.

"Yes and no, Mom," responded Will. "Yes, Dad was able to be a functioning father and husband before we moved into the little flat, and that all changed as soon as we arrived there. However, I still think he did his best work after we arrived in the flat. Maybe one day we'll understand it a little more."

"I'm with you, Mom," Wendy said. "I'll always remember Dad as the man he was before the flat. I'm too tired to understand the work he was obsessed with after we arrived there. It killed him for god's sake, and it nearly killed us. What good can ever come of that?"

"Mom, has anyone talked to you about what happened yet?" Will asked.

"No. The only people I've been interacting with are the doctors and nurses who've done a stellar job of piecing me back together," I explained. "They've kept everyone else away while I've been recovering. You two are the first real people I've spoken to since the fire."

"I expect the police will want to talk with us at some point," added Will.

"I hope they leave us alone," said Wendy. "Look at us. We've got no answers about anything apart from the fact Dad was mentally unwell. He needed to be in a loony bin, but we let him continue on his wild-goose chase."

"Hey, you two, let's focus on healing for now," I responded. "That's all that matters. One day, we may be able to make more sense of all this, but who knows."

CHAPTER 50

Lying in my hospital bed the next day, I wondered if I was the last person on Earth. I could hear doctors and nurses moving around, but they may as well have been aliens. No one could possibly understand all we'd been through. Even talking with Will and Wendy about it was challenging because we were all so hurt, and hurt people have a way of reinjuring one another without meaning to. So lying alone was the best thing I could do while I recalibrated the state of my life.

That afternoon, one of the nurses told me I had a visitor. I couldn't imagine who it could be given how cut off from the rest of the world our lives had been. I sat up in bed and waited.

A woman came bounding into the room full of energy and smiles. I gazed at her face, which I knew so well, but it took me a moment to recognize her. It was like seeing my own face from an earlier stage in my life, a time when I knew everything would be all right. It was my sister Angie.

"Hello, sis!" I smiled.

"Bell!" she squealed. "Oh my god, what's happened? Are you all right?"

"They are both big questions. Why don't we start by giving each other a hug?" I suggested.

Angie threw her arms around me with the abandon we hugged with as children. It was wonderful to be in her arms. I couldn't remember the last time I had been hugged by someone who loved me unconditionally. Benny had been beyond that for quite a while.

"How long has it been since we saw each other?" Angie asked mid hug.

"I know the answer to that one," I responded. "It's been over a year and a half, would you believe."

"I would, because it's felt like an eternity to me. Did I do something to upset you?" Angie asked. "I'm so sorry if I did. I can do better at being your little sister if you'll let me."

"Not at all, Ange. You did nothing to upset me. Please believe me when I tell you this one is all on me," I confessed.

"So tell me, what happened to you?" Angie asked with concern.

"We fell on hard times, really hard times," I explained. "And rather than being honest with you about it like a normal, healthy, big sister would, I decided to hide underground. I didn't want you to see the state my life, our lives, had become because I wanted to continue to be the strong big sister you knew when you were younger."

"Oh Bell, I'm so sorry to hear that," Angie responded, holding my hand. "Is that how you ended up in hospital? I know nothing about what happened to you. I just received a call from a Frenchman explaining you were in this hospital and in need of some family support. I came straight away."

"Gosh, there's so much to explain," I said. "And yet, I don't know most of the answers myself. Will, Wendy, and I are all here in this hospital recovering from injuries we incurred in a fire that burned through the flat we were living in."

"Oh my god! Are you all right? Are the kids all right? Is Benny all right?" Angie asked with growing urgency.

"The kids and I will be all right in time but . . . *we lost Benny in the fire*," I stated.

It was the first time I had said the words out loud to another human. They sounded unreal on the way out of my mouth, and they hung erratically in the air between us. I'd hoped I could release them without paying for it, but my tears wouldn't be held back. The moment I began crying, Angie joined me. She hadn't been close to Benny, but just as when we were kids, my pain was her pain.

"I can't believe Benny is gone," Angie finally responded, "He was so wonderfully, beautifully unique in a world full of average people."

I was surprised by Angie's response. The few times she and Benny had spent time together, I could tell she couldn't stand him. She never said anything to me, but as her sister I recognized her "What a twat!" expression that shone through every time Benny told her and everyone else that he was right, and they were wrong. People always talk kindly of the dead, but her comment implied she saw through to the real Benny at an earlier time in his life. I hope she did. Anyway, it was the best thing she could have said in that moment.

"So what's next for you and the kids?" Angie asked once we'd both stopped crying.

"We have a lot of work to do to figure out who we are without Benny," I answered. "In the past couple of years we've become such a close-knit team, so it's hard to picture who we are as individuals anymore. To be honest, I can't even remember who I was before I met Benny."

"I hear you, sis," Angie responded. "Please remember, you have a loving sister who wants to help you in any way she can. Maybe, just maybe, I'll be able to help remind you who Belinda Harry was before she became a wife and mother. Because she was pretty damn awesome. She still is."

Angie and I resumed our close and loving relationship from that moment onward. I was astounded by the way our relationship self-healed almost instantly. (Thank you for forgiving me, Ange.)

CHAPTER 51

The next couple of days ground by so slowly. All I had to while away the time with were memories of what had happened to us. And Wendy, Will, and I were allowed to see each other for around half an hour once a day. The doctors explained to us that Wendy and I were due to be released in around a week, while Will had a few-weeks stay ahead of him to treat his burn wounds. I struggled to imagine life after my hospital stay as I knew everything would change. There wasn't one part of our lives that Benny hadn't structured to optimally capture the data, so the idea of not caring about data anymore was both freeing and terrifying.

One afternoon while I was drifting in and out of sleep, there was a knock at my door. I wasn't used to anyone entering who wasn't a doctor and they never knocked, so I cautiously called out, "Come in." It was the Russian man and the posh gentlemen. My initial instinct was to run away from them as I regressed straight back to my street-stalking tendencies. But, of course, I couldn't run anymore. Those days were over. So I remained motionless in my bed and watched each of them approach one slow footstep at a time. The Russian man was wearing his favorite pair of brown suede shoes, and the posh gentleman was wearing a pair of brown loafers, which hadn't rated a mention in our data collection. I wondered how his shoes had escaped our all-watching eyes.

"So we meet again," said the Russian man with a different accent to what I remembered. "My name is Bruno."

"Hello again as well," said the posh gentleman. "I'm Sebastien."

"Hello," I responded, "I'm Belinda. But of course, you know that."

"We do," nodded Bruno as he sat down on a chair.

"So, who are you then?" I directed at both of them, intending the question to cover the entire group of Inexplicables.

"We can only answer that question by telling you a little of our story," responded Sebastien. "Would that be agreeable to you? We won't take up much of your time."

"I'm ready for some answers from you people," I said.

They nodded at one another and made themselves comfortable, which made me less comfortable.

"OK," began Sebastien, "so the first thing you need to understand is that the UK authorities have been increasingly concerned about a growing risk of terrorist activity for around three years now. The best intelligence available to the UK Government suggested the world's most dangerous terrorist groups were investigating ways to leverage the digital world while working more closely with one another to inflict serious damage upon the UK. It was believed that a number of terrorist groups were viewing the Brexit situation as an unusual opportunity to attack the UK while the government's eye wasn't on the ball."

I shifted in my bed. It was as though Benny was communicating from beyond the grave. He'd said something almost exactly the same to us only days earlier.

"The next thing you need to understand is that there is a group called 'Level B' within government intelligence who are part government and part private sector," Sebastien continued. "Level B's role is to ensure nothing falls through the gaps in terms of national security. What that means is we are searching for ways to address national risks when everyone else in the government is ignorant of what's really going on. We need to think outside the box, and we need to work with the best people in this country in any way possible. Oh, and by the way, Bruno and I are the co-heads of Level B."

My sense of unease continued to grow. I'd half expected them to tell me they were just members of the public who wanted to understand why we'd been acting so crazy. But this conversation was immediately heading in a direction I hadn't anticipated.

"Yes, that's right," interjected Bruno. "And to work with the best people in the security world means we have to investigate creative ways to enlist the help of people in the private sector. With that in mind, we came up with an innovative idea a while back to help us find the best of the best."

"Wait, so you guys are like undercover agents?" I asked.

"More like security experts who fly under the radar," Bruno responded.

"Don't tell me you wanted Benny to work for you?" I asked as a sense of dread suddenly entered my soul from all directions.

"We'll get to that," continued Bruno. "We became aware that many of Britain's best minds were competing on a TV program called The Connection Game. The program was designed to attract people with a unique ability to find the truth within a universe of randomness. We've found this valuable skill to be extremely rare because people who have it are often skirting very close to insanity. So we started viewing The Connection Game as an ideal opportunity to fish for talent, and we orchestrated a recruitment project around it. The idea was to run an individual version of The Connection Game to ensure we were exposing individual rather than team talent."

As Bruno spoke, Benny's demented face amid the fire popped uninvited into my mind—he was still shouting "Keep out!" at the door.

"The producers of The Connection Game loved the idea because it validated their business model which is focused upon identifying extraordinary talent," Bruno continued. "The show's host, Morgan Hill, was particularly enthusiastic to help us find the person we were looking for as he has a passion for excellence. In fact, he was the one who came up with the idea that the recruitment process should include a contractual agreement with the winner regarding a bigger role after the show. At first, we were against the idea, but we soon realized it was the only way to ensure we were establishing a productive longer-term relationship with the winner."

My blood was boiling. But I kept my mouth closed for the simple reason I wanted—no needed—to hear the truth. I'd waited far too long to hear it.

"You know what happened next," Sebastien interjected. "Benny won the show in spectacular fashion. And unbeknownst to you or Benny, that meant he'd signed a contract putting himself forward for a role in helping Level B better understand the terrorism risks facing this country."

I couldn't hold my tongue anymore when I heard this.

"What the fuck are you talking about? You never communicated with Benny about how he could help you. You never formed an agreement with him in any way!" I shouted in their direction.

Both Sebastien and Bruno paused at this point. They gazed nervously around the room as though they'd have done anything to avoid the question.

"This may be hard for you to hear," Bruno finally responded. "We'll tell you the truth out of respect for all you and your family have done. However, I warn you, as a civilian you may not understand the importance of our work and the high-risk context we are operating within."

It was like Benny was alive and well and once again talking to me about his important fucking work.

CHAPTER 52

"Just tell me the truth," I blurted out, unable to articulate all the thoughts rushing around my head.

"OK, Belinda," Bruno responded. "So we added a short clause at the end of the agreement Benny signed when he agreed to be a contestant on The Connection Game. The clause basically said: If you win the show you agree to be involved in a follow-up project with the production team and others. More importantly, there was explicit mention that the winner's life could be manipulated in the follow-up game in ways beyond their current comprehension."

He paused. My fury overflowed like lava from a volcano.

"You lying motherfuckers!" I screamed. "You're telling me that we were players in a twisted game that we were unaware of? What planet are you people from? You can't deconstruct people's lives and then piece them back together as you see fit. You should be ashamed of yourselves."

"This is why context is so important," responded Sebastien. "Because in our line of work the notion that anything goes is acceptable if it means we could potentially save the lives of millions of people. It will take you a long time to understand this, but I'm confident you will one day."

"No way. Toying with people's lives is unforgivable," I stated.

And then the implication of what they were telling me hit me like a ton of bricks.

"Hang on!" I seethed. "When you say Benny signed a contract committing him to having his life manipulated in ways beyond his comprehension, does that mean you were the ones who stole all our money and had us relocated to that flat?"

Again, Bruno and Sebastien looked nervous.

"Yes," Sebastien finally responded. "We can explain why if you'll only listen. We owe you the truth."

I was so shocked I could no longer speak, so I let him continue.

"After he won The Connection Game, we completed detailed psychological profiling on Benny and learned a number of key facts about him that informed how we could inspire him to do his best for us," Sebastian explained. "Key fact number one was that Benny's father instilled in him a deep-held inferiority complex, which meant he would go to extraordinary lengths to uncover the truth, and in his eyes, win any game he was playing."

"But it was a game," I interjected. "When you say 'in his eyes' . . . his eyes were spot on. It was the rest of us who had no idea you were controlling our lives like expendable puppets for your own twisted purposes. So why on earth did you steal all our money and force us into poverty?"

"That was a vital step to move Benny into the part of London where we suspected the terrorists were operating," responded Bruno. "It was more by luck than planning that led us to discover the flat you were relocated to. One of our team noticed the unique window looking onto the street from that flat, and we started piecing together a thesis as to how Benny would react if he could see nothing but the passing feet on the street. Our working theory was that his analytical brain would start connecting the dots whether he liked it or not. And by taking away your financial assets, we knew you'd have to spend enough time being supported by welfare and living in the flat for Benny's talents to showcase themselves. Both theories proved remarkably accurate in hindsight."

"Well, whoopty-do! Aren't you bloody geniuses?" I said with as much sarcasm as I could muster.

Bruno and Sebastien remained silent and uncomfortable.

"We are sorry you have to hear this, Belinda," Sebastien eventually said with a sympathetic look. "It must be incredibly painful to hear. Let's leave it there for today. We'll come back tomorrow to explain the rest. Please believe us when we tell you that causing your family pain was a necessary side effect of a strategy designed to protect our country from unfathomable damage. We are truly sorry for Benny's passing, and for all you and your family have been through."

Bruno and Sebastien stood and walked away in silence. I was in shock for quite some time. Then the tears came. I cried and cried. And then I started reliving everything we'd been through with the newfound perspective of what I'd just learned. There was no getting away from it: Everything Benny had said and believed was the truth. He was the only one who understood what was really going on. Yet, his family had—on numerous occasions—viewed him as insane and told him so. Then, despite it all, Benny died a gruesome death trying to protect us from the dangers he knew were lurking just outside our window. I was inconsolable. My grief for Benny's mistreatment and sacrifice took on a life of its own.

Eventually I ran out of tears and fell into a deep sleep. I dreamed I was in the audience again during Benny's infamous Connection Game performance. He was shining bright on stage, a magnificent man at the height of his powers. I was sitting next to Red High Heels and Black Business Shoes, but I could only tell that based on their shoes. Their faces were so average it was hard to recognize them as independent humans. Morgan Hill bounded out onto the stage like a coiled snake preparing to attack. I jumped out of my seat to warn Benny. "Run for your life, darling!" I attempted to shout out, but no words emerged from my mouth. My mouth was sealed shut and I was unable to communicate. So I tried shouting louder. "It's all an act that will destroy you!" I tried to call out, but once again no words came out. Morgan Hill began interviewing the contestants before the game kicked off, and my warnings to Benny evaporated into the ether, useless and unheeded.

A nurse shook me awake. "Are you all right, Belinda?" she asked urgently. "You were screaming hysterically."

"At least my voice works," I said as I drifted back to sleep.

CHAPTER 53

By the next morning, the awful truth had started to sink in. Benny had been right about everything—every single minute detail. And now he was gone. I knew I had a part to play in what had happened to him but understanding it was beyond me at that point. However, as I lay in that hospital bed, Benny's pain and suffering descended upon me as though it were my own. I'd have done anything to go back in time so I could thank Benny for all he did for us, for being brilliant, for being him.

Bruno and Sebastien returned to my hospital room mid-morning. By the time they walked in, my desire to kill them had subsided, but their presence remained far from easy. I knew I needed to hear everything if I was ever going to move on, so I forced myself to tolerate their presence.

"Morning Belinda. How are you feeling?" Bruno asked with genuine concern.

"Where are you from?" I asked, ignoring his question.

"I'm originally from France, but I worked in Russia for many years. It's my Russian persona and language-speaking ability that is often most helpful in this line of work," he explained sheepishly.

Once again, Benny had been right. I made a mental note to punish myself for all my stupidity.

"Now, Belinda," started Sebastien, "after yesterday's huge shock, we'd like to propose a slightly different approach today."

"Go on," I responded.

"We'd like you to ask us the questions you would like answered, all of them. As we mentioned, we know we owe you as much of the truth as you want or can handle. After all you've been through, we think it's time we let you drive the conversation," Sebastien suggested.

"OK, that works for me," I responded.

"One more thing before we start," continued Sebastien. "It's your decision whether or not we bring Will and Wendy into the conversation today. When they learn the truth is up to you."

"Not today, no way," I blurted out. "Will would attempt to murder you if he heard the truth like this today. I'll let them know when they are ready."

"OK," responded Bruno, "so what's your first question?"

"Who were the other Inexplicables?" I asked, knowing they knew our terminology as well as we did.

"Blue Joggers as you called him is a student who works casually for us. His specialities are creating diversions and encouraging people to follow him. I believe you got to know him in this way," Bruno began without a hint of humor. "Red

High Heels is Morgan Hill's girlfriend. She's an up-and-coming actress who works for us when we need a high-profile female presence. You may have seen some of her work in the latest series of Doctor Who."

I couldn't help but chuckle at how ridiculous the situation had been. They had been playing cat and mouse with us from the moment we arrived in the little flat. The more I heard, the more stupid I felt.

"And that leaves Black Business Shoes," continued Bruno. "We generally used one of our Level B colleagues for this role, but we occasionally experimented with different people. You may remember when you thought you'd mistakenly followed the wrong fellow at one point. You hadn't. We'd just changed people after the usual fellow clumsily noticed you trip on the steps and then laughed out loud. Luckily, we had a back-up actor at the ready that day."

I wondered if this was what it was like to enter hell with someone at the gates explaining to you what had actually been happening in your sorry life while you ran around like a headless, clueless chicken.

"Next question. Why did you offer us a way out a few months ago when we were working again? We received a letter offering us the chance to move out of the flat and we considered leaving at that point," I said, remembering our short period of normality.

"Yes, that's right," responded Sebastien. "When I mentioned Level B is part government, part private sector, it means we sometimes fall through gaps of our own because of the way government departments work. That letter was a bone fide communication from the housing office and a grave mistake on our part. When your family started getting on with your lives again and you received that letter, we thought the operation was over. In fact, someone lost their job over that incident."

"Poor you, poor them, what a disaster," I half whispered.

Bruno and Sebastien shifted awkwardly on their feet but remained silent.

"Here's another question: why on earth did you steal our laptops and other technology a few months ago?" I asked. "Surely that was in conflict with your own interests as it slowed our work down."

"Good question. We did that because Benny was too clever even for us," responded Sebastien. "We had installed tracking technology in all your laptops that allowed us to follow your work. After all, that was the whole point of the project. However, amid his paranoia that you were being watched, Benny vastly improved your digital security with a range of innovative and unique solutions. He did an excellent job of it and effectively blocked us from following your progress. It happened when you were all getting on with your lives again, so we were in the dark as to whether you were making any progress toward our goals. We made a team decision to confiscate your technology so we could extract the latest information."

"You bastards!" I couldn't help myself saying. "You were milking everything we did as though we were assets rather than humans."

The two of them diverted their gaze from my angry stare.

"Back up. Did you know we were listening into your conversation through Benny's computer that day?" I asked.

"We did indeed," confessed Bruno. "Our sophisticated antitracking software alerted us to the remarkably, well-hidden microphone inside the laptop."

"So why the hell did you own up to stealing our money when you knew we were listening in?" I asked.

Bruno took a deep breath.

"Around that time, our best intelligence suggested the Abnormals' attack was fast approaching. We were running out of time, so we had to take urgent action to accelerate Benny's work," he admitted.

I couldn't comprehend the full weight of that admission and what it meant at the time. I shook my head in silence.

"So we were right about the Abnormals?" I eventually asked.

"One hundred percent right," answered Sebastien. "They were a cooperative of the world's most dangerous terrorist groups working together to take control of the UK Government. Their mission was to turn the UK into a dictatorship under their leadership, which would eventually lead the world into war. And your final list of the twenty-two members of the Abnormals group was spot on. It was an extraordinary accomplishment to name every single member like you did. Well, except for one."

His reference to the Abnormals in the past tense hung heavy in the air.

"Who did we miss?" I asked.

"She found you actually," Bruno interjected. "The elderly lady known to you as Matilda. Her real name was Hilda."

"What about her?" I asked not ready to hear the answer.

"She was one of the most powerful and notorious members of the Abnormals group," Bruno explained. "We've been trying to figure out who she was for some time. While she spent her mornings monitoring the government's data center, she was up to a whole lot more in the background. We believe she was one of their main operatives. And she was incredibly successful at it for the simple reason she was an eighty-year-old woman whom no one suspected of doing anything apart from drinking tea. She was hiding in plain sight."

Once more, it was as though Benny's words were returning from the other side of the grave like an echo of the truth. I've never been so humbled.

"But what did she want with us?" I asked, suddenly uneasy. "Why did she willingly agree to come to the flat that day knowing what she knew."

"As the expression goes: curiosity killed the cat," Bruno responded. "Our intelligence suggests Hilda became fascinated by Benny's fame in the underground world she inhabited. We believe she was vaguely amused by his true-belief-revealing software project, and thought it was indicative of a man who didn't understand the complexities of human beliefs. But contrary to Benny's belief, the Abnormals had no interest in obtaining and using his software. They believed they were already streets ahead of him in their digital capabilities."

"So she came around for no reason other than nosiness?" I asked shocked.

"Yes, we believe so," Bruno continued. "We think she wanted to test her own brilliance against Benny's in a weird sort of way, a bit like a trophy hunt. And she was so confident, even arrogant, about her own abilities to remain hidden behind her mask that she genuinely believed she was safe around your family."

"Remind me to be careful who I talk to at cafés in the future," I said.

Both Bruno and Sebastien laughed lightly, but they thankfully held it back on my account.

"Do you know why this Hilda committed suicide in the fire?" I asked with growing seriousness.

"We suspect her beliefs demanded it of her," responded Sebastien. "The terrorist group she was most closely aligned with believed that to reach the afterlife you must make your own pathway toward it. So given the choice between dying in the fire or taking her own life, she chose her own pathway."

I was silent for a few moments. Matilda had seemed like such a nice person, and yet it was all a façade designed to hide her ugly truth.

"Hang on. Did she know about the game you kindly souls were playing with our lives?" I asked.

"We don't think so. That information remained airtight throughout the mission," answered Bruno. "Benny was known for his technology expertise all around the country. And the episode of The Connection Game Benny won so emphatically has become folklore among any groups with even a remote interest in data analysis, which includes most police and criminal organizations alike. He had become somewhat of a poster boy for what the analytical mind is capable of."

Some more tears arrived uninvited. The idea that Benny was at the pinnacle of analytical achievement highlighted just how underappreciated he had been in our lowly life under the stairs. His genius had been a burden that had not brought him any joy, only pain. So to know that others worshipped his talents was a hard pill to swallow. Why hadn't anyone told him just how special he was? I asked that question to myself as well.

CHAPTER 54

"OK, so enough beating around the bush," I said. "What was the outcome of our work, your work, whatever you want to call it?"

Bruno and Sebastien both took a deep breath. Bruno nodded at Sebastien.

"The mission was successful. Every single member of the terrorist cooperative has been arrested, and well, you know what happened to the infamous Hilda. She can't cause any more problems now. We took control of all the Abnormals' technology and uncovered the full extent of their work and plans. Between these four walls, we were shocked to discover how much progress they had made. Their technology was unbelievably sophisticated, and humbled our own expertise in that area," explained Sebastien with gravity.

"And it turns out we stopped them just in the nick of time," he continued. "They were planning their attack only five days after we apprehended them, which explains why Hilda was watching the data center so closely every morning. Controlling the data center was the first and most important step in their plan. For the entire plan to succeed, they needed that step to work, so Hilda was watching it like a hawk. If you hadn't struck up those conversations with her, which in turn sparked Benny's concern that an attack was imminent, this would have ended very differently. And if Benny hadn't traveled to the Docklands that day to meet Hilda, all our lives would be at risk. Benny was the true champion of the game he was so focused on winning."

I bowed my head for Benny and all he believed in. Bruno and Sebastien joined me.

"We know how much Benny sacrificed on behalf of others," added Bruno. "He will always be remembered as a hero."

It was almost too much to bear. Even now, it's hard for me to talk about how heavy the weight of the truth was. Rather than setting me free, it curled around my neck like a python looking for a guilty meal.

"OK, so you have been honest with me, but I have one more question," I said.

"Shoot," responded Bruno.

"Why didn't you communicate directly with us along the way? I now understand why you needed to set up the project—or whatever you call it—as you did, but why didn't you bring us inside the tent, particularly when Benny's mental health started deteriorating? A simple word from you would have proven to Benny, and to his family, that he wasn't crazy—that he was valued. It would have saved his life," I asked with more unlicensed tears escaping my eyes.

"We debated this one intensively," Sebastien responded. "If you remember, Bruno did attempt to steer you in the right direction at one point, but we concluded Benny couldn't know the entire truth until the very end. The reason came from Benny's psychological profiling. He was at the height of his powers when he thought the whole world was against him, due largely to the way his father had abused him as a child. We concluded that if we were to confess everything, his paranoia, which was his driving force, would have dissipated. And that would have jeopardized the entire mission."

"That's the worst answer you've given me yet!" I responded with my anger returning. "You had no right to play with a man's mental health like you did. You knowingly sacrificed my husband's life without his consent. You may defend your actions to yourselves by saying he signed a contract committing him to your bizarre game, but he wasn't a soldier. He was just a man. *He was just a man.*"

I became hysterical at that point. Bruno and Sebastien made more of their useless apologies. Then they left me to digest the dumpster full of truths they'd deposited at my door.

CHAPTER 55

And that's how I ended up on this blank page of my life. Well done, for listening all the way through. It was therapeutic to tell our story. You can still call me Bell.

I live in hope that one day Will and Wendy will forgive me, forgive their father, and forgive themselves for our respective roles in what happened. By hearing Benny's story, our story, in its entirety hopefully they'll understand its grayness, its inexplicability, and its beauty. And hopefully what's coming next for the two of them will be all the more fulfilling for the challenges we've been through and survived. I know I will use my remaining days to help others in ways I would never have considered prior to our time in the little flat. Did I mention we've decided to stay in Hackney, within the vicinity of the flat? I think it has something to do with holding onto our memories of Benny, both good and bad.

Who knows what's next for the Basilworths. Our future is full of promising uncertainty as we rebuild our lives one small step at a time. The kids will return to school, and I'll focus my energy on growing my baking business again, although I can't imagine I'll be doing any deliveries myself. There are just too many memories of those darker days when I stalked the streets in the shadows of humanity. It's time for us to appreciate all the light in our lives, both literal and metaphoric. Will and Wendy's one and only request as we start searching for a new flat is for floor to ceiling windows with views of anything but the street. How we've changed.

Speaking of light, Deidre is a godsend. She's become my greatest friend and inspiration throughout this experience. The epiphany stuck me while lying here that Deidre has been helping me become a better version of myself from the moment I met her amid the twisted game we were playing. She popped in to visit me the other day due to some kindly organization by Bruno and Sebastien who arranged for her to travel here in a limousine. After Deidre listened to my entire story with graceful acceptance of all my obvious flaws, I asked her if she could still see the good in me. I feared she'd change her mind about me and march out of my hospital room when she knew the truth. But she didn't. She carefully considered her words.

"Bell, after all you've been through, you have a choice," she eventually responded. "You can either focus on the darker parts of your story, of which there are many, and let them live on so they can control your future. Or you can celebrate all that's beautiful about your story while learning the many lessons it can teach you about how to become a better version of you. The best people I've encountered have survived the darkness and then thrived because of it. I know you'll make the right choice."

I live in hope that one day I'll believe in myself with Deidre's unerring faith. The data suggests I've got a good chance of getting there.

So that's our story. Sometimes, I hold myself partially responsible for Benny's death, and for his lack of peace when he was alive. But most of the time, I understand that Benny's life played out exactly as he always wanted it to. He was the leading player in the game show he always wanted to win, the game of his life. And while we were far from perfect, his family supported him on his journey to the best of our ability. Our lives will go on thanks to Benny, and his life ended because of Benny. And thanks to Benny, I'll always watch the passing feet on the street just in case there's a data anomaly no one else has noticed. Because there's always more going on than meets the eye.

Acknowledgements

I'd like to thank:

My wife Jess for your love and support.

My daughter Rosie for your joyful laughter.

My son Freddy for your generous smiles.

My publisher Lou Aronica and The Story Plant team for being so supportive and believing in life-affirming fiction.

Bill Fitzhugh for your kind endorsement quote after reading the novel.

The readers of *Secrets of a River Swimmer* who have been so interested in and supportive of *The Connection Game*'s launch.

The little flat below street level which I rented in London fifteen years ago for revealing the hypnotic powers of passing feet.

About the Author

SS Turner is the author of *Secrets of a River Swimmer*, an inspirational and humorous novel about finding the right pathway forward amidst the challenges of modern life. The novel was inspired by his experiences of swimming the River Tweed when he lived in Scotland.

Just like Freddy in *Secrets of a River Swimmer*, SS Turner worked in the global fund management sector for many years. But it wasn't for him. In recent years, he's been focused on inspiring positive change through his writing, as well as trying not to laugh in unfortunate situations. He now lives in Australia with his wife, daughter, son, one playful dog, two bossy cats, and ten fluffy chickens.